TROUBLE IN HIGH HEELS

This Large Print Book carries the
Seal of Approval of N.A.V.H.

TROUBLE IN HIGH HEELS

CHRISTINA DODD

THORNDIKE PRESS

An imprint of Thomson Gale, a part of The Thomson Corporation

Detroit • New York • San Francisco • New Haven, Conn. • Waterville, Maine • London

LIBRARY OF CONGRESS CATALOGING-IN-PUBLICATION DATA

Dodd, Christina.
    Trouble in high heels / by Christina Dodd.
        p. cm. — (Thorndike Press large print core)
    ISBN 0-7862-9000-5 (lg. print : alk. paper)
    1. Large type books. I. Title.
PS3554.O3175T76 2006
813'.54—dc22   2006026046

U.S. Hardcover:
ISBN 13: 978-0-7862-9000-0
ISBN 10: 0-7862-9000-5

Published in 2006 by arrangement with NAL Signet,
a division of Penguin Group (USA) Inc.

Printed in the United States of America on permanent paper
10 9 8 7 6 5 4 3 2 1

For Scott.
When I write about love forever,
I write about you.

ACKNOWLEDGMENTS

Some books come to fruition without struggle.

So I'm told.

My thanks to my editor, Kara Cesare, for holding my hand through the battle, and to Kara Welsh, for being so patient through disaster and flood. To my plot group, Lisa Kleypas, Connie Brockway, Susan Kay Law, and especially Susan Sizemore and Geralyn Dawson, who answered my panicked phone calls with brutal wisdom and witty banter. And to my agent, Mel Berger, thank you for being a sounding board, mentor, and friend.

ONE

Nashville, Tennessee
Fourteen years ago

Eleven-year-old Brandi sat in the open door of her bedroom with the floaty princess curtains and the pretty canopy bed, and listened to the sound of her mother's hysterical voice.

"But I don't know how to write a check."

"It's time you learned." Her father couldn't have sounded more disgusted.

"But you always did that for us."

"That's right." Daddy was sort of stomping as he packed. "I'd come home from a hard day's work at the office and I had to sit down and pay the utilities and the house payment and the credit cards and all the other bills. I had to make the reservations anytime we traveled and arrange to have someone mow the lawn. Taking care of you was a damned pain in the ass."

"But you wanted it that way!"

Daddy must have recognized the justice of her statement, because he sounded a little nicer. "It's not hard, Tiffany." Then he was back to impatience. "For Christ's sake, my secretary can do it."

"It's her, isn't it?" Mama's voice shook with suspicion. "It's Susan. That little slut is the one you're leaving me for."

"She's not a slut," he snapped. Then he took a long, audible breath. "And I'm leaving you because you don't do anything except . . . groom."

Brandi imagined her father waving his big hands at her thin, blond, immaculately coiffed and manicured mother.

"What do you want me to do? I can do whatever you want." Mama sounded panicked.

Brandi knew Mama *was* panicked, because Brandi was scared, too.

"You *can't* carry on an intelligent conversation. You *can't* discuss my business with me. The reason you always get picked for jury duty is because you don't know a damned thing about current events." He snorted. "A man like me needs an intellectual challenge, not an aging doormat."

Brandi had to know what was going to happen — to her parents, and to her.

Brandi's mother gasped. "I'm thirty-two!"

"As I said."

Why was he being so mean? Tiffany was beautiful. Everybody said so. All Brandi's friends at ballet envied her for having a mother who looked like a movie star. Brandi didn't think it was so hot having people talk to her all the time about Tiffany and ask if she was proud to have such a pretty mother, but she always smiled and nodded her head, because then they always said, "And you'll look just like her when you grow up!"

"You never wanted to talk to me about your business before." Mama's heels clicked on the hardwood floor as she followed Daddy around their bedroom. "You said you left Jane for me because she was always talking about that stuff when all you wanted was a peaceful home where you could relax."

Daddy grunted.

"Look around you. I've consulted feng shui experts and brought in decorators to make this a home that you could be proud of —"

"And I paid through the nose for that fool Japanese guy —"

"Indonesian!"

"And for some idiot decorator to change my curtains in my office four times a year."

11

Daddy was getting hostile.

"Drapes. They're drapes. And you bring clients into that office, Gary, and we had to get them right!"

Brandi loved that when it came to something she really cared about, Mama got in Daddy's face.

"Besides, our house headlined in the Frontgate catalog —"

The spread in Frontgate catalog had been Mama's pride and joy, and had given her great cachet among her friends.

"That catalog brought you a lot of work. The Dugeren murder case and" — Mama's voice quavered — "that high-profile divorce case. . . ." She was right.

So Daddy attacked from a different direction. "Do you think I don't notice the bills to the dermatologist and the plastic surgeon? Your discreet little visits for your facial buffs and your body peels?"

"What's wrong with that?" Honestly bewildered, Mama asked, "Don't you want me to be beautiful?"

"I want something more than an empty shell who smiles vacuously and babbles about how Vicky at tennis has to do something about the cellulite on her thighs! And your daughter's just as bad."

Brandi wanted to cover her ears, to not

hear her own father disown her by saying *your daughter,* but it was like listening to a car wreck — the insults and the rejection commanded her attention as surely as the screech of brakes and the crumple of metal, and for one wild moment she wondered if she would come out alive.

"All that girl does —"

"Brandi." Mom took a deep breath, and Brandi pictured her squaring her shoulders. "Her name is Brandi."

"All Brandi does is take ballet and gymnastics and cheerleading classes. She's a mini-you. Why couldn't she be more like Kimberley?"

Kim was his first daughter, his daughter with Jane.

"Kimberley plays softball, and she does it damned well." His voice rang with pride. "She's got a sports scholarship to UT. She's going to be an engineer and make something of herself. Not like that kid of yours. Brandi is stupid."

Stupid. Daddy thought she was stupid. Brandi closed her eyes to try to contain the anguish, and when that didn't work she put her fist against her mouth and shoved, holding back her shriek.

She wasn't stupid. He was. *He was.* She wanted to go down to her parents' bedroom, stomp her foot, shout and rail at her father for throwing her and her mother away as if they were trash.

But Brandi didn't make scenes. Brandi followed the rules in the hope that being good would somehow make everything okay.

Everything was not okay, but if she just tried a little harder . . .

"She is not stupid!" Mama said.

"How would *you* know?"

Brandi gasped. How could he be so cruel to Mama?

"She's your daughter as much as Kimberley. She's smart, too. She's never had anything but straight As, even in math." Mama didn't pay a bit of attention to Daddy's insult to her, but leaped into the fray to defend Brandi.

Of course, Mama's strengths weren't taught in school. She was really good at making their house pretty and knowing the right thing to wear and smiling at men so they got flustered and turned red.

"Brandi's probably going to be some kind of freaking English major and a drain on my wallet for the rest of my life." He sounded so disgusted, as if being good in English were a waste.

"She's the best in her class in gymnastics and ballet."

"A bunch of skinny little girls in tights!"

Brandi gritted her teeth. She wasn't skinny or little anymore. She had a figure, and at five-foot-ten she was an inch taller than Mama and four inches taller than any of the rest of the girls in her class. But around the house Daddy hardly glanced at Brandi, and he had never bothered to come to her recitals.

"Kimberley plays real sports," he said. "Competitive sports."

In a prissy tone, Mom said, "If you ask me, Kimberley is a lesbian."

With a soft groan, Brandi dropped her forehead against the wall. It was true. Of course it was true. Kim had told Brandi herself. But Daddy was homophobic, and he sure didn't want to know that his sports-inclined daughter was gay. Mama had just messed up big by telling him.

Daddy shouted, "Why, you jealous little —"

Mama gave a little cry of fright.

He was going to hit Mama.

Brandi started to her feet, picking up her beloved ceramic dragon to use as a weapon.

She heard the sound of glass shattering.

Heart pounding, she ran into the hallway, dragon upraised.

In a guttural tone Daddy said, "For

15

Christ's sake, Tiffany, don't be stupid."

"I'm not stupid!" Mama stomped her foot. "I just think things like manners and pleasure are important, and you shouldn't have broken that vase."

Brandi skidded to a stop.

Mama continued, "It took me months to find the right vase for that table!"

Slowly Brandi lowered the dragon. She crept back toward her room. If they knew she was listening they'd make her shut her door, and no matter how her stomach churned, she had to know whether her daddy had destroyed their lives.

"That's the problem," Daddy said. "You always cared more about vases and manners than about ideas or work — or me."

"That's not true!" Mama whimpered like a kicked puppy.

It *was* true, but to Brandi's childish eyes, it had seemed that that was all he required of her mother. Only in the last year had he grown restless and contemptuous.

Mama's quiet sobbing must have made Daddy uncomfortable, for he tried cajoling her. "C'mon, Tiff, you'll be all right without me. Jane is doing just fine."

"B-but J-Jane had a prenuptial agreement. Y-you didn't want me t-to get one."

"That was your mistake."

Brandi recognized that tone in her father's voice. Guilt was hotly prodding him — and he blamed Mom.

"Y-you said . . . you said you'd take care of me forever."

"For shit's sake, would you stop blubbering? It's disgusting." He slammed his suitcase closed. "I'll have my lawyer call your lawyer."

"I don't have a lawyer!"

"Get one." Daddy's heels slapped the polished hardwood floor as he walked down the hallway.

Brandi tensed as she waited to see if he would stop to hug her before he left.

But he passed without a glance in her direction.

Brandi swallowed her disappointment. She knew how. She'd done it for years.

Mama ran past her and after him, crying with ever more desperation. "I don't have a job. How will I support Brandi? We'll starve!" She caught him as he opened the door, grabbed at his arm, and tried to hold him back.

Even Brandi recognized high drama at its best.

Quietly she shut herself into her bedroom and left them to it.

Her stomach hurt, roiling with distress.

She absently rubbed the pain and looked around her bedroom. Mama had decorated it with white-and-gold furniture and pink-and-gold upholstery. When Brandi was young she had felt as though she were living in a Barbie dream house, and she'd loved it.

Now that she was older she felt as if she were living in a Barbie dream house, and she wanted it changed. But she hadn't wanted to hurt Mama's feelings, so she'd added a few touches herself. A stained-glass window done in shades of blue that looked like her favorite print in *The Hobbit*. Her shiny green dragon with sparkling gems for eyes. Three black-and-white posters of the Hadrien Boys from England. But peering through the stained glass, running her fingertips over the dragon's scales, and looking at the boys did nothing to ease the ache in her chest. In her heart.

She opened the window and looked out at the soft green unfurling in the trees. Nashville was beautiful in the spring. Their huge yard was tiered and landscaped and usually the sight made Brandi feel warm and secure. Today it wasn't working. Nothing was working.

Downstairs she heard the front door slam so hard it shook the house.

Her throat hurt, so she took big breaths of

the fresh air, desperate to hold back . . . no, not tears. She wasn't going to cry.

She was going to fix this. Somehow she had to do something that would make it better.

Walking to her painted desk, she pulled out a tablet, one engraved with her name, and at the top she wrote, *Things to Learn.* She drew a line beneath the words and numbered down the lines, and wrote:

How to Take Care of My Mother.

1. Learn how to write checks.
2. Find out what a utility is.
3. Figure out how to make the house payment.

Then she tore that list off, set it carefully to the side, and on the top of the clean sheet, wrote:

How to Take Care of Myself.

1. Learn how to write checks.
2. Get scholarships so I can go to school.
3. Play baseball.

She frowned at that one and chewed on the end of her pen. No, that wouldn't do. She wasn't good at baseball; to Kim's annoyance Brandi ducked when the ball came in her direction.

Brandi crossed off *Play baseball* and replaced it with *Become a lawyer.*

She didn't know exactly what a lawyer did — a girl who attended ballet, gymnastics, and cheerleading classes in every spare moment learned remarkably little about the real world, especially when her father never talked to her about his job — but she knew he made a lot of money. And her father had required her mother to look beautiful and Brandi to be charming when Mr. Charles McGrath and his wife visited, and Mr. McGrath was an important Chicago lawyer.

That was what she wanted. She wanted to be important. She wanted the power to make her father behave, and the ability to get her mother a prenuptial agreement.

Whatever that was.

Learn how to make a prenuptial agreement.

Two

Chicago
Fourteen years later

If Brandi's caller ID had been working, she would never have picked up the phone.

But it wasn't, and she did, and that just figured, because it had been one hell of a week.

Not that Brandi hadn't expected it. Anybody with a lick of sense could predict that moving from Nashville to Chicago in the dead of winter would be difficult, and Brandi prided herself on her good sense.

But she'd picked the coldest winter Chicago had seen for a century, which made the pipes in her apartment building freeze for the first time ever, which meant that her movers had had nothing to drink, not that that had stopped them from using her toilet, which for the lack of water didn't flush and probably wouldn't for weeks, and using it with such typical male abandon that she didn't dare sit on it even in the most dire circumstances because there was no way to clean the seat. And one guy caught her talking to herself while she tried to wipe the seat with a wadded-up Kleenex out of her purse, and the son of a bitch had the gall to inch away as if she were crazy.

She didn't think much of men right now, and the movers' backpedaling only increased her ire — and her sense of isolation.

She didn't know anybody in this town except Alan and Mr. McGrath — for years now she'd called him by the honorary title of Uncle Charles — but where were they while she crammed her entire life into a one-bedroom apartment?

In a lovely piece of irony, the icy roads had sent the truck carrying her new sofa and armchair careening into an empty Marble Slab Ice Cream Shop. The delivery men wrestled the furniture up to her fourth-floor apartment by tilting it sideways in the freight elevator, a maneuver that made her cover her eyes and pray to the gods of furniture placement.

Her entreaties must have worked, because they planted the sofa and the chair in front of the small propane fireplace, put the ottoman between them, and moved her end tables into place.

Surely her luck had turned. The sofa wasn't damaged. The colors and fabrics were exactly the way she had ordered them. They would fit perfectly in the new apartment she and Alan would move into when they married. It was only later that night, when she stopped unpacking long enough to drop into the chair, put her feet up on the ottoman, and look, really look at the furniture, that she realized the sofa was eighteen inches too short.

She'd received the love seat, not the full-size sofa she'd ordered.

She spent the whole night on her hastily made bed, worrying about making the phone call to Amy, her salesperson at Samuel's Furniture.

That, at least, went well. Amy was apologetic, behaving just as well as Brandi could have hoped, but the fact was that she had to wait another six weeks until the actual furniture she'd ordered arrived, and for a few minutes it seemed as if that sucked more than anything else that had happened in this horrific, endless week.

Until the phone call she picked up because she thought, honestly thought, that Alan was calling to tell her he was coming over at last.

Instead, it was her mother.

"Well? How did the move go?" As always, Tiffany sounded like a cheerleader bolstering her team's spirits before the big game.

Brandi stared around at the endless parade of boxes. Empty boxes piled catawampus against the wall. Flattened boxes stacked by the door. Boxes, far too many boxes, still taped shut and scratched with black Magic Marker from her last two moves. An endless supply of boxes, no stereo system in sight, and pizza for dinner again. "Well, I've been unpacking for a day and a half and I haven't seen Alan. Not once."

"Now, sweetheart, I'm sure he's busy. After all, he is a physician." Mother's Tennessee accent sounded soft and tender.

Brandi didn't know why she'd bothered to complain. It was pure exhaustion and loneliness that made her give in to her irritation and criticize her fiancé to, of all people, her mother. "He's not a physician. He's a resident."

"That poor boy. I saw on *60 Minutes* how those hospital administrators work their residents ninety-six hours at a time. And you said he was brilliant. Remember? You told me he was the top of his class and all eyes were on him."

For once Brandi wished her mother would

take her side. About anything. "He hasn't called, either. He may have e-mailed, but I don't get connected to the Internet until next week."

"I hope you didn't call him. A nagging woman is an unpleasant creature." Tiffany was the personification of 1950s Southern womanhood.

"Yes, Mother, I know, although if he'd remember me long enough to do as he promised, I wouldn't be seized by this overwhelming desire to nag him." Brandi scratched her nails against the grain of the fabric on the couch, watched as the brocade rose in four welts, and wondered which one of them she wanted to scratch — her mother or her fiancé. "But I'd like to point out that I'm a lawyer who relocated from a lovely, soft, *warm* city to be close to my fiancé. I'm about to start my first full-time job at a major Chicago law firm, and *I'm* going to be working all the time. He could at least call to see if I've frozen to the side of the Dumpster taking out my trash."

Mother's voice took on that pious tone that made Brandi want to shriek. "To keep her man, a woman always has to give one hundred and ten percent."

"How did that work out for you?"

The sound of her mother's shocked inhalation brought Brandi to her senses. She loved her mother, she really did, but Mother had been Daddy's first trophy wife, and he'd left her and the quietly anguished eleven-year-old Brandi for his twenty-three-year-old secretary and a new baby, a son guaranteed to give him what he needed — a football-uniformed mirror image of his youthful self.

Except, of course, Brandi's half brother was now thirteen and supremely uninterested in sports. Instead Quentin was a brilliant computer programmer.

Brandi felt sorry for Quentin; she knew what it was like dealing with a panicked mother who was losing that dewy glow of youth, a father who didn't bother to hide his disappointment in his child, and their rapidly disintegrating marriage.

"I'm sorry, Mother. I'm a bitch."

"No, you're not."

"I'm pretty sure I am." Not always a bad thing, in Brandi's opinion. "Let's face it, with his current troubles Daddy has proved he doesn't know what he wants. Not in a wife. Not in his kids."

"Your father is a good man."

Brandi smiled bitterly and stroked the slick scales of her treasured old dragon. No matter how much Daddy screwed Tiffany over, she never said a nasty word about him. When Brandi was a teenager she might have been conflicted if Mother had badmouthed him, but those days were long gone.

Daddy was not a good man. He was self-centered, abusive, and manipulative, and no one knew that better than Brandi.

"When you get off the phone with me, call him. He'll want to hear that you got there safely."

"Oh, Mother. He'll barely remember I moved."

"And tomorrow's his birthday."

"Ohh. I forgot." He'd probably forgotten, too, but Tiffany kept up the pretense that he was a normal man who celebrated special occasions, probably because that way Brandi was forced to communicate with him on a semiregular basis.

When Brandi thought of talking to him, of the chance that he would yell at her, or, worse, of the possibility that he wouldn't have time to speak to her, her stomach hurt. She always put it off as long as possible.

That was why she'd gotten engaged to Alan. He might not be a man of fire and passion, but he was steady and dependable — or he had been until she needed him.

And Mother was right about that, too. He probably had a whopper of an excuse. But

Brandi — who'd broken a fingernail down to the quick, whose deodorant had failed hours ago, who was dehydrated and didn't dare drink her bottled water because she couldn't flush — wasn't in the mood to hear it right now.

"Alan'll be by soon." Mother used a conciliatory tone. "Maybe he'll come tonight to take you out to dinner."

"I don't want him to take me out. I want him to help me unpack." Yep. Definitely bitchy.

"No, go out! You should seize every chance for a good time right now, while you're young." About this, Tiffany sounded fierce.

And that made Brandi squirm with guilt. The reason Tiffany hadn't been out there kicking up her heels was because she'd been trying — not succeeding, but trying — to make a living for Brandi. "Mother, you're not exactly old. You're not even fifty. *You* could get out there and have a good time."

"Men my age want women your age, and men who want women my age are too old to have a good time. In every way." Tiffany's voice was droll. "But actually, I've been thinking. . . ."

"What?"

Tiffany hesitated.

"What?" It wasn't like her mother to be

coy. Quite the opposite.

"I wish *I* could be there to help you!" Tiffany burst out. "I miss you!"

Brandi would have sworn that wasn't what Tiffany intended to say. But she was too tired, too dirty, too disheveled to dig for the truth. "I haven't lived at home for seven years. You can't miss me that much."

"I know, but it's different with you so far away. When you were at Vanderbilt you were right across town, and I thought if you needed me, I could get to you right away. Now . . ."

"I'm okay, Tiffany. Really. I'm good at taking care of myself." *A lot better than you are at taking care of yourself.*

"I know. You are capable. I'm proud of you." But Tiffany sounded fretful. "I just wish Alan were there. He's so reliable."

Except now. "Tomorrow night he's going to take me to a party at Uncle Charles's." And if he did this disappearing act and didn't show for that, she didn't care what excuse he came up with; she was going to kill him.

"A party?" Tiffany inhaled with excitement. "At Charles's home? Oh, that is a showcase. He recently had the foyer remodeled. Do you know that when they stripped the paint off the curved stairway, they found

29

that underneath it's solid mahogany? Can you imagine? I wish I could see it! Do you like Charles?"

Her mother's leaps from one subject to another made Brandi blink. "Sure. I've liked Uncle Charles since he used his legal expertise to wring child support out of Daddy."

"Your father was confused by that woman he married."

"So we're hoping he's pussy-whipped instead of morally corrupt?"

"Don't use that term, Brandi. It sounds bitter, and that's not at all attractive in a young woman."

"Yes, ma'am." Interesting that when Tiffany got motherly, Brandi felt more secure.

"Tell me all about the party."

"It's a charity ball to raise money for the museum. There'll be a silent auction, and during the entertainment — by the way, Uncle Charles got Elton John — I'm sitting at the McGrath and Lindoberth corporate table." Of course she was. She might be new, but she'd earned straight As out of Vanderbilt Law, and that was no small feat. Even without Uncle Charles's influence she would have been interviewed, and she'd aced that. She'd won this job fair and square. She was good, and she knew it.

"What are you wearing?" Tiffany asked.

Uh-oh. "That black sheath I bought for parties at law school."

Tiffany didn't say, *Oh, but you bought it at Ann Taylor,* or, *But that's two years old.* Instead she said, "Darling, black? That's so New York. Show those Chicago lawyers how good a Southern girl can look!"

"I look awful in pink." Brandi slithered down to sit on her backbone.

"Wear red. Men adore red."

"I don't care what men adore," Brandi snapped, then took a long breath. Tiffany had never changed her mind. She'd lived through fourteen years of miserable existence, and she still thought a man was a woman's best friend — a man and the gifts she could get from him.

"But the sheath doesn't show off your figure."

"Thank God. Do you know how hard it is to dress for business with a chest like mine?"

"Women pay good money every day for a chest like yours. Marilyn Monroe made a fortune with a chest like yours. With a figure like yours!" Tiffany laughed, the kind of throaty purr that said she knew a lot about how men and women played.

Unwillingly, Brandi laughed, too. It was true. If she hadn't become a lawyer, she could have been a Las Vegas showgirl. She

31

was all hourglass figure. During interviews she'd mashed down her bosom so the women wouldn't immediately hate her and the guys would look at her face. "I can't afford a new dress right now. This move cost a fortune."

"I thought Charles paid for the move."

"The firm paid for the move," Brandi corrected. "But I bought furniture" — furniture that was the wrong damned size — "and paid first and last month's rent on the apartment. And starting this month I'm paying Daddy back for my student loans."

"Your daddy would want you to have a new dress."

My God. Tiffany was like a dog with a bone. She never let go.

"Your daddy likes pretty young girls to have pretty things."

"Only if the pretty young girl is his secretary and he's screwing her." Before Tiffany could object, Brandi added, "Besides, with Alan there I don't need to worry about catching a man."

"No, but you need to make sure his gaze is riveted to you and he never leaves your side for fear that the other men will whisk you off!"

Brandi laughed again, but wryly. "Alan's stable. He's professional. He knows he can depend on me. He's just not the jealous type."

"Given the right incentive, every man is that type."

No use arguing. Tiffany did know her men.

"But I don't want that type. I consider marriage a meshing of equals, a . . . a calm in the midst of the storm of modern life." Brandi's modern life — a life whose touchstones were good sense, moderation in all things, and a logical progression toward her goals of not being like her mother, proving her father wrong, paying back her debts, and being a model citizen.

She wanted nothing about *Desperate Housewives* to taint her.

"Good heavens," Mother said blankly. "You don't mean that you and Alan are calm in bed?"

"No, don't be ridiculous." Although since Alan had entered medical school he was brief and businesslike, and lately, on the infrequent weekends he managed to get time off, too tired to perform at all. "We have our moments. But there's no shrieking fights or huge dramas."

"You're annoyed with him now, but you're not going to shriek at him?"

"How often have you seen me shriek?"

"Never." In a tone that indicated total cluelessness, Mother said, "You were almost frighteningly calm, even as a child."

Because her parents were playing out the big dramas. "When I see Alan I'm going to explain that he needs to be more sensitive to my needs." Brandi injected humor into her voice. "You can't have it both ways, Tiffany. I can't be sensible enough to know that he probably is too busy to remember that I moved this week *and* cherish such a huge passion for him I can't survive without his very presence."

"No, I . . . no, I suppose not. It's just that those first few years when your father and I got together in bed we erupted into flames —"

Brandi pulled the phone away from her ear. "Ew, Mother, don't tell me that!"

"It seems so early in your relationship to be so cavalier." Tiffany's voice brightened. "And that's why you need a new dress!"

Brandi sighed deeply. "I'll think about it." For about three seconds.

"Get your hair highlighted, too, honey. You've gone a kind of mousy brown."

"I'd call it dishwater blond." Brandi fingered the split ends — Tiffany would have a spasm.

"Dishwater blond is just as attractive as it

sounds. Get highlights."

Someone beeped in. Thank God. "Tiffany, I've got to get this." She cut off her mother and answered with a snap, "Hello?"

"Brandi? It's Alan."

"Yes, Alan, I know your voice. Let me hang up on Mother." She switched to her cajoling tone. "Alan, promise you'll hold on."

"I'll hold on." He sounded sullen.

Great. It would be one of *those* conversations. But she couldn't take the chance he'd ditch her and later say it was a medical emergency. He'd done it before and this time she really did need to talk to him.

She clicked back to her mother.

"Speak of the devil, there he is! Let me take this call, Mother. I'll talk to you later!" When she wasn't so tired and could control her irritation a little better.

She cut Tiffany off in the middle of her good-byes and said to Alan, "Where have you been? I've been worried about you!" Which sounded better than *I've been irritated at you.*

"I'm in Las Vegas." His normally flat Massachusetts accent vibrated with some violent emotion.

"Las Vegas?" She was so dumb. She didn't suspect a thing. "What happened? Is someone sick or something?"

"Sick? Is that your best guess?" So much for the calm in the storm. Alan was shouting.

"I —"

"My girlfriend's pregnant. I just got married. And this is *all your fault.*"

THREE

Brandi stood with the phone held loosely in her fingers, staring at the apartment she'd rented and paid too much for so she could be close to the medical center and Alan, and tried to absorb the message.

She was a smart woman. She was a lawyer. Words were her weapons and her tools. But she couldn't comprehend him. There was — there had to be — some kind of mistake.

"Alan, are you drunk?"

"A little bit. I needed some liquid courage before I called you. Can you blame me?"

Blame him? She didn't even know him. "I don't understand. Y-you've got a girlfriend?"

"Not anymore. Now she's my wife. I tell you, none of this would have happened if you'd moved to Chicago when I did." That made even less sense than anything else he'd said.

"But I got accepted to Vanderbilt Law and you got accepted to University of Chicago.

How could I come with you and get my degree?"

"For shit's sake, I'm going to be a doctor. Do you think I couldn't support you?"

"I think it wasn't about you supporting me. I think it was about me being fulfilled in my work. You *said* you understood." The numbness was wearing off. Alan was married. Married.

"Oh, blah, blah."

"You've been sleeping with someone on the side." Married with a baby on the way. Alan. The guy who used a condom and insisted she use contraceptive foam all at the same time.

"On the side, on the back, on the front . . ." He lowered his voice like he didn't want to be overheard. "Listen, this isn't what I wanted either, but she's pregnant. I have to marry her, or I'm a jerk."

"That ship has sailed," she said with a bite in her voice.

Obviously he didn't like that. His voice got sharper and he dug deeper with his nasty little insinuations. "And another thing. If you'd been a little less of a cold fish, I wouldn't have been such an easy catch."

Yes, the numbness was wearing off, and temper was starting to stir. "This is crap. You're not blaming me because you couldn't keep your zipper closed!"

"I sure as hell am."

"Let me rephrase that. I'm not accepting the blame." She tightened her fingers around the receiver as if it were Alan's neck.

"Alannnn." Through the phone Brandi heard the high, satisfied tones of a woman who'd just gotten her way.

"Is that *her?*" Brandi asked.

"Yeah. That's Fawn." Alan didn't sound any happier than Brandi.

But Brandi took damned little comfort from that.

"Alannn, don't forget . . ." The bitch must have covered the receiver, for all Brandi could hear was a low murmur.

Then Alan abruptly spoke into the receiver, dropping the imitation of an injured party and sounding just like he always did when he spoke to Brandi — like a doctor giving advice on how to shed excess pounds.

Why hadn't she realized that before? Why hadn't she realized that he wasn't too tired to make love to her; he was uninterested . . . and getting satisfaction elsewhere?

"Brandi, I need my ring back."

"Your ring?" Brandi was back to not understanding.

"I'm a resident. I can't afford another diamond, so you need to give me my ring back." When she didn't reply, he said impatiently, "My engagement ring."

Brandi glanced at her finger. She'd removed it to protect the diamond while she unpacked. Because it was precious to her. Because it represented careful planning and logical life decisions and true love and all that crap.

She curled her hand into a fist. "Alannnn." If she did say so herself, she did a pretty good imitation of Fawn. "It's not *your* ring. It's *my* ring. And let me give you a little legal advice. In a situation like this, possession is nine-tenths of the law."

She hung up. She hung up softly, without a hint of the ire that roiled in her belly, but she did hang up.

Still holding the cordless, she hurried into the bathroom.

The phone started ringing. And ringing. And ringing. She had to find her answering machine and hook it up. Alan needed something to talk to.

Opening the medicine cabinet, she stared at the shelf where the diamond nestled in its black velvet box. Protected and cherished. She knew her diamonds — when you had a mother who was a trophy wife, you learned these things — and this was a good diamond. Alan had insisted on taking out a loan to get her just the right stone, just the right setting. A marquise-cut, one-carat, pure white diamond that blinked with bits of ancient blue sky and new yellow sun. The platinum setting displayed its simple grandeur.

At the time she had thought he realized how much she wanted it. Now she wondered if it had been nothing more than a symbol of his own good taste. It sure wasn't a symbol of his good sense.

Abruptly irritated with the constant chime of the phone, she answered, then cut Alan off, then opened the line again. She hesitated, her finger over Tiffany's number.

Telling her this, tonight, seemed like an admission that Tiffany was right. Tiffany said no man was interested in a sensible, intelligent, well-organized lawyer with the ability to support herself and be fulfilled in her work. Tiffany said every man wanted a high-maintenance wife dependent on his approval. In fact, that bastard Everyman wanted Marilyn Monroe in a red silk dress.

Brandi's finger smashed down on the autodial. She counted the rings, then heard her sister's voice say, "I can't come to the phone right now. . . ."

Of course not. It was Thursday night. Kim was a coach, and there had to be some kind of game at Smith. Volleyball or softball or whatever-ball season it was.

"Please, Kim, call me as soon as you can." Brandi hesitated, not sure what else to say. Finally, she worked up, "I sort of need you," and hung up.

Had her voice trembled? She hoped not. Kim would think she'd been crying, and she'd never been so far from crying. All this churning in her gut was a combination of rage, humiliation and, well, humiliation.

Yanking the ring from the box, she tossed it like garbage at the toilet.

Luckily, the lid was down and it bounced off and skittered across the tile floor.

Yes, she was mad, but not so mad that she tossed a flawless diamond ring down the tubes.

Besides, even if she succeeded in hitting the bowl, she couldn't flush. The pipes were frozen.

She chased the glittering, glorious symbol of her romantic folly into the corner by the tub. Picking it up, she cradled it in her palm . . . and smiled, a Machiavellian smile that, if he'd seen it, would have made Alan sweat.

No, it was better, so much better, if she made use of the ring — to make herself happy.

■ ■ ■ ■

As Brandi walked along, huddling close to the buildings in an attempt to avoid Chicago's blistering cold wind, her cell phone gave a series of sharp rings. She wanted to ignore the summons; answering would involve peeling off her glove, digging into the capacious pocket of her black London Fog, and pushing up her wool hat to put the phone to her ear — all activities guaranteed to turn her already flash-frozen flesh into a solid Popsicle.

But that was Kim's ring tone, and after a night spent awake and fuming, Brandi needed to talk to *somebody.* It took her a minute of frantic fumbling before she managed to pull out her cell and flip it open.

"What is wrong?" Kim's deep voice demanded an immediate response.

"Wait a minute; I'm going inside." Brandi opened the door of Honest Abe's Pawnshop, the one her landlord had recommended as the most reputable in the area.

The heat hit her cheeks and she moaned with joy.

"Why are you making that noise?" Kim sounded even more coachlike and commanding.

"It's cold outside. It's warm in here." In the last twelve hours, Brandi had gone through anguish, embarrassment, and rage and now had reached the moment where she relished imparting her news just to hear Kim's reaction. "I'm pawning my engagement ring."

"Why?"

"Alan jilted me."

"You're shitting!" Kim shouted. "*Alan* did?"

It was a small shop, crammed with large goods against the wall and small goods inside the glass counter, and everything had a fluorescent tag on it with the price written in black Magic Marker. Brandi smiled at the Asian man behind the cash register and at the two handsome young men lounging by the gun counter.

This was almost fun.

Well, except for the fact she had to go to a major charity function tonight . . . alone. But she had a plan. Man, oh, man, did she have a plan.

"Mr. Nguyen?" she said to the man behind the counter.

"Yes." The owner was short with black, black hair, dark eyes, and beautiful golden skin.

She placed the black velvet box on the

counter. "Eric Lerner at my apartment building said you were honest and would give me a fair price."

"I appreciate the business. Thank Eric for me," Mr. Nguyen said.

"So how much?" She pushed the box toward the pawnshop owner. Into the phone she said, "Alan got his girlfriend pregnant and had to marry her in a quickie Vegas wedding."

"Was Elvis involved?" Kim shot back.

"Dunno."

"Wait, wait, wait," Kim said. "That bloodless little weenie Alan got a girl pregnant and had to get married?"

Now Kim had surprised Brandi. "Didn't you like him?"

"You know how doctors always have this cachet, this intensity, this certainty that makes you pay attention to their every word?"

"Yeah."

"Alan would have made a good accountant."

Brandi gave a spurt of laughter.

The pawnshop owner wasn't really old, maybe in his sixties, but he had that palsy that some people get. His fingers were shaking as he placed the jeweler's glass in his eye and peered at the diamond.

"You don't sound particularly broken-hearted." Kim sounded cautious.

"I'm sure brokenhearted will come later. Right now I'm just furious. I guess it's the prospect of pawning my diamond and knowing that Alan will have to pay through the nose to get it back."

"Hmm. Well. That's good."

Brandi knew Kim had made some judgment, the sense of which escaped her, but she didn't care. As long as she got her revenge. Because no matter what they taught in ethics class in law school, revenge tasted really good.

"A fabulous diamond in a popular setting," Mr. Nguyen said.

"You can easily resell it," Brandi agreed.

In her ear, Kim asked, "What did Tiffany say about Alan and his new wife?"

"I haven't exactly told her."

"You didn't tell your mother?" Kim sounded incredulous.

"I can't. She's going to say, 'I told you so. I told you you have to cater to a man. I told you you couldn't act as if your career is as important as his. I told you to be a Stepford wife.' "

"I think you're doing your mom a disservice." As usual when they talked about Tiffany, Kim sounded calm and wise.

"Last night when I hadn't heard a word from him since I moved, she was defending him." And while that had riled Brandi last night, today it made her furious.

"Last night you intended to marry him and she wanted desperately to make sure *your* marriage worked, so she counseled you the best she knew how."

"I suppose." Kim could be right. Probably was right. But Brandi wasn't in the mood to be fair.

"Have you talked to our father?" Kim used the deeply mocking tone she always used when she talked about Daddy.

"About Alan? I don't *think* so." Brandi ladled on the sarcasm.

"No, for his birthday."

"Damn. I forgot again." And Tiffany had reminded her.

"Don't blame you. I girded my loins and made the call. Bastard didn't even bother to pick up, so I left a message."

"Aren't you lucky?"

"That's what I tell myself."

Mr. Nguyen was staring at the diamond as if deep in thought and tapping his chin.

"I have the paperwork," Brandi told him. She'd searched half the night for the sheet that rated the diamond's clarity and flaw-lessness.

He barely glanced at it. "Okay, I'll give you eight thousand."

"Dollars?" Brandi was stunned. Alan had paid ten thousand; he'd made sure she saw the bill of sale. In fact, he'd demanded she *appreciate* the bill of sale.

The asshole.

As Tiffany's jewelry had had to be sold to support them, Brandi had gained experience with pawnshop owners. They never paid more than twenty-five percent of appraised value, and *then* they acted as if they were doing you a favor. And they never, ever appraised the jewelry wrong.

Haggling was a fine art in a pawnshop, and Brandi had been prepared to bargain. But maybe while she'd had her head down studying in law school, diamonds had taken a hike in value. Hastily she said, "Sure. Eight thousand. It's a deal."

"That's good," Kim said appreciatively.

Mr. Nguyen slipped the diamond into a box and slid it into the case. "A pretty girl like you needs jewels to decorate your neck and ears. Yesterday I got in diamond earrings —"

"I don't care if I never see another diamond as long as I live." Brandi had never meant anything as much in her life.

"Who are you and what have you done

with my sister?" Kim gasped in simulated dismay.

"Shaddup," Brandi said into the phone.

"Sapphires to match your beautiful eyes." Mr. Nguyen smiled at her, but he had white lines around his mouth and a birthmark on his cheek . . . or a bruise.

She glanced at the two guys. They'd moved to the computer counter. They were chatting in low voices, seemingly focused on the array of iPods in the case. They weren't standing close, and they seemed unconcerned about her transaction, but both had their scarves wrapped over the tops of their heads and over their mouths. A niggling unease worked its way up her spine. It almost looked as if they were trying to disguise themselves.

"Kim, hold on a minute. . . ." She leaned across the counter. "Sapphires might be just what I need." In a lower voice, she said, "Do you need help?"

"What's happening?" Kim spoke softly in her ear.

Mr. Nguyen smiled even more broadly as he placed a small white box on the counter. "No. I'm hiring no one right now. It's too cold and business is not good."

"What's wrong?" Kim repeated.

"Nothing. I think." Brandi picked up the

box and asked Mr. Nguyen, "Those guys aren't bothering you?"

"They're in the neighborhood all the time. They came in to get warm and to see what I have in electronics." He shrugged. "They're hackers."

"Hackers?" That wasn't good.

"Maybe I said that wrong. They're computer geeks." Leaning across, he flipped open the lid.

What met Brandi's eyes made her catch her breath. Held upright on the tiny white velvet showcase, the sapphires blinked in a glorious shade of blue.

"Whoa." They must have been a carat each, set in yellow gold. Brandi forgot how to haggle, how to play hard to get. She was almost salivating on the counter when she said, "Gorgeous."

"I swear to God, Brandi, if you don't talk to me . . ." Kim sounded pissed.

"Sorry. I got distracted. There are these sapphires —"

"Good ones?" Kim liked her jewelry and had been a willing student when Tiffany taught the girls how to tell the real from the dross. "No, wait! You can't divert me. Is there something wrong in that place?"

Brandi glanced at the guys again. They were pointing down at an antique tiara and laughing. They looked youthful and carefree, and one laughed hard enough to start coughing. He sounded sick, like he had bronchitis, and the other pounded on his back. Brandi supposed the scarves might be because they were cold or ill. She didn't know why Mr. Nguyen wouldn't tell her if there was a problem.

And the sapphires drew her gaze like hot coals. "Everything's fine. Now let me look at these stones." Brandi accepted Mr. Nguyen's offer of his jeweler's glass. She wiped it carefully, then held it to her eye. "Cornflower blue," she pronounced.

"From Kashmir," Mr. Nguyen said.

"From Kashmir," Kim echoed. "The best."

"One has an inclusion partially covered by the prong. The other has a blemish. I think they're real."

"They are real! Ask around. I have a good reputation. I don't rip off anyone!" Mr. Nguyen was obviously indignant. "One thousand!"

"Apiece?" she asked, incredulous about the price.

"For the pair!"

The sapphires were real, with the flaws only genuine stones contained. They were cornflower blue, the most desirable shade.

He wanted only a thousand, and just as pawnbrokers were known for buying low, they were also reputed to sell high.

Kim reflected Brandi's suspicion. "A thousand for the pair? Why?"

"It is my birthday, and a Vietnamese tradition to treat the first guest with honor on that day." Mr. Nguyen, who so far had been speaking and acting like an American born and raised, bowed like an Asian.

Caught by surprise, Brandi bowed back. "Happy birthday."

With a return to his businesslike demeanor, Mr. Nguyen said, "So I owe you seven thousand dollars — that's the eight for the ring minus the thousand for the sapphires. I'll cut you a check and wrap the earrings for you."

"Yes. Thank you." Into the phone Brandi said, "Maybe my luck has changed."

"I'll say!" Kim's enthusiasm was contagious. "What's the plan now?"

"What makes you think I have a plan?"

"Honey, you're a lawyer. You don't take a shit without a plan."

"Hey! That's not true. I can be spontaneous!" Sometimes. Once in a while. Occasionally.

"Yeah, yeah. You and your master lists and your daily lists and your daily planner and your PDA."

"You are such a bitch."

"Yes, I know, and what you are is the antithesis of *spontaneous*." Kim sounded wry, amused, and not at all offended.

After the divorce, Kim had been the older sister who helped Brandi through the trauma of losing her father, of seeing her mother fall apart, of eventually losing their house and of dealing with the slow, difficult drift down into poverty. Kim had been the one who insisted Brandi look forward and see that someday she would be able to take control of her own life and no longer be driven by circumstances.

Brandi scrutinized Mr. Nguyen as he slid the earrings into the holes in the display insert. He affixed the backs to the posts; then, noticing the way she watched him, he smiled and lifted the insert out of the box. "Do you want to wear them?" He held it out.

She did. They were so beautiful, and sapphires were reputed to bring good luck. Or bad luck; she couldn't remember. At this point, who cared? She would survive. She would prosper. She would make that son of a bitch Alan sorry.

She leaned over the mirror and inserted first one post, then the other into her pierced ears. "My God, Kim. They're fabulous." They *were* the same color as her eyes. Smiling into her reflection, she groped for the display insert and handed it back to Mr. Nguyen. She heard the click as he shut the case, and tore herself away from the enthralling sight of her ears in those gorgeous earrings. Straightening up, she accepted the small velvet box from Mr. Nguyen and stuck it into her pocket.

"Who do I make the check out to?" Mr. Nguyen asked quietly.

"Brandi Lynn Michaels." B-R-A-N-D-I L-Y-N-N . . ." Brandi spelled each name slowly and carefully.

"The plan," Kim demanded.

"I don't have any water at my house. I'm dirty and I'm tired of peeing in a frozen toilet. I'm taking this money. I'm going to a five-star hotel."

"Okay, I'll buy that." But Kim sounded cautious, as if she heard something awry in Brandi's tone.

"I'm getting myself a suite on the concierge level. I'm going to bathe in a huge tub; then I'm going down to the shops on the Miracle Mile and I am buying myself the best dress ever. Red. I'm going to buy red, one that shows off my cleavage."

"If I had your cleavage I'd show it off all

the time," Kim said.

"With touches of blue so I can wear my sapphires." She smiled as she contemplated her next move. "I'm going to buy great underwear. Fancy, lacy panties and a bra that would make a statue drool."

The guys at the end of the counter stopped laughing and stared at her. Stared as if they were memorizing her figure.

She must have been talking a little too loud.

She didn't care. "Great shoes. I'm going to wear the highest heels, the most impractical fuck-me shoes ever created."

She accept the engraved check Mr. Nguyen handed her. It was for the right amount, and she shook it at him and beamed. "I'll be back!"

"Go on now." He made a shooing motion at her. His hands were really shaking now.

"Are you sick?" Brandi asked.

"Yes. Sick. You should go. Go!"

"Thanks. It's been great doing business with you." She headed for the door.

"I'm not going to like the next part of your plan, am I?" Kim asked.

"You always told me I was old before my time."

"Now I *know* I'm not going to like this."

Brandi stepped outside. The blast of cold

air felt as if it scoured the flesh off her face. "You always said I should do something wild while I was still young."

"*Now* you listen to me?" Kim moaned.

"I'm going to have a massage and a pedicure and a manicure and get dressed in all my glory." Brandi pulled her scarf close around her ears. "And I'm going to a huge, prestigious charity party at Charles McGrath's home."

"Don't do this," Kim warned.

"I'm going to pick up a man."

"This is not right," Kim said.

"And I'm going to have one fabulous night of sex to remember for the rest of my life."

FOUR

As the cab drove Brandi deeper into Kenilworth's wooded streets, a pang of guilt
struck her. With its old-fashioned lamp-
posts, its huge estates, and the mansions set
back among the trees, Kenilworth was the
epitome of the classic old-money neighborhood. "Wow," she murmured. "Mother
would love this."

"What?" As he'd been doing since he
picked her up from the Tirra Spa on West
Erie, the driver glanced in his rearview mirror, then apparently decided he didn't care
about restraint or public safety, and stared.

Not that she didn't appreciate the proof
that the spa makeup artist and hairstylist
had both been brilliant, but she truly didn't
want to hike the miles to Uncle Charles's
house because the driver had hit a lamp-
post. Not in stiletto heels. "Look out!" she
said.

He whipped his head around and stared

into the evening shadows. "What?"

"Oh. I thought I saw a dog." Not true, but at least he was peering forward again.

"A . . . dog?" He swerved, his already awful driving exacerbated by her warning. "These people in here are so rich they'll get your license taken away for hitting their dog. Can you imagine?"

Yes, she could imagine very easily. To take her mind off the peril she faced with every screeching turn, she took out her phone and cradled it in her hand.

She still hadn't called her father. And she had to. And if she did it right now, he would probably be at dinner and wouldn't answer, and if by bad luck he did, she could be on the phone only until she got to the party.

Part of any plan for calling her father always included an impending reason to hang up and the good possibility that she could leave a message.

"Are you warm enough?" The cabby's hand crept toward the heat to turn it off.

"Barely." Tiny gold straps curled around her feet and up her ankles, and she used her bare, red-polished toes as the excuse to demand warmth. Actually, with her London Fog buttoned and belted, she was comfortable, but she wasn't about to admit that. The heater had two speeds, full-blast and off, and when it was off the windows frosted over so quickly the driver couldn't see.

Not that that seemed to worry him.

Closing her eyes for a moment, she took a few calming breaths and punched Daddy's number.

He answered. *Bad luck.*

"Daddy, it's Brandi." She kept her voice cheerful and warm, a direct contrast to the cold roiling in her belly.

"Oh. Brandi. What do you need?"

She'd obviously caught him in the middle of something. He had that I'm-too-busy-to-bother tone going. "I don't need anything, Daddy. I called to wish you happy birthday."

"Yeah. Thanks."

Keep the conversation rolling, Brandi. "What are you doing to celebrate?"

"I'm working."

"Oh. Well." What a surprise. When she was a kid, he'd missed more birthday parties — hers, his, Tiffany's — than he'd made. "I arrived in Chicago safely."

"You did, huh?" She heard him shuffling papers. "How's the job going?"

"I haven't started yet. I start on Monday."

He grunted. "That'll be interesting. I'll bet they've never had a ballerina working at McGrath and Lindoberth before."

"I haven't taken ballet lessons since I was

thirteen." When Tiffany had run out of the alimony money and they'd had to make a choice between ballet and eating.

"Bullshit. You took it in college. Stupid thing to do. Why didn't you take a sport? That would have taught you some back-bone, some competitive spirit."

"Dance isn't stupid, Daddy." Of course, it wasn't dance that he considered stupid. It was her, and he took every chance to make sure she knew it.

She didn't know why she cared; she knew it wasn't true. Yet when he used that cold, lashing tone, he took her back to that moment fourteen years ago when he'd walked out on her and her mother, and all the anguish she'd felt rushed back and she shivered with the pain of an abandoned child.

"Yeah. How's McGrath?"

"I'll see Uncle Charles tonight. Shall I give him your regards?"

"Sure. The old coot doesn't like me, but what the hell. It's always good to keep up connections." Someone spoke to him. A woman. His secretary, maybe, or his newest lover, or both. "Listen, Brandi, I'm busy. Call me back after you've started the job and let me know whether you're putting that damned expensive law degree to use."

Sometimes she just wanted to wring his fat neck. "Daddy, *you* convinced me to borrow the money from you rather than use a student loan. You said it made sense because you wouldn't charge me interest."

"I didn't say I didn't want to get paid," he shot back.

"I'll pay you," she said softly.

"You bet you will."

The driver said, "Hey, is this where I turn in?"

He veered so suddenly that her shoulder hit the door. "I hope to God." She had never meant anything so devoutly. She wanted out of this cab. She wanted off this phone call. And not necessarily in that order. She spoke into the receiver. "Daddy, I have to go. Talk to you later."

But he'd already hung up.

The cab passed through the open iron gate and tore up Uncle Charles's long, softly lit driveway at thirty miles an hour.

Viciously she shoved her phone into her bag. She could feel her cheeks burning. Damn her father. He always made her feel like some kind of shiftless no-account mooch. She should never have borrowed the law school money from him. Even when she'd done it, she knew it was the wrong thing, that he had offered it only so he would keep the power to manipulate her. But like the sucker she always was about him, she hoped that this time he'd offered because he'd realized, at last, that he cared about her.

Sucker.

The driver slammed on his brakes ten feet past the wide, curving stairway that led to the front door. "Thirty-seven twenty-five," he said, pointing at the meter.

"Back up to the door." She articulated each word in tones so clear they rang like struck lead crystal. She was in no mood to take shit from any man, much less a cab-driver who tried to cheat her by going the wrong way and then kill her with his ineptitude.

He started to object, but he looked in the rearview mirror one last time, and something of her simmering rage must have shown through her still mask, for he slammed it in reverse and got her to the right spot.

A man in a long, dark coat and dark hat decorated with an escutcheon waited to assist her. Was he . . . a footman?

He was.

He opened the door.

A blast of cold air hit her.

He extended his gloved hand. "Welcome,

Miss . . . ?"

"Miss Michaels. Miss Brandi Michaels."

He touched his gloved hand to his hat. "Miss Michaels, Mr. McGrath asked that I extend a special welcome to you. He's looking forward to seeing you."

"Thank you." Oh, yes, Tiffany would *definitely* enjoy this.

Brandi handed him her brand-new Louis Vuitton duffel bag and shoved two twenties at the cabdriver. "Keep the change."

"Hey, that's only three bucks tip. I got you here in a hurry!"

"And I wanted to be late." Taking the footman's hand, she lifted herself out of the warm cab and into the frigid Chicago winter.

In these shoes she was over six feet tall — five inches taller than the footman and two inches taller than Alan. Not that she cared about *that,* but for the first time in four years she didn't have to cater to some man's ego.

She looked up at the well-lit exterior of the stone English Tudor home.

The house spread its wings wide in both directions. Its conical towers rose four stories, and the stones were arranged in fantastic patterns, with half-timber work and roofs and gables that swooped and rose to delight her eyes.

She knew Uncle Charles's history; he'd bought the house for his wife — they'd delighted in decorating and entertaining — and when she'd passed away over ten years ago, he'd mourned sincerely. He'd called to talk to Tiffany occasionally; he seemed to feel she understood, and in some ways Brandi supposed she did. After all, death was a kind of abandonment, too.

"Go on in, Miss Michaels," the footman advised. "It's thirty below and the wind's starting to kick up."

She shuddered at the report and hurried up the steps. A tall, burly man with a shaved head and frosty blue eyes surrounded by pale eyelashes held the wide door open for her. She sighed in delight as the heat of the foyer enveloped her.

"May I see your invitation, please?"

Brandi glanced at his name tag. Jerry. Security. And everything a security man should be: He was muscled, his suit was black, his shirt was white, his tie was gray. Two black men and one Asian woman, all dressed precisely like him and with similar impassive expressions, stood in the foyer waiting to welcome other guests.

That, more than anything, told Brandi how many important people were attending this event to raise money for the Art Institute of Chicago. Uncle Charles feared party crashers, and wanted no violent incidents involving his very wealthy clients and friends.

Brandi stood, poised and calm, while Jerry examined her invitation, the guest list, and her face.

Behind her, a well-groomed older Hispanic couple stepped into the door and were treated to the same scrutiny by another security man.

"Miss Michaels, would you mind if I went through your, er, satchel?" Jerry indicated her bag.

"Feel free." She handed him her duffel.

The other couple shed their coats and watched curiously as her guard placed her bag on the elegantly fragile Queen Anne table against the wall and popped the latch.

This place was beautiful. Everything was big, tall, expansive — the shining parquet floor, the Old World portraits of stiffly posed, bewigged nobles, the wood-paneled walls. As she admired the newly discovered mahogany on the curved stairway, the crystal chandelier sparkling two stories above her head, and the carved Chinese rugs, her toes curled. The house was as glamorous as Tiffany had hoped.

She made note of the details to tell her

mother — the mother she had yet to inform of her broken engagement.

Of course, Brandi had spent the day luxuriating in a much-needed bath, massage, manicure and pedicure, spray tan, haircut and -style, the biggest shopping spree in which she'd ever indulged. . . . It was amazing how quickly one could spend seven thousand dollars when one was determined.

Oh, and she'd spent time arguing with Kim about the execution of her plan. Kim, who'd become surprisingly stodgy when it came to her younger sister's morals.

Who'd had time to call Tiffany?

The faint sound of choking brought her attention back to Jerry.

His broad shoulders stiffened. A slow, bright red crept up his pale skin from his necktie to his receding hairline.

Good. She hoped he was embarrassed. She understood the need for him to search her bag, but she didn't have to like it.

He swallowed as he lifted the brief, thin scrap of silk and lace that would cover her breasts so erotically. She knew it would; she'd tried it on in the shop, as well as the other various sheer undergarments and bits of hedonistic sleepwear.

He tried to refrain from looking at her,

but he lost the battle. His brown gaze darted over her bosom.

He saw nothing but a woman huddled in her black London Fog. As much as she would have liked to appear swathed in a gossamer cape, she refused to go out in this godforsaken Chicago deep freeze without her heaviest coat — and even it wasn't heavy enough.

He pulled his hand free of the bag as if escaping some fatally baited trap. "Okay. Do you want to, um, check the bag? I mean, do you want to check it so you don't have to carry it? You know, get a check tag so you can have it when you leave?"

"That would be delightful." She kept her voice pitched at that tone she'd heard her mother use so many times when she wanted a man to do something for her. "Jerry, would you take care of that for me?"

"Yeah." He pulled at the collar that circled his linebacker-size neck.

"And my coat, too?" She fluttered her eyelashes, the ones with the mascara the makeup artist had promised was like tar.

"Oh, yeah," he said.

When the other guards coughed and shuffled, he realized how he'd been manipulated. Looking stern, he said, "The checkroom is right over there. . . ."

She smiled into his eyes.

In disgust he said, "Oh, never mind. Just give me the coat. I'll do it."

She unbelted the coat. Unbuttoned it. Taking a deep breath, she slid it off her shoulders and down her arms.

The silence in the foyer was profound.

She looked around. Jerry's mouth was hanging open. One black security guy had his arm braced against the wall. The other had taken a step forward. The Asian security guard was smiling as if she'd just had a vision — Brandi hadn't realized she was a lesbian, but obviously she was. And of the Hispanic guests, the husband looked enthralled and the wife furious.

So Mother was right. A red dress worked.

A long, silk, sleeveless scarlet dress with, as Mr. Arturo said, "Two really elegant design features, darling, and both of them hold up the bodice."

Of course she was wearing underwear — a thong — and her stiletto heels, and a crystal blue bracelet and those sapphire earrings, those great sapphire earrings. But she hadn't been absolutely sure whether she'd achieved the effect she sought.

Until now.

Yes, it appeared this dress, this body, and these shoes could stun every race, every economic strata, and both sexes. In any language, she called that success.

Unfortunately none of these men were candidates for her plan.

She'd made a list of her requirements.

She wanted a man who was handsome, mature, rich, discreet, and most important of all, from out of town. That way, with any luck, she would never see him again.

Even if she did, she was determined not to care. Nobody cared about their honor or their reputation anymore — witness Alan — so she sure as hell didn't, either.

A large arch led to a broad hall, and from beyond Brandi heard the chatter of men's and women's voices and the clink of glasses. She strolled through and into the reception.

The crowded room was painted a creamy gold, with one wall of bookcases rising to the tall ceiling. A log fire blazed in the immense stone fireplace on the far wall. Large, gilt-framed mirrors reflected the beautiful people who mingled, smiling, holding champagne glasses, and posing for photos. The men were in tuxedos, the women in black and sometimes a subdued blue. She was the only one in scarlet.

Good. Let them notice her. Let them all notice her.

As she stood in the doorway, conversations faded first nearby, then rippling out from the epicenter that was *her.*

She took a long, slow breath that allowed her breasts to swell above the low neckline and eased the breathlessness that came with knowing that she stood here alone when she should have been on the arm of her fiancé. Alone because she'd been a fool. Because she had believed she could write a grocery list of the qualities she required in a man and check them off as if he were a hothouse cucumber.

She took another long breath and smiled, a smile that glittered and beckoned, a smile she hoped would disguise her rage and project sexual readiness to all the eligible men in the room.

And it must have worked, for a dozen tailored suits started in her direction — then halted when Uncle Charles broke free of the crowd with his hands outstretched.

Her smile became one of genuine pleasure, and she took his hands.

Charles McGrath was a dapper seventy years old with a shining bald head, sagging jowls, and a glorious smile. Years of criminal law hadn't dimmed his enthusiasm for life, and the spring in his step and his frank appreciation for beauty attracted both friends and women. He was a bit of a chauvinist —

he'd been amazed that Brandi could succeed so well in law school, and then that she wanted to work after marriage. But he had gamely subdued his male protective instinct and assigned her to Vivian Pelikan, one of the nation's foremost — and most ruthless — criminal lawyers.

Now he spread her arms wide and looked at her with a twinkle in his brown eyes. "You are stunning. Forgive me for saying so — I know no young woman should be compared to another woman — but you'll permit an old man a little reminiscence."

"Of course." She already knew what he was going to say.

"You remind me of the first time I saw your mother. She was eighteen and the most glorious creature I had ever seen. I would have swooped in, but I was married at the time and had foolish ideas of fidelity."

"Good for you." She must have been a little fierce, for he looked taken aback. She stepped forward and pressed her cheek to his. More quietly, she said, "I mean, that's rare these days."

He misunderstood. Of course he did. He didn't know about Alan.

"Your father's a fool. To leave a treasure like Tiffany for another woman —" He broke off. "But none of that tonight. You *do*

71

look stunning. Who would have thought when I first met you at the age of three pirouetting around your father's office in a leotard and tutu that you would grow so tall and so beautiful?"

"Oh, yes. Ballerina Brandi." The memories that gave Uncle Charles such pleasure made her want to writhe. "I danced up until the time the boys complained they couldn't lift me because I was taller than them." That wasn't strictly the truth, but this was neither the time nor the place for her more truthful and bitter reminiscences.

Uncle Charles threw back his head and laughed aloud. "Now you have the revenge. What happens to this magnificent dress if you let out your breath?"

"Your party gets a lot more interesting."

"Breathe in," he advised. "I'm too old to handle a stampede in my house. Now where's your fiancé? I expected to see him."

She gave the response she'd been practicing, the one that said so much and so little. "You know he's a resident."

"He'll be sorry he missed you looking like this!"

"He already is sorry." *A sorry, deceitful son of a bitch.* "He just doesn't know it yet." Time to change the subject. "Uncle Charles,

I haven't been to your home before. It's stunning!"

"Thank you." Uncle Charles tucked her hand into his arm and walked her into the crowd. "It's a work in progress, but it's so big. Most days I rattle around here all alone. I miss having a special someone in the house."

"I'm sorry." She hesitated, then presumed on an old family friendship. "Perhaps it's time to find someone else."

"I think you're right. Now have you viewed my coup d'état?" He beamed and steered Brandi toward the far wall.

Spotlights were focused on some exhibit.

"What is it?" she asked.

"You'll see." Uncle Charles worked his way inward, carrying Brandi along in his wake. "Excuse me."

"It's gorgeous, Charles." A contemporary of Uncle Charles's clapped him on his shoulder.

"Thanks, Mel," Uncle Charles said. "I didn't know if I was going to get it until the last minute."

"Wow! That was freaking wonderful. Great job, Mr. McGrath." Eyes shining, a young woman grabbed Uncle Charles's hand, shook it hard, then wiggled her way toward the bar.

He looked after her and shook his head, smiling. "I have no idea who that was."

The crowd grew more tightly packed, the comments more numerous.

"Beautiful exhibit, Charles."

"Extraordinary to see it up so close."

At last he and Brandi reached the front. A velvet cord held the guests back from a glass case surrounded by spotlights, and inside the case was a necklace, the kind of necklace that would make any sane woman's heart beat more quickly.

Brandi was very sane.

Set in antique platinum and surrounded by white diamonds, massive in their own right, was the most immense sparkling blue stone Brandi had ever seen.

"It doesn't even look real," she said in awe. "What is it?"

"Oh, it's real, all right," Uncle Charles said. "That's the largest blue diamond in the Russian royal jewels. That, my dear, is the Romanov Blaze."

FIVE

"The Romanov Blaze is part of the traveling exhibition currently on exhibit at the Chicago Museum," Uncle Charles told an awed Brandi. "It was given to Empress Alexandra by Czar Nicholas when she told him she was pregnant with their fifth child. It's reputed to be bad luck, and indeed, seven months later Crown Prince Alexis was born with hemophilia."

"Which helped bring about the fall of the royal family," Brandi whispered.

Everyone in the crowd was whispering as if they were in church, as if the presence of such beauty required reverence.

The diamond's cold beauty and dreaded curse mesmerized and beckoned.

But four burly men who looked like Jerry stood on each corner of the exhibit, and she didn't have a doubt that if she, or anyone here, made a move toward that jewel all hell would break loose.

"It's extraordinary, Charles." A middle-aged woman in an elegant black sleeveless gown and her own glittering stones couldn't keep her gaze off the Romanov Blaze. "How much is it worth?"

Uncle Charles tucked his thumbs into his lapels. "Colleen, in its present incarnation, with the weight of its history behind it, it's priceless. If it were stolen and cut into a few smaller stones, it could be worth forty million, more or less."

"Surely no one would cut that magnificent diamond!" Colleen protested.

"It can't be sold as is except to a collector, and the chances of being caught with it are too great. If it's cut, it's not easy to identify, and there's a market for stones of this purity."

Brandi was impressed. Uncle Charles knew his stuff.

He turned back to Brandi and lowered his voice. "Security was a bear, but at the last minute I managed to bring in enough guards to satisfy the Russians and the museum. Even with that, I had to tell the museum directors the Blaze would double the donations to support the exhibits. Those people know this stuff; I don't know what got into them to think of refusing."

The grim edge to his mouth told her more

clearly than his words how poorly Uncle Charles had taken their rejection, and she suspected he'd bludgeoned them with the threat that he would withdraw his support unless they yielded. This was a side of Uncle Charles she never saw, but she knew must exist.

His guests sucked up to him. The museum and the Russians had capitulated to his demands. He was, after all, a very powerful man, and used to getting his own way.

"Might as well leave room in front for the newcomers." Taking Brandi's arm, he led her out of the crowd and signaled to the man they'd met on the way in. "Brandi, have you met Mel Colvin, one of our senior partners?"

"No, we haven't met," Brandi said. "But I've admired his work on Nolan versus Chiklas."

"How kind of you!" Mel smiled broadly and took her hand. "Charlie, you old rascal, is this the lady you were telling me about?"

"No! We've hired Brandi to work criminal law." Uncle Charles glared at Mel.

"Oh. Oh! Good to meet you, young lady." As if he'd lost interest, Mel gave her fingers a perfunctory squeeze, leaving Brandi confused by his sudden change in mood, and turned back to Uncle Charles. "But is the lady you told me about coming?"

"Not tonight. Not yet." Uncle Charles quickly turned Brandi to another guest, a petite, toned, attractive female in a full-length black Vera Wang knockoff. "This is Shawna Miller, McGrath and Lindoberth's able head receptionist."

Shawna shook Brandi's hand, but the chill she projected rivaled the deep freeze outside. She did *not* approve of Brandi. "That dress you're wearing would be fabulous at, say, the Academy Awards!" Shawna said.

Meaning, of course, that it was a bad choice for a charity dinner hosted by a law firm.

But Tiffany had imparted many lessons to her unwilling daughter, including how to handle short, hostile women.

Brandi leaned close to Shawna's ear and in a whisper advised, "Try ABS next time. They make divine knockoffs at a reasonable price."

She had to give Uncle Charles credit: He recognized undercurrents when he saw them, and before Shawna could give vent to her swelling fury, he dove into the fray. "Have some champagne." He handed Brandi a glass from a passing tray, then directed her to an attractive, older, African-

American woman. "You know Vivian Pelikan."

"Indeed I do. It's always an honor, Mrs. Pelikan." Vivian Pelikan was one of the first black women to break through the glass ceiling and become a senior law partner, and she'd done it solely with sheer brilliance and drive. She wore her graying hair cropped short, and her lively brown eyes danced; she'd obviously heard the exchange between Shawna and Brandi.

Mrs. Pelikan shook Brandi's hand. "You've come just in time, Miss Michaels. We're starting an exciting new case on Monday, and I've put you on the team."

"I look forward to that," Brandi said. "It's an honor to work with you."

"Let me introduce my husband, an architect with Humphreys and Harper."

"How good to meet you, Mr. Pelikan."

"Mr. Harper," he corrected, but he smiled and introduced her to his partner, Mr. Humphreys, who fit all her criteria for a lover except that a) he lived in Chicago and b) he looked like a bug-eyed frog.

Brandi's wild, flaming affair would be conducted with the bedroom lights blazing, and for that she needed a man who lifted weights, who had a dusting of dark hair on tanned skin, and whose chest hadn't descended into his drawers. So she smiled, allowed Uncle Charles to mention her fiancé, and when he had moved off to welcome more arrivals, she continued to work her way deeper into the crowd, searching for the jewel of a lover hidden somewhere among the tuxedos and metrosexuals.

She met a lot of fellow employees at the law firm. Tip Joel, Glenn Silverstein, Sanjin Patel. Sanjin had been friendly until she'd made it clear she wasn't interested in an affair with a coworker. Tip and Glenn had taken one look at her and decided she'd traded on her sexuality or her family friendship with Uncle Charles or both to get her position in the firm.

When she went in to work, they would learn. They were men. Men like Alan. She'd crush them like bugs beneath her pointed heels.

She moved with the ebb and flow of the pack into the next room, a large reception hall where the caterer was setting up the buffet. The huge mirrors on the walls reflected the china, the silver, the dancing motions of the waiters as they waltzed through the crowd offering hors d'oeuvres. A bar was set up in each corner, and there Brandi lingered, searching for the Man.

She met a lot of lawyers and businessmen

from across the city and the country. Something was wrong with each one. They were local, they were unattractive, and if they were handsome, then they were married. . . .

Most of them were married, and seemed very willing to sleep with her regardless. The deceitful bastards.

After two hours of serious searching, she found herself leaning an elbow on the bar, sipping her second glass of champagne and morosely conversing with Gwynne Durant, a junior lawyer from the firm whose physician husband was at this moment delivering a baby. Gwynne thought she and Brandi were alone for the same reason, and felt sorry for them both.

Brandi didn't disabuse her. Gwynne would find out the truth soon enough. Everyone would find out that Alan had been sleeping with Fawn, got her pregnant, and got married while engaged to Brandi. Brandi could hardly wait for the snickering to start.

Feeling vaguely ill, she put down the champagne and stared as the golden bubbles detached themselves from the side of the glass, rose, and popped.

Her feet hurt, and for what? For nothing. Among all the wealthiest, most handsome, most educated men in Chicago, she could find no one to help her forget Alan. To forget his deceit, her humiliation, the incredible disappointment.

She smiled bitterly as she listened to Gwynne's rambling commentary on marriage to a doctor and the sacrifices she'd made for his career, and reflected that Kim would be relieved to hear that Brandi would spend the night alone huddled under a comforter in a chaste bedroom in Uncle Charles's house.

"They're starting the buffet," Gwynne said. "I had hoped Stan would get here in time to eat with me. I know it's not a big deal, but it's nice to have a guy to stand with you so you don't look like the world's biggest loser — *Oh, my God.* It's the count!"

Gwynne's tone made Brandi straighten away from the bar. "The count?"

"Roberto Bartolini. He's an Italian count."

"You mean like Count Chocula?" *A count. C'mon.*

"No. How can you look at that man and think children's cereal? All I can think is slow hands and hot sweat."

Brandi had been disappointed so often tonight, she couldn't work up the energy to turn and take a look. She just hunched a shoulder and took another sip of her drink.

But Gwynne burbled on. "I heard him talk on the news. He has this voice like Sean

Connery, only Italian. He has only the faintest accent" — Gwynne measured his accent between her thumb and forefinger — "but you know he's not American because of the words he uses."

"Italian words?" Brandi asked sarcastically.

"No, English words, but . . . you know . . . *long* words."

"Like spaghetti?" *Wow.* Sarcasm was becoming a way of life.

"*No.* Flattering words. Words you don't hear every day. Like magnificent. And postmodernism. And . . . I don't know . . . ancestry. He uses words like an artist uses a brush."

"All right. Fine." Gwynne was in such an ecstasy of awe, amusement and genuine panting lust, Brandi took a chance, swiveled on one her of stiletto heels — and froze.

The crowd had parted, and there he was — sex in an Armani suit. Roberto Bartolini was tall, at least six-four, with shoulders that made ballerina Brandi imagine how easily he would lift her, spin with her, hold her. . . .

"See? What did I tell you?" Gwynne fiercely poked Brandi in the ribs.

He was Johnny Depp without the eyeliner. Like a pirate, he stood and surveyed the room from beneath dark, hooded eyes that looked amused and unsurprised by the interest he roused. His shoulder-length dark hair was swept back from his tanned face, leaving the stark compilation of features unadorned and glorious, like a harsh and savage mountain range. His mouth was a wide slash; his lips were full, firm, supple, the kind that made Brandi, and every other woman in the room, shiver with anticipation.

More than that, he carried himself like a man who knew his worth and was certain of his welcome. He had more than money, more than breeding, more than looks.

He radiated charisma. And power.

"Is he married?" Brandi demanded.

"No, but what difference does that make? You're engaged. I'm married. We can only look at the menu; we can't order off it."

That's what you think.

"Not that I'm complaining or anything. I mean, Stan's a good guy, but he can't compete with Roberto Bartolini. Look at him. He's rich. He's foreign. He's a world traveler, and he just got in from Italy."

Uncle Charles walked toward Roberto with his hand outstretched, pleasure in every step.

With a slight smile, Roberto shook his hand, and Brandi caught her breath at another glorious aspect of Mount — or rather, *Count* — Bartolini.

Gwynne moved closer and wiggled as she prepared to impart the most important piece of information. "And *get this* —"

"Sh." Brandi laid her hand on Gwynne's arm. "Be quiet and let me enjoy the view." And soak in the fact that fate had, for once, played fair with Brandi.

He was the one. He was the Matterhorn and she was going to scale him.

Placing her glass on the bar, she stood the way they'd taught her in ballet class: arms softly curved, back straight, chest out. Her scarlet gown glowed like a jewel among the black fashions. She glittered with rage and the need for revenge. And she looked at Roberto Bartolini. Compelled him to look back at her.

His head turned as if he heard her summons. He sought her in the crowd.

She knew he would see her.

The instant he focused on her, a thrill shot up her spine.

He took in the sight of her quickly, then with lingering appreciation.

Then he looked into her eyes.

Gwynne's babbling faded from Brandi's consciousness. She brought air into her lungs. Her heart pumped. Her sexuality stirred. She was, for the first time in her life, a creature of instinct, concentrating on one thing and one thing only — the satisfaction of her own body. And without words, this man with his smoky sensuality and smoldering eyes promised he would give it to her.

Noticing nothing, Uncle Charles stepped between them and waved a hand toward the diamond's display case.

Roberto's response was all that a host could wish, but he stepped aside so once again he could see all of her.

She smiled at him, a faint, feminine taunt.

"Love 'em and leave 'em . . . reputation in the 'love 'em' part is terrific." The volume control on Gwynne's voice must have been broken, because Brandi could hear only a few phrases.

"Yes," Brandi breathed. "I know." Deliberately she turned and strolled slowly toward the corridor that led to the private living quarters. She paused in the doorway. How long, she wondered, would it take him to find her?

Six

Roberto wondered what the woman wanted.

He wondered if he would give it to her.

If it was what he was hoping, he would. Who could resist a magnificent creature like that? Her hair was caught in a loose chignon at the back of her head, and strands of bright gold brushed her cheeks and kissed her rosy lips. Her scarlet gown stood out among the sleek sophisticates with their everlasting, dreary black. Her body made him catch his breath — all long, long legs, rounded hips, narrow waist, and a bosom that would have made Botticelli weep with joy. From this distance, Roberto couldn't discern the color of her eyes, but the expression in them challenged him. Beckoned him.

"Thank you for coming, Roberto."

Roberto jerked his attention to Charles McGrath, the head of his law team.

"Your presence will add a most interesting element to the mix here." Charles's eyes twinkled with mischief.

"No, thank *you* for having me. Not all men would have the courage to court such notoriety."

Charles laughed. "The promise of meeting you and your notoriety got many of these guests here and their wallets opened."

"For such a good cause, I am honored to be of assistance." Roberto liked the older man. Charles McGrath was a remarkable combination of kindness and ruthlessness, shrewdness and hospitality. Certainly he knew how to summon stunning women to his parties.

"Shall I let her at you?" Charles asked.

For a moment Roberto thought Charles meant the lady in red. But no, a female in her late thirties stood not far away, staring at him in the manner of a ravenous crocodile.

"Of course. I'm here to meet your guests." Roberto glanced again at the lady in red and allowed himself a moment of cold logic.

Fate was not usually so kind as to offer, without strings, an anonymous woman of beauty for his delectation. So the strings must be there. Invisible, but there nonetheless. "As you have instructed me, I must be careful what I say to reporters. How will I recognize them?"

"All of them are wearing their press identification badges," Charles said.

"Ahhh." The lady in red had not been wearing a badge.

"The badges are big, they're white, and they're obvious. I personally made sure of that, and made it clear the consequences to their newsgroup should anyone remove them. The women aren't happy about that — they complain the badges ruin the cut of their gowns — but I say that's the price of doing the job." Charles lowered his voice. "I know I'm an old curmudgeon, but I liked the days when men had the tough jobs and women were more decorative."

"Ah, didn't we all? Now so many of them insist on using their brains for things other than pleasing their men. It is a disgrace." Roberto chuckled, amused by his own chauvinism.

But Charles didn't chuckle. He nodded. He was, like Roberto's father in Italy, of a different generation.

With an eye to the magnificent creature in the red gown, Roberto said, "But I do beg your pardon. I may have to retire early. I fear I suffer from jet lag."

"Of course. An hour of genial conversation should do it."

"I'll make the hour count." Roberto

exchanged a smile with Charles. He glanced toward the lady in red and saw her disappear into the depths of the house. He took a step after her.

Then the best of Chicago society rushed him. They did so elegantly, of course, with more class than the paparazzi, but still they rushed.

Charles introduced Amanda Potter, one of Chicago's leading architects. She flashed her smile and her bosom. "Mr. Bartolini, I'm so pleased. I've never had the pleasure of meeting a real . . . Italian count before."

The woman was too old to successfully carry off *coy,* but Roberto bowed over the hand she extended to him — the hand sporting a ring with a handsome emerald in a white-gold setting.

"What a striking stone." He touched it lightly. "From Colombia and, of course, two point one carats."

She gasped in amazement. "That's . . . that's absolutely right."

While the crowd murmured, Roberto allowed his gaze to touch each face and then each jewel. Some guests stepped back. Most pressed forward.

A party trick. He performed nothing but a party trick, but it impressed them.

And when his duty was done, he would

follow that gorgeous lady in red.

More women greeted him with flutters and flattery. Men shook his hand and expressed their admiration. The press followed, cameras at ready. Everyone wanted to pose with him for photos.

Charles steered him toward the right people, introducing him to the mayor of Chicago, two senators, and the fashionista who hosted a reality television show teaching American women proper fashion sense.

He did not like her. She despised her audience. She was insolent and rude.

But she liked him. She fawned on him, putting her stamp of approval on him. "Mr. Bartolini, you look fabulous in that suit. Armani, isn't it?"

For *this* he was not pursuing the woman in scarlet? "I don't know. I don't pay any attention to names. It's so bourgeois, don't you think?" He smiled into her eyes, mocking her pretensions.

She drew back. She didn't like him anymore, and she attacked like the beast she was. "So, Mr. Bartolini — or should I call you Count?"

"Mr. Bartolini will do."

"Are you going to go look at the Romanov Blaze?"

"The Romanov Blaze?" He cast a deliberately bewildered glance around him. "What is that?"

As he intended, the crowd laughed. He walked toward the display case, away from that dreadful female, and he found himself anticipating his first glimpse of one of the grandest diamonds in history. He enjoyed seeing the guards tense as he approached, and quickly assessed the security they'd rigged up. Very impressive. Lasers and pressure pads, not to mention the heavy-set, cold-eyed guards. He acknowledged them with respectful nods — his grandfather had taught him to show respect to those assigned to futile missions.

They nodded back, hulking men who itched to tackle him on any pretext.

And there it was, glittering beneath the spotlights — the Romanov Blaze. It sparkled with hypnotic splendor, and for one moment he forgot his surroundings and smiled to see such beauty.

But while he admired the diamond, it was cold and hard . . . unlike his magnificent creature. He wanted the woman in scarlet.

He had given Charles and his guests fifteen minutes. Fifteen minutes of being suave, continental, mysterious, everything they wanted and expected.

Now he excused himself and walked down

the hall after the mystery wrapped in scarlet silk. He glanced into one doorway after another until he saw her, gleaming like a ruby in the dim setting of McGrath's library. She stood by the fireplace. She gazed into the flames, a faint smile on her lips, and in profile he could see the different facets of her beauty. In the firelight, her pale skin glowed like burnished gold. She'd taken off her shoes, yet she was still tall, the kind of woman with whom he could dance — among other things — and still look in her face. Her hand clasped the mantel, and her upraised arm proved she took her health seriously, lifting weights to sculpt her bare shoulders. The silk gown caressed her body, outlining the lift of her breasts and her bottom.

His eyes had not misled him. She was, indeed, a magnificent creature.

Turning her head, she observed him with such amusement it was clear she had known he stood there, and posed for him. And she wore only a thong beneath that silky gown — or if he were lucky, nothing at all. One-carat sapphires at her ears, yet her eyes contained a warmer blue flash than any cold stone.

"Glorious," he said.

"Thank you." She knew what he meant

and acknowledged it without false humility.

Stepping into the room, he shut the door behind him. "I think you want to talk to me."

She glanced down at the floor as if she sought the right words. Then she straightened her shoulders, turned fully to face him, and lifted her chin.

She looked, suddenly, less like the dream he'd been seeking all his life and more like a professional. A professor, or more likely a lawyer.

Or FBI?

Yes, of course. An agent from the FBI.

Abruptly his pleasure in the encounter cooled. Tucking his hand into his jacket pocket, he waited.

"For tonight, I would like to sleep with you," she said.

Roberto's hand clenched into a fist inside his pocket, and the flare of excitement lit again. Not FBI. Not unless they'd significantly changed their tactics.

"I have my reasons. I don't expect you to inquire about them. But I need . . . a night . . . a man . . . I need *you*. I've never done this before, so you don't need to worry about wearing a number or being a notch on my belt. You don't have to worry that I intend any kind of entrapment. My purpose is solely for my own pleasure. And yours, of course, I hope." She waited for a response with a stillness that betrayed fierce emotions tumbling beneath the surface.

Not FBI.

A groupie?

Possible.

The first spy placed by the Fosseras?

A theory worthy of note.

Or perhaps she was a gift from fate to offset the ruin of his good name.

She grew discomfited by his silence. Looking down, she searched out her shoes and donned them one at a time. "But before I continue, perhaps I should ask whether you're interested."

"Interested?" There wasn't a straight man in Chicago who wouldn't give his right arm to stand where Roberto was standing now. The crackle of the flames and the faint sound of her breathing broke the silence in the library. He strolled toward her, and when she lifted her head and shook the golden strands of hair away from her face, he smiled with all his charm. Lifting his hand, he let it hover an inch away from her chin. "May I?"

He had thought she would relax toward him. Instead, like a spinster schoolteacher allowing a liberty, she gave a stiff nod.

Ah. Not experienced. Not a groupie.

She smelled good, like a flower that bloomed in the night. Like a woman with secrets. Slowly he slid his fingers under her chin toward her right ear, taking pleasure in that first, all-important contact with her skin. The texture was as velvety as it looked, and warm with the heat of the fire and the heat of her need. He touched her earring, a gorgeous sapphire, then caressed her lobe, tucking her hair back. Like a cat, she turned her cheek into his hand.

A sensuous creature who liked to be stroked.

She watched him from the most amazing cornflower-blue eyes, her expression solemn, as if he were her teacher and she an earnest student. She had a way about her that nourished his ego — an ego his mother regularly told him needed no feeding.

Leaning over, he kissed her lightly, a brief brush of the lips. He wanted the slightest taste, an exchange of breath, to see if they were compatible . . . and with that, he wanted more. He pressed his finger on her full lower lip. "Are you worried that your lipstick will smear?"

"The makeup artist promised that when all the rest of me has turned to dust, the lipstick and the mascara will be left."

He grinned. She was funny.

But she didn't grin back. She was stating a fact. She pressed her hand to his chest — a touch firm with determination. "I would like a kiss. A real kiss. I want to know if it will be as good as I think, or if good sex is a myth fostered by movies and fed by loneliness."

A deliberate challenge? Perhaps. And perhaps she was ingenuous. Certainly love had cheated her somehow.

He still grinned as he leaned toward her again and gave her what she wanted. Lips parted, tongues meeting, sliding . . . for the first time in years, a mere kiss took the world away. He closed his eyes to better savor the taste of her — champagne first, then as he explored, her own flavor. Sweet brown sugar melted on uncertain yearning. Cool cream poured over warm desire.

She was like a grand cru wine from the vineyards of Bordeaux — expensive and worth every sip.

He forgot deliberation. He forgot restraint. He pulled her close, crushing the delicate material of her dress, craving the slide of silk against her bare skin. His other hand slid beneath the nape of her neck to hold her in place. He bent her back, holding her weight against him, and experienced her through his mouth, through his body, through the scent of her and her hold on his lapel.

A primitive part of him clawed to be free, to shove her skirt up, to push her down on the floor, to take her quickly, with all the need thrumming in his veins.

Some remnant of the gentleman he had once been made him release her, steady her with a hand on her elbow, and ask huskily, "Does that answer your question?"

She stood looking at him, blue eyes wide, fingers pressed to her lips. "Not a myth," she whispered.

"No." He wanted to laugh, but the effort of freeing her had strained something chivalrous inside him and he didn't dare push the issue. "No, good sex is not an illusion, but what's between us isn't good sex. It's more like a force of nature . . . or a trick fate has played on us both."

"Funny. I thought . . . *fate*. . . I thought that when I saw you."

"We are agreed. This is fate." How pleased his grandfather would be to know that Roberto proved himself half Contini after all! Wild. Reckless. Incorrigible. "So we'll spend the night together. You don't have to tell me why. I don't have to pretend to love you. And in the morning we'll part, never to see each other again." He'd never been rash before. Why now?

Ah, yes. Because his life had tilted sideways and everything he had known, everything he had been, had been knocked askew.

"All right. It's a deal." She extended her hand to shake his.

When he took it, he realized she trembled. He hoped not from nerves; he hoped from suppressed desire. Lifting her hand to his lips, he pressed a lingering kiss on the palm, then closed her fingers on it.

"But I don't want to be seen leaving together." For a woman who had been thoroughly kissed, she showed a practical streak.

For that matter, so did he. "I have to stay longer. To do less would be ungrateful to Mr. McGrath. So I'll call my driver. He'll pick you up when you step out the door. I'll tell the concierge at my hotel that you're coming." He handed her his passkey.

She looked down at the card in her hand. "Aren't you worried I'll steal something?"

With all the people who were watching him? "That is the last thing I'm worried about."

"Somehow I can't imagine that you're a trusting soul."

And she was a discerning soul. "Tonight I

will trust you with myself."

She inclined her head, not because she believed him, but because she accepted his right to prevaricate. She strolled toward the door, each motion of her body beneath the scarlet gown an enticement. "Don't change your clothes," he said.

She turned back in surprise. "But I bought the most gorgeous negligee."

Suspicion — some would call it good sense — rose in him again. "For me?"

"Yes. Well . . ." She shrugged. "For the man I found tonight. Luckily, it *is* you. The negligee is a cream silk with lace inserts here and —"

"I want to remove your gown," he whispered huskily. At his own instructions, desire hit him hard and low. The thought of seeking out the zipper of that enticing dress, sliding it down, seeing what was beneath it . . . He took a step toward her.

She saw his craving and chuckled, low and warm. "Remember, Roberto, you must stay at the party for another hour."

He did have to. He was in Chicago for one reason. No woman, however attractive, could change that.

"At midnight, you can turn into a pumpkin." Again she strolled toward the door.

He remembered what he didn't yet know,

and called, "What's your name?"

She leaned against the door frame, her body a beckoning silhouette, and smiled. "Brandi. I'm Brandi."

"Brandi?"

"Yes?"

"You go to my head."

Gwynne and a weary-looking man in a rumpled suit had engaged Uncle Charles in conversation. Gwynne's husband. Gwynne leaned against him, holding his hand, secure now that he was there, and Brandi worked her way across the floor toward them.

Gwynne and Stan turned away as Brandi approached. Gwynne tried to stop, but Stan tugged her toward the buffet table, and she gave Brandi a helpless wave and followed.

Brandi had Roberto on her mind, so when Gwynne looked back with pity in her eyes, Brandi didn't know what to think. Pity? For the woman about to spend the night with Roberto Bartolini? With a dismissive shrug, Brandi said, "Uncle Charles, I'm going to take my leave. I know I was going to stay, but the move . . . I have so much to do before Monday . . ." She tried to arrange her expression to weariness, and not show the guests, and certainly not Uncle Charles, that she'd just experienced the kiss of a lifetime. When she thought of it, of Roberto, she wanted to put her hand over her heart to feel it race and know, at last, that she was alive.

To her surprise, Uncle Charles didn't object. "I'll walk you to the foyer."

She was so relieved, she didn't notice the somber cast to his eyes. She got her things from the checkroom, and as he helped her into her coat, he said, "I was just talking to Stan Durant. You know he works at University Hospital."

"Yes." She buttoned her coat and wished Roberto were departing with her. Of course, they couldn't leave together, but it felt odd going to an assignation by herself.

"Stan says there are rumors flying around the hospital that your fiancé . . . that Alan . . ."

Uncle Charles had succeeded in capturing Brandi's attention.

". . . married some female in a Las Vegas wedding."

Busted! Busted, and now Uncle Charles was going to figure out why she was leaving, too. She probably had guilt written all over her face. "I . . . I didn't want to tell you. . . ."

"Dear, dear girl." He straightened her collar. "You were so brave to come here tonight when your heart is breaking."

"Breaking. Yes." Maybe guilt looked like suffering. Certainly she didn't feel as if her heart were breaking. More like she couldn't wait to make love with Roberto Bartolini.

"I'll let you go without another word" — Uncle Charles took her hand — "but promise you'll come to me if I can do anything to mend your grief."

"If I think of something, you'll be the first to know." Or not. Uncle Charles would never find out how she mended her grief; on that she was determined.

"Let me bring my car around for you."

"No!" She swallowed. "I mean, I've made arrangements for a car. But thank you; you've been very kind."

He held her in place and looked into her eyes. "Promise you won't be like your mother and let one bad apple spoil the whole crop. That lovely woman should have remarried years ago, and she won't take a chance and trust another man."

He was comparing her situation to her mother's. It was inevitable, she supposed, but how she hated it! "I won't. Good night, Uncle Charles." She kissed his papery cheek and picked up her bag.

"Your car's waiting, Miss Michaels." Jerry opened the door.

A blast of frigid wind took her breath away. She gasped, then hurried out. A long black limousine stood at the bottom of the steps. The driver stood holding the door. He must be freezing. As she slid in, he tipped his hat, then shut the door and hurried around the car.

A dim overhead light illuminated the interior of black leather and polished wood. The clean, new-car smell intoxicated her. She sank back and let the seat heater thaw her bones.

"I'm Newby, miss. I'll have you to the hotel in about a half hour." The driver had a British accent, and just like in the movies, he wore a billed cap. "Can I get anything for you before we start? A drink? Something to read? A phone or computer? We have satellite connection if you'd like to check your e-mail or surf the Net."

She was impressed. Of course she was impressed. "No, thank you, I'm going to sit back and enjoy myself."

"During the drive, if you desire anything, let me know."

"I will, thank you."

"There's a button right there to summon me." He rolled up the window between the seats, put the car in gear, and, unlike her cabbie, drove her smoothly down the road.

The luxury and the lack of reality enfolded her. She was on her way to an assignation with the man of her dreams, the assignation she'd successfully arranged for herself. Perhaps she had a career in labor negotiations. She'd made a bargain . . . but when Roberto had taken her hand, when he'd kissed her, he made it feel like more than a bargain.

Fate had given her just what she asked for.

Why did she choose this minute to remember that fate always required payment for her services?

SEVEN

The concierge didn't flinch when Brandi requested iced champagne, a bowl of fruit, and three dozen white candles. He asked only, "Scented or unscented? In jars? On stands?"

"Not scented, and a few in jars if necessary, but mostly I think simple pillar candles will do. Bring them in and place them . . ." She surveyed her temporary domain. Roberto occupied a corner suite on the top floor of the fifty-eight-story Resolution Hotel on Michigan Avenue.

She didn't like being up so high. Heights made her queasy. But as long as she didn't look out the window, everything was fine. More than fine. The ceilings in the sitting room and the bedroom soared two stories, and skylights showed the stars glittering bright and cold in the black of eternity. In the sitting room, the gas fireplace bathed the walls in a flickering golden glow.

Roberto's laptop, a marvel of technology with its custom case, sat on the antique desk. In fact, all the furniture looked antique, yet the seats were comfortable and included a backless sofa upholstered with a striped satin fabric and standing on clawed feet. "I think I'd like you to place them there on the table." She gestured toward that sofa.

"Behind the fainting couch?" the concierge asked.

"Yes. Exactly there. I'll distribute them. I'll need them in the next half hour."

"Of course." He bowed his way out.

Brandi waited until he'd shut the door before picking up her bag and tearing into the bathroom. She had her ablutions all planned out, and in less than forty-five minutes she had showered, shampooed, and slipped back into her scarlet dress and her gold shoes. She dried her hair and clipped it atop her head. She dabbed her neck and wrists with sandalwood- and orange-scented perfumes. She lit the candles and posed on the fainting couch, reclining on her side, her head propped up in her hand, the flames flickering around her, bathing her with sultry intent. She was confident she'd done everything to make this her night of sensual debauchery with the sexiest man in Chicago — a man of her choice.

Then Roberto walked in, and she realized she could control everything tonight . . . except him. In her carefully plotted scheme of revenge, he was the unknown element.

He stopped short at the sight of her. His hands flexed. His eyes narrowed.

A pirate.

He looked like a pirate.

He moved into the room, discarding his bow tie and jacket, and he didn't swagger, but he did . . . stalk. And he looked hungry.

Suddenly she felt less like a seductress and more like a maiden to be ravished.

But he sounded mild enough. "Do you like your accommodations?"

"I've never seen anything so lovely in my life. The view . . ." She gestured at the two gigantic corner windows where the lights of Chicago spread out like candles on a cake, and beyond that Lake Michigan was a dark blot in the icy night.

"Good." His already deep voice deepened more. "I want you to be happy."

"I am happy." She sat up a little straighter. "Very happy. That bathroom is the epitome of decadence. I could perform the solo from *Swan Lake* right there between the tub and the vanity." She was chatting, and all because her heart was beating faster.

This was what she wanted, wasn't it? The

chance to make love with a man every woman dreamed of?

Of course it was, but she hadn't taken into account that women dreamed of dangerous men. Surely an Italian count with a reputation for great sex wasn't dangerous, but right now, in the dark, knowing that soon their bodies would meld, he *seemed* dangerous.

In fact, now that she thought about it, he'd seemed dangerous at the party, but her own fury had insulated her from apprehension.

Now, torn between trepidation and a rapidly increasing awe, she chewed her lip and watched as he unbuttoned his shirt.

Clothed, he gave the impression of being tall and healthy, but his suit hid the cascade of muscled ribs, the ridged belly, the bulging arms. This man took working out to an art, and that surprised her. Most men who exercised to such a state of fitness worshiped their own bodies and had no time to admire a woman.

All Roberto's attention was fixed on her. It was almost intimidating to be the focus of so much attention. Intimidating . . . and exciting.

"On the way here, I convinced myself that my eyes had deceived me. I told myself there was no way you could be as magnificent as I remembered. But you . . . with your golden hair piled high on your head and the red silk caressing your glorious curves" — he smiled, and dimples pressed deep into his cheeks — "and those frivolous gold sandals, you look like a Roman feast."

"Do I?" Odd how easily her cold feet warmed under the sunshine of his praise.

He returned her to the time when she was eighteen, at college, and just learning of her potent sexual appeal. Tiffany had told her that youth was the greatest aphrodisiac of all, but until Brandi saw the senior frat boys sauntering toward her, one by one trying desperately to impress her, she hadn't realized how right her mother could be.

Then she'd met Alan, the sensible choice, and she'd done the right thing. She'd accepted his proposal. She'd been with him for four years, and somehow during that time the thrill of knowing she could smile and turn a man into a willing slave had vanished, leaving behind a female prosaic and almost weary.

Now Roberto caressed her with his deep voice, and called her magnificent, and she believed him.

Recalling her plans for seduction, she slithered back on the couch and stretched, her arms a graceful arch over her head, her breasts almost — almost! — slipping free of their restraint.

His harsh inhalation was a balm to her soul.

She released the clip that held her hair in place, and shook her head. The newly highlighted strands tumbled around her shoulders.

She barely saw him move, yet suddenly he was kneeling at her side.

"You're a Roman feast, and you convince me I'm a conquering gladiator." The warm, rich timbre of his voice had changed. He sounded guttural with desperation. With need. Catching her head in his broad hands, he held her still for his kiss — a kiss of rough desire, of tender desperation.

Where had he learned to kiss like this, with just the right pressure of his lips on hers, with a tongue that stroked the cavern of her mouth so expertly she felt a growing warmth between her legs? He lifted his lips, and she pressed her thighs together, trying to preserve the sensation.

But he was only moving up to kiss her eyelids, then over to suck her earlobe, then bite it with a gentle nip that made her gasp and struggle briefly.

"Did I injure you?" he murmured. When

she didn't answer right away, he drew back and wet his finger on his tongue, then slid it along her lower lip. "Darling, you have to instruct me. I never want to harm you. To tease you, to titillate you, to make you cry aloud with ecstasy. But hurt you, never."

"No. No, you didn't hurt me." Yet the sudden change from pure slick recklessness to the sharp edge of his teeth reminded her to be wary. She didn't know this man. He was big, far taller and broader than she had remembered. And the way he watched her, as if he were a predator and she his prey . . .

Yet when he said, "I only want to take you to the brink of pleasurable insanity," she learned she trusted him to take care of her — her body and her feelings — far more than she had trusted Alan for a long, long time. And she realized, also, that Roberto's voice, his accent, his words, and his care for her created warm havoc in her body.

Grasping the edges of his shirt, she pulled him up to her and kissed him. Kissed him as she had never had the nerve — or the interest? — to kiss Alan. She captured Roberto's tongue and sucked on it, needing the taste of him in her mouth, needing the intrusion of his body into hers. When she finally let him go, she asked, "*That* brink of pleasurable insanity?"

112

He ripped the remaining buttons off his shirt. Actually ripped them.

They bounced across the floor. He gestured at them, at himself. "You make me a beast."

"I do, don't I?" And how pleased that made her! She pushed his shirt off his shoulders, down his arms . . . everywhere she touched his skin flushed and burned with fever.

He shook himself free of the shirt and cupped his hands over her bare shoulders. "I savor the silk of your skin, the strength of your arms."

She looked at him: at his face, his chest, his waist. In awe, she whispered, "You are so beautiful."

"Beautiful? Me?" He chuckled in resonant amusement. "Men are not beautiful."

"You're beautiful like a statue, like art, like" — she looked up at the skylight — "like the stars in the midnight sky. You're so much more than I expected . . . but you're everything I deserve."

"I like that you have such expectations, and that I fulfill them. Most American women, they can't say what they wish." His Italian accent was strong and tender. "They haven't the words, or they're too shy to use them. I always pitied them for that deficiency. But you . . . you speak to me and I am mad with passion. Do you want a madman?"

"I want *you.*" In a leisurely gesture, she stroked the straining neckline of her dress. "I want you to undress me." *My God.* She was actually purring.

"I know a few things about undressing a woman, and somewhere on this gown there must be a zipper." His gaze roamed over her, but he wasn't looking at the dress. He was looking at *her.*

"Somewhere there is." She trailed one finger down his breastbone and over the ridges of his stomach.

His erection pressed against his zipper, and he sucked in his breath, still and waiting.

But not yet. Not yet. She smiled a Mona Lisa smile, and walked her finger back up to touch his lips.

"You're a tease. I hope I survive the night," he said hoarsely. "And if I don't, well . . . what a superb way to die."

"A man with a sense of humor. More than that, a man with a sense of humor about *sex.*" Tilting her head back, she laughed aloud with joy. "I didn't know such an animal existed."

"What kind of animals have you known?"

Oh, no. They weren't going to have this discussion. Not now. "The zipper," she reminded him.

"The zipper," he repeated. He explored the back seam on her dress, trying to find the elusive pull.

"It isn't there. Of course not. I'm desperate, and the damned zipper is hidden." Hooking his finger in the neckline, he tugged lightly. "I don't want to tear your dress."

"It doesn't matter. I won't ever wear it again." She had never meant anything as much as she meant that, and she smiled at the success of her plan to chop Alan from her life in a grand — and expensive — gesture.

"You smirk like a cat with a canary feather drooping from its mouth." Taking her chin, he held it until she looked at him. "About whom are you thinking?"

So. She had to tell him something. "My ex-fiancé."

"Ah. That explains . . . so much." He projected charm, demand . . . seduction. "Think of me instead."

"That's very easy to do." She gave in to curiosity, and her hands dropped to his belt. She unbuckled it, then tugged it free of the belt loops. Taking her time, she loosened the button, then dragged the zipper down.

Her knuckles dragged across his erection, and she felt his heat through two layers of cloth.

When their flesh touched, she was alive as she had never been in her life . . . What would it be like to experience that heat inside her? The anticipation was so great that every inch of her felt exposed, nervy, anxious . . . craving.

He watched her from beneath lowered lids, and again that sensation of danger lapped at her. He wanted her so badly his breath raised and lowered his chest in painful increments. He had red along his cheekbones, and his hand hovered over the top of hers as if he wanted to grab it and force her compliance right now. Yet still he waited, a powerful man yielding to her wishes.

Flirting with danger, she discovered, had a piquancy of its own.

His pants sagged on his hips, and she slid her fingers inside the waistband of his shorts. Her fingertips brushed lower and lower, not really seeking . . . tormenting. When at last she brushed the tip of his erection, he braced himself against the sofa and closed his eyes to better absorb the pleasure.

Watching him accept her servicing was a potent aphrodisiac. In a breathy voice, she said, "I think you'd better locate my zipper pretty soon or *I'll* tear my dress off."

"I thought you'd never ask." He ran his fingertips over her neckline, barely touching her skin, leaving a thread of sizzling flesh behind. He found the zipper on the side, and it slithered down with a faint hiss.

She was so tight with tension, so sensitive with euphoria, the slick silk seemed to abrade her skin. Her nipples ached and she could barely breathe.

He slid the material off her breasts like a man unwrapping his most anticipated Christmas present.

The cool air whispered across her nipples. With a faint sense of dread, she watched Roberto's expression. After all, Alan had complained about her breasts — they were too abundant, the nipples were too large, too rosy, too sensitive. . . .

Roberto groaned aloud, and dipped his head to lick her as if she presented him with flawless diamonds set in pure gold.

His tongue, rough and expert, created sensations so intense her fingertips tingled with the need to stroke him.

Placing her palm on the side of his head, she turned his face up to hers. His skin burned beneath her hand.

He had a fever, and she'd given it to him.

She was young. She was beautiful. She had gifts men would kill for. That Roberto would kill for. Turning his head, he kissed her fingers and banished the cold that had possessed her since she landed in Chicago. He made her heart dance, her blood warm. His perfect body exuded power, and she controlled that power.

She exulted in her supremacy. "Watch," she said.

With her hands on her hips, she slinked out of the silk dress.

He observed, his lips slightly parted, as she revealed her body to him.

She kicked the dress away.

He groaned aloud. "*Bella, bella!* You are . . . so beautiful. So beautiful!"

She had brought a flush to his cheeks, a flame to his dark eyes.

And except for a lacy bit of a thong and her stiletto heels, she was naked, more naked than she'd been in her whole life. She wanted to cover herself with her hands, but how ridiculous was that? The die was cast.

He stood. With a grin that bared his straight, white teeth, he dropped his pants to the floor and stepped out of them.

She waited, breathless with anticipation. Tickling her brain was the memory of her first sight of him at the party. Would she be as amazed now?

He pulled down his underwear.

The answer was simple, succinct . . . and anything but short. He was a big man, and nothing about him disappointed. His belly rippled with muscle, his hips were tight, his thighs bulged like those of a man who rode and rode hard . . . She took a long breath and wondered if she could bear it if he rode her hard.

Or if she could bear it if he didn't.

"Tell me, *cara.* Tell me if I please you."

His glorious voice and exotic accent masked, for an instant, the meaning of his words. Then she realized — he wanted *her* approval. This magnificent man didn't assume anything about her. He was taking the time to find out, and to have him at her mercy intoxicated her.

She placed her index finger on her tongue, then slid it, wet and warm, down the ridge of his thigh. "You please me very much."

Without art or deliberation, he shed his shoes and socks. He slid her thong down her legs without disturbing her shoes, then held the tiny, lacy thing in the air and examined it with a smile that both mocked and worshiped its brevity.

Dropping it, he placed his knee between her legs, bent over her, touched her throat, slid his fingers down her breastbone and her belly. He swirled his thumb around her navel, then kissed it . . . and thrust his tongue inside.

The spark he sent through her made her arch off the couch.

And he laughed softly. She almost thought he laughed in Italian.

Scooping her legs up in his arms, he went down on her.

The first brazen touch of his tongue made her fight him. She wasn't used to such intimacy . . . or the concentrated rush of passion that hit her like a runaway train.

But he paid no attention to her struggles, holding her for his ministrations until she fought not for freedom, but for passion. His tongue shredded her composure, left her without masks, without defenses, teetering on the edge of control. He pushed, and orgasm ripped through her.

She writhed. He encouraged. And she soared beyond restraint, in the freedom of knowing her joy pleased him, enthralled him.

When she finally finished, she found him on top of her. He let her feel his weight, and she reveled in it.

Everything was so different than it had been with Alan. Alan sulked if she made suggestions, backed away from acts he considered disgusting, defined by anything that gave her pleasure. Roberto was bigger, broader, taller, tougher . . . she didn't worry about breaking him. She could say nothing, do nothing that would hurt his ego. He was so sure of himself. . . .

She wanted to be sure like him.

Taking his shoulders, she looked into his eyes. In her most commanding tone, she said, "On the bottom, mister."

He laughed, a short, pained gasp of amusement. Slipping his hands underneath her, he flipped them.

Suddenly she found herself dominating a man who gladly gave up supremacy. She lifted herself above him, looked down at him, saw him watching her from beneath lowered lids. He smiled, a slight, challenging smile, and she responded with all her competitive spirit. She placed one stiletto on the floor, then the other.

"Don't hurt yourself," he said.

It was a taunt, a challenge.

She smiled back at him. "Don't worry. I was in ballet and gymnastics. I'm very . . . limber."

He closed his eyes as if absorbing the implicit promise into his mind and his body. When he opened them, she could see the painful anticipation that held him in thrall. And she proceeded to show him a side of herself she never knew existed.

EIGHT

Brandi's cell phone rang, a silly little tune, waking Roberto from a pleasurably exhausted doze to the full light of morning. Late morning, by the looks of the sunshine beaming in through the skylights.

She lifted her head off his shoulder and looked toward her purse with an expression that was a mixture of helpless affection and annoyance. Touching Roberto's chin, she smiled wryly. "I have to get this." Sliding out from under the covers, she grabbed her phone and flipped it open. "Hi, Tiffany. I know, I should have called you with a report on the party." She was talking fast, making excuses to someone who had the right to know.

Tiffany . . . she hadn't mentioned a Tiffany.

Of course, the two of them hadn't done a lot of talking.

Interested, Roberto lifted himself up on one elbow.

Brandi stood bathed in the sun, gloriously naked and unself-conscious. Strands of gold hair tumbled around her shoulders. Her breasts were superb, with full pink nipples that had almost hummed when he touched them. She was tall, not some tiny fragile thing he had to worry about crushing, with legs that wrapped around his waist and a body that lifted to his, demanding her due.

"Good for Uncle Charles," Brandi said. "Yes, it was fabulous. Important people, lots of reporters, *great* clothes. It was worth moving to Chicago for, even with the frozen pipes and no Internet."

He lifted his eyebrows. She'd just arrived in Chicago? "I wish you could have been there. You would have loved it." She listened. "Did he? Well, Uncle Charles is right. If I do say so myself, I was gorgeous."

Roberto lifted his thumb to her.

She grinned back at him. Whereas last night she had been unsure in her sexuality, today she was confident.

He had done that.

"No, Alan was busy." Brandi turned toward the window.

Alan. The ex-fiancé. Roberto didn't know what the hell difficulty Alan had had realizing what a treasure he possessed, but Roberto was grateful to the idiot. If not for him, Roberto wouldn't have spent a night of decadent pleasure in Brandi's arms.

He looked at her left hand, the hand that held the phone. There was a pale mark and an indentation where she'd taken off a ring. So the engagement had only recently terminated. Yesterday, perhaps? That would explain so much.

She looked out across Lake Michigan, then glanced down. Down the fifty-eight stories to the ground. She stared as if mesmerized, then suddenly, hastily, she paled and backed away.

Roberto recognized the symptoms. His mother was like that — not really afraid of heights, but not willing to look down. She had gone up in the Tower of Pisa, but the whole time she had kept her hand on her heart and her eyes on the horizon.

Brandi unzipped her bag. "I didn't stay at Uncle Charles's. I was tired and I left early."

So whoever this Tiffany was, Brandi wouldn't confide in her. Didn't tell her where she'd spent the night, or with whom.

"But I wish you could have seen the Romanov Blaze." She rummaged in the bag. "It's so *big*. I never heard for sure, but I think it's probably fifty carats —"

Brandi had a good eye. Forty-eight point eight carats.

"— with a sparkle and a purity that would tear your heart out. It's a beautiful clear color, violet almost, with a fire in its heart." She pulled out a thin, long strip of sheer rose-colored material. "No wonder it's called the Blaze." She slipped one arm into it, then the other.

Roberto realized she was putting on her robe . . . if that transparent wrap with lace inserts could be called a robe. The winter sunshine beamed down on her from the skylights, penetrating the material, hinting at her outline and giving her skin a rosy glow.

Or was the glow the result of his lovemaking?

"Uncle Charles has a great house. The refinished foyer is gorgeous." She walked into the sitting room and lowered her voice.

Roberto had good ears and a healthy interest in hearing her end of the conversation.

"Say . . . Mother? Did Uncle Charles tell you anything about me?"

Mother? Roberto sat straight up. She had had to answer her mother's call, of course. That was good. But she called her mother by her first name?

126

"No?" Brandi kept her voice perky. "I was just trying to get a feel for how he really felt about hiring me."

Hiring her? Roberto leaped out of bed and walked to the doorway. This woman who looked like a model or a socialite or, for God's sake, a high-priced call girl, *worked* for Charles McGrath?

As a secretary. Please, as a secretary.

"There seemed to be some resentment among his employees about me." Another pause, and while she stood beside the desk, she caressed his laptop with one elegantly polished finger. "Well, because they think I got the job because we know him or because of my looks, or both. Yes, I know, Mother. I don't undervalue myself." Her voice contained a snap that surprised him.

If he had ever spoken to his mother in such a tone, she would have smacked the back of his head.

"Graduating magna cum laude from Vanderbilt Law was enough to get me into all the top firms," Brandi said. "But the other employees don't have to be fair, do they? Especially when they haven't worked with me yet."

She was an attorney. A newly hired attorney with the best grades from one of the top law schools in the United States.

But . . . but . . . her sapphires were large and real, and her gown was couture. She had said she would never wear it again. That kind of careless disdain for something so expensive always signified that there was money in the family.

Not that a wealthy background precluded her own success, but wealth coupled with her looks meant she shouldn't have that drive to get to the top . . . and he was being a presumptuous ass. He'd had the advantages of a privileged background and a handsome face, and in his thirty-two years, he'd done well for himself. Very well for himself.

And when life had brought a reversal of fortune, he had done what he must to find his way back. Right now he was paying the price, but it would be worth it.

Yet Brandi worked for McGrath and Lindoberth.

He looked away from her. He had to look away from her. He needed to think, and that was impossible when she stood silhouetted against the windows and all her peaks and valleys called to him.

Had she known who he was when she beckoned him? She'd known his name. Of course she had to know the cause of his celebrity. His picture had been in all the papers.

But apparently she'd just moved to Chicago. If she'd been unpacking, if she'd had no water, if she had no Internet, it was possible she hadn't heard about him. Perhaps the gossip at the party hadn't reached her ears. Assuming that was all true, and that she wanted her job at McGrath and Lindoberth, then last night had been a hell of a miscalculation — on both their parts.

Should he tell her?

What good would that do?

The damage had been done.

They couldn't go back.

So why not enjoy themselves and pay the piper when the time came?

Was he making this decision out of logic or desire? As she said good-bye and shut the phone, he slowly paced toward her. It didn't matter. Nothing mattered . . . as long as he could have her one more time.

He caught her around the waist from the back. "I would like to extend my invitation to remain here for the weekend."

He felt her spine straighten. She was going to say no.

But he had powers this *piccola tesora* could barely imagine.

He opened her robe, then ran his hands

down her thighs and up to linger on the golden fluff of hair that barely concealed her lips.

She caught her breath.

Bending his knees, he pressed himself against her, and whispered in her ear, "I haven't shown you what I can do with my . . . tongue."

"Yes . . ." She cleared her throat. "Yes, you have."

"There's more. So much" — he slid his tongue along the shell of her ear — "more."

She wasn't easy. She tried to think about it. About her resolve to take only one night for herself. "I have to unpack," she said faintly.

"So you can go to your cold apartment with the frozen pipes and work to finish unpacking — the unpacking that you can easily do next week — or you can spend the time with me being warm and bathed and pampered . . . and loved." He opened her to his fingers and tenderly explored her, touching all the right places, making her melt against him. "I can show you such pleasure as you've never imagined. You'll be insensible with joy. You won't be able to stop smiling. Come, *cara,* be mine for one more day."

Her phone rang again, a series of sharp

rings. She still held the phone in her hand, but she looked at it as if she didn't understand what she should do. Then she shook her head as if coming out of a daze and lifted it to her ear.

Accidenti! He had almost had her.

"Hi, Kim. Everything's fine. Yes, I did." She listened. "I know you didn't, but you were wrong. It was everything I could have wished. In fact" — she cast a long, even look over her shoulder at him, a look that teased and revealed — "I'm going to have to call you back on Monday, because I'm spending the rest of the weekend with him."

As Brandi walked down the hall toward her new apartment, she couldn't wipe the smile off her face. It was Sunday. Sunday night. She had spent the entire weekend in the arms of a man who made her forget what's-his-name. Roberto had everything any woman could ever desire — smoky sensuality, sexy accent, great cheekbones, muscular body, slow hands — and best of all, she would never see him again.

Her smile slipped.

She would never see him again.

But that was what she wanted. She sighed only because he'd introduced her to decadent pleasures she'd scarcely imagined, and she knew she would miss watching with hungry eyes as he strode from the bathroom to the bedroom to the sitting room.

She fumbled to insert her key in the lock.

Clothed, he was glorious. Naked, he was —

Before she succeeded, the door swung open on its hinges.

For a long, long moment, she stared, not understanding. She had locked the door. She knew she had. Yet she examined the lock. It was smashed.

Someone had broken into her apartment.

Stunned, she pushed the door open and stared, hands limp at her sides.

The cushions on her new sofa had been tossed. Papers were strewn everywhere. The boxes she'd left packed were opened and dumped. The glasses she had put in the cupboard were shattered on the floor. Across the cream-colored wall, red paint dripped a message — DIE BITCH.

And her dragon . . . she whimpered and rushed inside. She knelt beside the green shards and touched the sharp edges with tender fingers. All these years, she'd kept her dragon pristine with nary a chip on him. She'd dragged him from the home where she'd lived with her parents through a series of smaller and smaller apartments, then to the college dorm, then to the law school . . . and now someone had come in and broken him.

She stared around at the mess with disbelieving eyes. She'd been robbed.

And how dumb was she to be inside? The criminal might still be here.

She rushed back into the hallway and called 911.

NINE

"I might point out, Miss Michaels, that it's not a good idea to be late the first day of work." Mrs. Pelikan stood at the head of the conference table, her team assembled before her, and reproved Brandi as she slipped in the door.

"It's okay when Mr. McGrath is your family's best friend." Sanjin Patel smirked.

Brandi considered how pleasant he'd been Friday night when he'd been hoping to get into her pants, and supposed that a firm smack across his handsome chops was out of the question. "I apologize, Mrs. Pelikan. My apartment was vandalized. The police left about midnight. The locksmith left at one. I had to clean enough to get to the bed, so I didn't crash until three. This morning I did call with a message." Which she'd given to Shawna Miller knowing full well it would never be passed on.

"You could have e-mailed," Sanjin said.

"They smashed my laptop." They didn't steal it. They smashed it.

"I'm sorry." Mrs. Pelikan sounded sincere. "Not a good introduction to our fair city."

Your fair, freezing-ass-cold city.

"What did the police say?"

"They said the security in the building is actually very good. The apartment manager was completely apologetic." So apologetic he'd arranged to let her insurance agent in today to take pictures of the damage and was paying for a crew to clean up the mess. Eric did *not* want to give his other tenants reason to worry. "He gave the police the video from the cameras at the doors. They're going to study it and see if they recognize the perp, but usually in cases like this, one of the tenants was being 'nice' and let him in."

"What was stolen?" Mrs. Pelikan asked.

"Nothing appears to be missing. It looks like an act of pure vandalism." Somehow, that made the situation worse. To think someone attacked her things, slashed her new, wrong-size couch, dumped her drawers and the boxes she hadn't yet unpacked, for no reason except spite seemed vindictive and far too personal.

Last night after everyone left, Brandi had tried to sleep, but every time she had drifted off, she jerked awake. Then she lay in the darkness, her eyes wide, waiting to hear the soft sound of a footfall or see a dark form move across the window.

"You could have stayed home, Miss Michaels." Mrs. Pelikan frowned as she looked Brandi over. "Perhaps it would be better if you *went* home."

Obviously Brandi hadn't done a good job with the concealer on the circles beneath her eyes. "Of course, thank you, Mrs. Pelikan. But I have been looking forward to working with you and your team, and I didn't want to miss the chance to be in on the ground floor of this exciting new case." She stood there, clutching her briefcase in sweaty palms and hoping she maintained some semblance of professionalism, while she sounded like a major suck-up.

But she couldn't bear the idea that on her first day everyone was sniggering at her, gossiping about her behavior at the party, taking the opportunity to make snotty comments about her connection to Uncle Charles. So she'd dragged herself up, put on her best booby-mashing bra, dressed in her most conservative, least wrinkled black suit, and indulged in a cab to get her to McGrath and Lindoberth as quickly as she could. At least now Sanjin could make his snotty comments to her face.

"Good." Mrs. Pelikan turned crisp and businesslike. "You know everyone here. Tip Joel, Glenn Silverstein, Diana Klim . . ."

Brandi wished she were back in the suite with Roberto, safe and warm and loved.

Not loved, exactly, but certainly cherished. Although he'd made no attempt to find out her last name or where she lived. He'd been content to let her walk out of his life forever . . . and that was right. That was just what she had wanted. In fact, a weekend had been far more than she'd wanted, and his indifference — for that was what it was — had kept her from calling him when she'd discovered the break-in. Thank God she still had her dignity.

Instead she had this room of coworkers who stared at their organizers, their notebooks, or their Palm Pilots. Anything to avoid looking at her and murmuring pleasantries.

Maybe that was the way they greeted people in Chicago, but Brandi was from Nashville. In Nashville, good manners were the standard, not the exception, and she wasn't going to let them get away with it.

She marched up to Tip. "Tip, Friday night I thought you were fighting a bit of a cold. I hope you're feeling better."

Tip was an old lawyer, probably not the best because he was sixty and not a partner, but he knew how to play the game. He shook her hand. "I'm better, thanks."

"Diana, how good to meet you again," Brandi said. "I hope you'll give me the name of your hairdresser. The guy who cut mine slaughtered it."

Actually he'd been an artist, but Diana was thirty-something, married, with highlights that shouted "Beauty School" and a cut that accentuated her plump cheeks. A little flattery wouldn't go amiss there, and didn't. Diana's brown eyes lit up, and she said, "Sure, I can do that."

Glenn cleared his throat.

"Later," Diana added.

"Sanjin —" Brandi offered her hand, but she didn't think Southern charm would get far with him. Never mind a woman scorned — he was single, intelligent, from India, and didn't like the fact she hadn't been interested in a man who worked at her firm.

He touched her hand and inclined his head with a chill that told her she'd made an enemy.

"Miss Michaels, if you're done with the chitchat?" Mrs. Pelikan managed to sound severe and look as if she knew exactly what Brandi was doing. "Glenn is the team leader on your first case, so you'll be working for him."

Brandi saw Glenn nod pontifically and knew she faced trouble. He was fifty, balding, and fighting it with a bad comb-over. Friday night after he'd slavered over her like a rabid dog, she'd spent ten minutes joking with his wife about old fools. Perhaps it hadn't been wise, but in her opinion a man who was willing to cheat on his wife should be put down and then neutered, and not necessarily in that order.

"Glenn, why don't you outline our case for Brandi?" Mrs. Pelikan sat down and crossed her arms over her chest.

Brandi opened her notebook and held her pen at the ready.

"I'll try to be succinct, since everyone here already knows the details and our client will be in soon." Glenn rose and spoke directly to Brandi while everyone else looked disgusted. "He has dual citizenship, American and Italian. The FBI claims he's a jewel thief. They assert his specialty is diamonds, big diamonds, and that he's stolen from museums and private citizens in New York City, San Francisco, and Houston. The CIA also has an interest in him, claiming he's committed similar crimes in Rome, Bombay, and London. But the FBI landed him first."

Brandi nodded.

"Would you like to take notes, Miss Michaels?" Glenn looked pointedly at the blank notebook in front of her.

Everyone in here already hated her, so she told them the truth. "I have a photographic memory, Mr. Silverstein, but I will take notes when necessary to verify the details." She smiled toothily at him.

Glenn took a long, patient breath that clearly expressed his doubt. "The FBI has videos of our client in two of those locations prior to a robbery, and most important, an audiotape of him speaking to the owner of the jewel a mere hour before the robbery took place. He's renowned for romancing females before he allegedly steals their finest pieces —"

"Their finest pieces?" Tip gave a snort.

Brandi endeavored to keep a straight face.

"And this woman, Mrs. Vandermere, says she saw him take her eight-carat diamond necklace before he left for the night. The FBI is prosecuting on circumstantial evidence and one woman's accusations." Glenn swayed like a cobra preparing to strike. "They might be able to make it stick . . . if our client were poor. But he's not. He can

140

afford the best defense, and that's us."

"Of course," Brandi said.

"He's independently wealthy and a respected businessman." Diana smiled with reminiscent pleasure. "The fact that he's an Italian count doesn't hurt, either."

The hair on the back of Brandi's neck stood up. She drove her pen tip into her notebook. The top page tore, but she barely noticed. Wildly she looked from one attorney to another. "What's his name?"

"Don't you ever read the papers?" Sanjin asked.

"His name!" Brandi rapped her knuckles on the table.

Her fierce demand took even Glenn aback. "It's Bartolini," he said. "Roberto Bartolini."

TEN

"Surely you saw Mr. Bartolini." Mrs. Pelikan observed Brandi's horrified expression from sharp brown eyes. "He was at Mr. McGrath's party."

"She left early. She'd already filed us away in her photographic memory." Sanjin's voice held a wealth of spite.

The door opened. Mrs. Pelikan's secretary stepped inside and in a breathless voice announced, "He's here."

Before Brandi could collect her composure or lift her jaw off the floor, Roberto strode in.

He looked delicious even with his clothes on.

No wonder he hadn't asked her last name. She'd told him where she worked. Whom she worked for.

The silky black hair she had so loved to run her fingers through had been trimmed into a businesslike cut.

He knew she'd be on his case. He knew he'd meet her again.

His dark gaze swept the room, lingered on Diana. . . .

She had to recuse herself.

Oh, God. Oh, no. She had to recuse herself . . . and she had to tell them why.

He looked at Mrs. Pelikan. Glenn.

Brandi wanted to fall off her chair and hide under the table.

Dear God. She was going to be fired from her first job. Her father would snort about how useless she was and how she would never pay him back for college. And . . . and maybe she wouldn't, because she had committed the cardinal sin: She'd had an affair with a client.

Distantly she realized introductions were being performed.

"Mr. Bartolini, I think you've met everyone here," Mrs. Pelikan was saying. "Glenn, Sanjin, Diana, Tip . . ."

They were standing up as their names were called.

Roberto shook hands with each one.

"I don't think you met Brandi Michaels?" Mrs. Pelikan asked.

"Miss Michaels." The smile he offered her was polite, admiring, and basically that of a man who was meeting an attractive woman for the first time. "How good to meet you."

She was insulted. After their weekend together, he dared pretend he didn't know her?

No, wait. She was pleased, because this gave her a moment to think what she should do. Recuse herself, obviously. At Vanderbilt she'd taken Ethics and the Law. It had to be done.

Someone poked her in the back. Glenn. He glared and indicated she should stand.

She scrambled to her feet. "Mr. Bartolini, I look forward to working with you."

She didn't know where that had come from. She wasn't going to work with him. She was going to recuse herself. The fact that it would be unpleasant and grossly embarrassing and the end of her career and she'd have to work at McDonald's for the rest of her life serving Happy Meals made no difference.

Interesting that he was offering her the choice, keeping their relationship a secret. Was he ashamed of her?

No, it wasn't that. He hadn't known she was a lawyer at his firm until she told him. She remembered how he'd scrutinized her — as if he weren't sure what to think.

Someone poked her in the back again.

Glenn. Everyone was seated now.

Roberto sat at the head of the table with Mrs. Pelikan, listening as she explained their defense plan.

Brandi sat, too, and tried to think what to do. Regardless of whether Roberto gave her the chance to avoid telling the truth, she had to. If their relationship ever became known, it would jeopardize his defense. But she didn't have to blurt it out here. Not with Sanjin shooting her the evil eye. After the meeting was over, she would follow Mrs. Pelikan into her office —

Sanjin's voice jerked her attention back to the meeting. "I say we send Brandi. She needs to meet the judges in the city, anyway, and her inexperience won't matter, because what can go wrong with this sort of meeting?"

She glanced around. In her turmoil she'd missed something very important. "I'd be glad to do whatever needs to be done." An innocuous statement.

"Fine," Mrs. Pelikan said. "Tip, you and Diana see what else you can dig out of your sources at the FBI. Sanjin, the research — it's all yours."

Sanjin's face fell. *That* served the little weasel right.

"Glenn, you're with me. Brandi, you go with Mr. Bartolini to meet Judge Knight. It should be simple enough. He's a pushover for a pretty face." Mrs. Pelikan stood up and nodded briskly.

The whole team stood up and nodded briskly.

Brandi imitated them, but . . . she had to go with Roberto to meet a judge? How had that happened?

That's right. She'd been distracted by the plan for the ethical and required murder of her own career before it had even had the chance to draw breath.

Everyone seemed to be waiting for her to lead the way out, so she did, with Roberto close on her heels. The team split for their offices.

Brandi started after Mrs. Pelikan.

Roberto caught her arm. "Where are you going?"

"To tell her —"

"You can do that later. Nothing will be harmed if you go with me to a meeting with Judge Knight. You heard Mrs. Pelikan. He likes a pretty face, and he's not disposed to like me at all, so you'll be my protection."

She looked down at his hand. The last time that hand had been on her, she'd been kissing him good-bye, and that kiss had ended on the floor before the fire in the hotel bedroom. She looked up at him. The last time she'd been this close, she'd buried her nose in his chest and smelled the clean, fresh scent of him as if it were an aphrodisiac.

Now she could smell the scent of him again, and she didn't know whether to run into his arms or away.

But he seemed oblivious to her flight-or-fight reaction. He let her go and in a sensible tone asked, "Where's your coat?"

"In my cubicle."

"You'll need it. It's cold out there."

"Ya think?" That was sarcastic. But she hadn't insisted she go to Mrs. Pelikan. That would have been the right thing to do. Yet she was scared, and Roberto was right. Wasn't he? It wouldn't do any harm to go with him to charm a judge.

She let him help her on with her coat. She put on her gloves in the elevator. She didn't look at him. Didn't look at the people who got on with them. Didn't even glare at the woman who did a double take and checked him out.

But she did think it would be fortunate if the elevator dropped all forty stories to the ground and ended Brandi's cowardice and indecision — and while it was at it, finished off that slut who winked at him.

Roberto's limousine stood illegally parked

at the curb, and Newby stepped out. He doffed his hat to her and opened the door.

A witness. Newby was a witness that she and Roberto had had an affair. The concierge at Roberto's hotel was another witness. So was anybody who'd seen her walk into the hotel. Oh, and Jerry, the bodyguard at Uncle Charles's, had seen the car she had slid into. Putting her hand to her face, she imagined their depositions in the case disbarring her.

"It's okay." Roberto took her arm and herded her toward the car. "You're making it too complicated."

"I don't think I am."

He shoved her inside the car and followed her in.

"I think it's very clear-cut. I am just too much of a coward —"

He grabbed her shoulders and spun her to face him. "You are not a coward. Of all the things I learned about you this weekend, that is the number one truth. Please do me the favor of not disparaging yourself in such a manner again."

She'd forgotten. During their weekend of overwhelming, completely fabulous monkey sex, she'd found herself liking Roberto. Rallying her defenses, she said, "Well. Thank you. But you're a jewel thief, so how good a judge of character can you be?"

"First — I am not a jewel thief until a jury convicts me."

Which, as his lawyer, she knew.

"Second, a jewel thief must be a very good judge of character." He leaned across her.

She shrank back from his warmth, his scent, the pressure of his body against hers.

Taking her seat belt, he buckled it for her. "It's almost more important than being able to hold myself by my fingertips on a ledge five stories over the street."

The car started, and she stared at him in horror and fascination. "Hold yourself by your fingertips on a ledge five stories over the street? You could be killed!" She flinched at the idea of this beautiful man plummeting toward the pavement. . . .

Unbidden, a memory popped into her head . . . Roberto, unbuttoning his shirt, revealing that rippling, muscled chest . . . No *wonder* he had such a buff body. Hanging by his fingertips required conditioning, practice . . . "No. Wait." Remembering that, and what followed, was the last thing she should do. "You just admitted to being a jewel thief. Don't ever say that to anyone else. *Ever.*"

"What have I done, sweet Brandi, to make you think I am foolish?" His accent was rich and full in a way she had never heard it . . . except when they made love. Then each word he murmured in her ear was opulent with the tones of Italy, and when his body moved on hers, she could forget Chicago, the cold, her furniture, her ditz of a mother, her bastard of a father, and that son of a bitch who had spent their engagement screwing another woman. This weekend had been the best of her life . . . and this Monday was the worst day *ever.*

"I don't think you're foolish." That was the last thing she thought about him. "I think you're immoral. Why didn't you tell me who you were?"

"What did you think I did for a living?"

"I don't know. You're an Italian count!"

His mouth twisted wryly. "*Count* doesn't pay as well as it used to."

"No, I suppose it doesn't come with a salary." What *had* she been thinking?

"You knew my name. You didn't seem to know what I was accused of, but I saw no reason why that would matter to us."

Oh, fine. He was just like Alan. He was shifting the blame to her.

He continued, "Not until you were speaking to your mother and mentioned going to work for Charles McGrath did I realize we had committed a legal impropriety."

"Oh." He wasn't blaming her. He wasn't blaming either one of them. How refreshing. "Then it was too late."

"Exactly."

"Wait. That was Saturday morning." She remembered the conversation with Tiffany very well, for immediately afterward he'd come to her and proposed they stay together, and she'd melted all over him like hot fudge on ice cream.

He smiled at her, his dark eyes alive with amusement, his lips quirked knowingly, and waited for her to come to the same conclusion he had.

"Okay, so the damage was done," she admitted begrudgingly. "Couldn't you have told me?"

"And have you call Charles McGrath and tell him you had to quit? I think not. Besides" — he leaned forward and whispered — "I wanted to sleep with you."

He sounded just like he did when they made love. *Oh, no.* She looked down at her lap as she knit her gloved fingers together. She needed to concentrate. She could *not* jump his bones. "Look. I didn't have the nerve to tell Mrs. Pelikan the truth right away" — her voice trembled and she steadied it — "but I won't jeopardize this case. When we get back, I will do what's right

151

and recuse myself and . . . and take the consequences."

It was good for her peace of mind that she didn't see the expression on his face.

"Now why are we going to meet a judge?" she asked.

"Weren't you paying attention?"

She turned and glared at Roberto.

"Okay!" He lifted his hands as if trying to stop a punch. "Judge Knight wants to meet me. He's been assigned my case. My instructions are to be earnest, to remind him of my reputation as an international businessman with ties to Chicago" — his voice hardened — "and to ease his case of the ass."

"This shouldn't be difficult. You're very charming. I'm charming, also." She practiced a Southern belle smile at Roberto. "We should be out of there in half an hour."

ELEVEN

"How could you have said those things to Judge Knight?" Brandi stalked down the broad corridors of the courthouse toward the door.

"He's too sensitive." Roberto strolled beside her, his hands in his pockets, his collar unbuttoned, his tie loose around his neck.

"You told him the American justice system was a farce. You told him the FBI can't tie their shoes without reading the instructions. You as good as told him you were guilty and should have been caught years ago except that the CIA was a bunch of incompetents." She was hissing. She knew she was. But she couldn't stop. "This has been the most mortifying three hours of my life."

"But at least we get to stay together." They were nearing the outer doors.

She struggled to stick her arms in her London Fog.

He caught her collar and helped her into the sleeves.

"What is Mrs. Pelikan going to say when she finds out you've been remanded into my custody? She's going to fire me. I don't have to worry about recusing myself, because" — Brandi's voice rose — "she's going to fire me!"

People walking down the corridor stared.

Roberto shrugged at the police manning security and indicated he didn't know what she was carrying on about. "See? You didn't want to explain why you had to recuse yourself, so everything came out for the best."

"For the best? I've screwed up the first thing she asked me to — Wait!" Suspicion struck, and she stopped cold.

Roberto jerked her clear of oncoming traffic.

"What did you say?" she asked.

"I said, 'Everything came out for the best.' " He slid into his overcoat.

"No, before that. You said, 'At least we get to stay together.' " Her voice rose with her indignation. "Did you do this on purpose?"

"Cara." He faced her. Put his hands on her arms. "You really do think I'm stupid. I adore you, but I wouldn't risk a lifetime in jail for a few weeks in your custody. That

doesn't make sense."

"No." She calmed. "No, it doesn't. But neither does what you did in there." She pointed back at the judge's chambers.

"He's an American judge. I'm an Italian count." Roberto slouched against the wall. "He was insolent. I reminded him of his place."

Roberto's snobbery reminded her all too clearly that they had nothing in common. Nothing. "You certainly did. While you were out of the room visiting the men's room, Judge Knight told me that he grew up on the streets of Chicago to become the most respected official in the city."

"To impress a pretty girl, I'm sure he exaggerates." Roberto dismissed the judge's claim with an airy gesture.

She buckled her belt so tight she could barely breathe. Or maybe it was rage that constricted her chest. "He thinks he has the right to interrogate a man of your privilege who has turned to crime."

"He does not have that right." Roberto wasn't joking.

And to think she used to admire arrogance in a man.

She pulled her gloves out of her pocket. The white velvet case from the pawnshop came tumbling out with them.

He picked up the case and handed it to her. "I hope there's nothing valuable inside."

"No, I'm wearing the earrings." She shoved it back in her pocket, put on her gloves and her hat, and headed out the doors.

He followed.

When they stepped outside, the frigid wind whipped at her. The limo. The limo was heaven. She headed toward it.

He didn't. He stopped on the courthouse steps and looked up and down the street. His gaze lingered on two guys huddled next to the huge monument Picasso had presented to the city.

They were dressed up like polar bears with hats, mittens, boots, scarves over their faces, yet they had to be freezing their keisters off.

Then Roberto said the stupidest thing she'd ever heard. He said, "Let's walk."

"Walk?" Her lips were already numb. "Are you *insane?"*

"You already think so. I might as well confirm your opinion." He draped his scarf around her neck and over her ears, and smiled at her pinched crankiness. "Come. Let's tell Newby. He can follow us in the car."

"The office is miles from here!" The soft cashmere wrapped her in his warmth, his scent, his self-assurance.

"We're not going back to the office. We're going to a restaurant. I haven't eaten."

She glared at him.

"It's not far," he assured her. "Only a few blocks."

She wanted so badly to tell him that she would watch him walk from the car, but Judge Knight had been furious at his treatment at Roberto's hands, and his anger had spilled over to McGrath and Lindoberth, and specifically on Brandi. He'd been very detailed about what would happen to her and her budding career if she misplaced Roberto, so she didn't have the nerve to leave him. Not in front of the courthouse. Probably not until the case was over. "All right. We'll walk."

Roberto spoke to Newby, then joined her, setting a brisk pace down the sidewalk.

She marched along with her head down, muttering, "I hate this. This isn't winter. Winter is hot chocolate and marshmallows. Winter is snow lightly falling on a hill. Winter is sledding. It's too damned frigid to snow. It's too damned glacial to do anything except freeze to death walking through Chicago."

"Here. Let me keep you warm." Roberto wrapped his arm around her.

She knocked him away.

He didn't look offended. Worse, he didn't look cold.

Only a few people cared enough to fight the wind and walk the streets. For the most part, pedestrians waited for summer and warm weather — even those two guys at the statue had apparently decided it was too bitter to stay out on the plaza, because they were trudging along about a block back. One of them was coughing — something must be going around.

"Why did you move here if you hate winter so badly?" Roberto asked. "It's not as if Chicago hides its reputation. It *is* the Windy City."

"Fiancé." He needn't think she was over that stunt he'd pulled in the courthouse. Her rage was the only thing that kept her from freezing.

"You moved here to get away from him?"

"I moved here because he lives here." She knew where the questioning was going, and she didn't want to tell him the truth. Finding a gorgeous Italian lover had removed the sting of Alan's rejection. Discovering her gorgeous Italian lover was a jewel thief had created a whole different range of humiliation. "How much farther to the restaurant?"

"A block." He glanced back at the car, then glanced back again. "Newby's right behind us with the car. You can get in."

She glanced behind them, too. Newby was cruising along at the same speed they were, blocking traffic without any apparent thought to the other drivers' convenience. "No. As soon as I turned my back, you'd make a dash for it."

Roberto laughed at her. Actually laughed at her. "If I wanted to make a dash for it, how would you stop me? Hang on to my ankle to slow me down?"

"You'd be surprised," she said darkly. Actually, ballerina Brandi could kick him right in the back of the head, but he didn't need to know that. She might need to do it sometime. Or at least, she might want to. "Where is this restaurant?" The only place she could see was a good ol' American greasy spoon with fluorescent lights that flashed advertisements for Budweiser and Old Milwaukee.

"That's it," Roberto said. "The Stuffed Dog."

The greasy spoon it was. "That doesn't look like your kind of place." Not the kind of place a full-of-himself Italian count would frequent.

"You'd be surprised. So . . . you moved

here last week and you're no longer engaged this week?"

Wow. He was sort of like a boomerang, flying out, then coming back to the same spot. "That's right."

"Who broke it off?"

She timed her answer so that he was opening the door when she replied, "His wife."

The place had black-and-white linoleum on the floor, padded booths, and stuffed animals — poodles, chows, German shepherds, golden retrievers, yellow Labs — hanging on the walls wrapped in cellophane. The chairs didn't match, the table legs were metal, the tops were lacquered wood, the lunch counter was chipped, and the aromas were divine.

Brandi hadn't eaten since last night when she left Roberto. At the onslaught of mouth-watering aromas, a sudden loud complaint from her stomach told the grizzled waitress about it.

"Sit down, honey, before you fall down." She waved them toward a booth, then did a double take and stared at Roberto. "Say, aren't you that guy? The one in the paper? The guy who stole all those great jewels from those society women?"

He was in the paper? Everybody knew about him?

"The jewels were gifts." He bent all his attention to the plump, worn-out waitress and flashed her a smile.

She put her hand to her chest. She blushed. Blushed for probably the first time in forty years. Fervently she smiled back. "I'd believe it."

Yeah, his smile lit up the restaurant. It seduced a simper out of a woman wearing orthopedic shoes, a burn on her left arm, and an expression that said she'd seen it all and it hadn't impressed her. For sure it could seduce jewels out of any woman.

Roberto looked toward the back corner, toward the long table where men sat huddled over their plates, smoking, eating, and talking. No other customers sat around them.

Because of the smoke, Brandi supposed.

"I see friends of mine back there," Roberto said. "We'll join them."

The waitress started to object, then took a long look at Roberto. "It's your funeral."

Brandi recognized the feeling that she'd been played for a sucker. She ought to — she had been often enough in the last three days. "Are *they* why you wanted to eat here?"

"*They're* famous for their hot dogs."

Which was no answer at all. "What kind

161

of friends are these?" she asked.

"Old friends of the family."

They'd already been spotted. At the sight of Roberto and Brandi advancing on them, the men rose to their feet. In fact, she was going to be the only woman here, and the way they were looking at her, as if she were a . . . a moll, made her feel out of place.

Some guy of around fifty-five with broad shoulders and a rotund belly stepped out from behind a plate of two hot dogs and a huge mound of fries. He advanced on them, arms wide. "Bobby! Bobby Bartolini! How good to see you. You're all grown up!" His Italian accent was stronger than Roberto's, and his voice rumbled in his large frame.

Brandi's eyebrows rose. If he dared called Roberto "Bobbie," then these people *were* old friends of the family. But other than him and another guy at his right hand, they were all about Roberto's age. About thirty, various heights, and in good shape, with muscular arms sticking out from rolled-up shirtsleeves.

"Mossimo Fossera, what a pleasant surprise." Roberto embraced him heartily. "Who would have thought I would meet you here, now?"

Yeah, right. They'd come in here to meet them.

"We Fosseras hang out here a lot," Mossimo said.

Roberto patted Mossimo's belly. "As I can see. Greg, is that you, man?" He shook hands with a guy almost as handsome as he was. "Dante, hey. You still going out with that gorgeous girl, Fiorenza?"

Dante beamed. "No, I stopped going out with her . . . when I married her."

The men laughed.

Dante and Roberto exchanged fake punches.

"Fico, hey, your complexion finally cleared up. Ricky, when did you lose all that hair? Danny, great tattoo. Son of a bitch must have hurt like hell." Roberto had lost the faint Italian accent and sounded like any American man. He acted like an American man, too, all con and horseshit — although maybe Alan had made her a little prejudiced against the gender.

"What's this?" Mossimo talked to Roberto and indicated her with his head.

"Brandi, let me take your coat." Roberto unwound his scarf from around her face.

"Whoa." The exclamation slipped from Fico as if he were unaware.

Roberto slid her London Fog off her shoulders and hung it on the coatrack.

The men stared without subtlety, making

Brandi all too aware that her booby-smashing bra and conservative suit weren't hiding her figure as well as she'd hoped.

Slipping his hand around her waist, Roberto pulled her close against him. "*This* is Brandi Michaels. *This* is my lawyer."

Much cackling and jabbing of elbows followed the introduction: "Hey . . ." "Yeah, sure." "Leave it to Roberto, heh?" "That's a new name for it. Your lawyer."

The men denigrated Brandi right to her face and laughed as if she weren't there. As if she were some superficial blonde.

As if she were her mother.

She smacked Roberto hard in the ribs with her elbow, and when his breath *oof*ed out of him, she stepped forward and offered her hand to Mossimo. "My name is Brandi Michaels. I work for McGrath and Lindoberth, and not only am I his lawyer; he's been remanded into my custody."

The younger men stopped chortling and gaped at one another as if they didn't know how to respond.

Mossimo bowed over her hand. "I should have expected Bobbie to have the best-looking lawyer in the business." Like Popeye, he talked out of the side of his mouth. She was surprised he wasn't eating spinach and popping biceps. "Sit down, Miss Michaels."

Danny pulled out a chair.

She seated herself, and Roberto shoved his way in next to her. Right next to her, almost on her lap, like some guy protecting his territory. She was tempted to elbow him again, but the waitress slapped menus on the table before her and Roberto, then stood with her pad at the ready.

A single glance told Brandi what she wanted. "A Coke and a garlic kielbasa." Garlic sounded like just the thing to ward off vampires . . . and Italian lovers.

"Grilled onions and sauerkraut?" the waitress asked.

"Oh, yes." Brandi smiled sweetly at Roberto. "And fries. Lots of fries."

"I'll have the same," he said.

The way he looked at her, she got the feeling that he wouldn't care if she smelled like garlic and sauerkraut, which was bad for her plan to stay away from him — and way too flattering.

"So, Bobbie, how's your grandfather?" Mossimo grinned, a lopsided grin that matched the way he talked. "Sergio doesn't get out much. I haven't seen him for a long time."

"For a man who's eighty-one, he's good.

A few aches, a few pains. When the weather's cold, his hand hurts." Roberto tapped his forehead. "But the mind's still sharp."

"Good. Good. As for the hand" — Mossimo pulled a long face — "it was too bad, but it had to be done."

The conversation died as the men looked at one another, then looked at her.

You'd think they never dined with a woman.

"Are you from Chicago, Miss Michaels?" Mossimo asked.

"No, I just moved here." No one said anything, and she added inanely, "It's cold."

The Fosseras shuffled their feet under the table. Roberto leaned back in his chair, apparently relaxed, his thumbs tucked into his pockets, and not at all interested in upholding his end of the conversation.

Why had he insisted on dining with these people if he didn't want to talk to them?

Yet Tiffany had instilled in Brandi her womanly duty, so she asked, "Have you lived here all your life, Mr. Fossera?"

"I was born in Italy, but I came here with my brother Ricky when I was eleven. These kids were all born here." Mossimo shut his mouth as if he'd inadvertently revealed state secrets.

Carrying on a conversation with these

guys was the heaviest social burden she'd ever had, and when her phone rang, she gratefully pulled it out of her purse.

Then she looked at the number, and she wasn't grateful anymore. "Excuse me; I have to take this. It's McGrath and Lindoberth." Pushing her chair back, she walked away from the table. She heard the buzz of conversation behind her as she left, but what those guys were saying *about* her wasn't nearly as important as what McGrath and Lindoberth was about to say *to* her. Taking a breath, she answered.

It was Glenn, and the tone of his voice froze Brandi as surely as did the weather. "What happened?"

"I was going to call you. We had a little trouble with Judge Knight." *Euphemistically speaking.*

"I just got off the phone with Judge Knight, and that's not what he told me."

Brandi should have anticipated that. She would have if she hadn't just suffered through Roberto's transformations: from Roberto the charming to Roberto the jewel thief to Roberto the aristocrat to Roberto the common jerk. Her brain was confused. "The judge took exception to a few things Mr. Bartolini said."

"Miss Michaels, in deference to your

inexperience, I gave you the easiest job on the case — getting Mr. Bartolini down to meet Judge Knight so the judge would be predisposed to his case. And you failed."

What a balding, pompous windbag! She would take credit for being stupid and sleeping with a stranger — although not to Glenn — but she wasn't taking the fall for Roberto's behavior. "Mr. Silverstein, I am hardly capable of directing Mr. Bartolini's conversation, and in fact, if Judge Knight told you everything, he told you that I kept him from immediately putting Mr. Bartolini in jail."

"Instead you got him remanded into your custody. Every woman here would kill to be in your position." Glenn's voice rose. "Do you think I'm a fool, Miss Michaels?"

She wished he wouldn't ask leading questions. Not when she was this tired, this hungry, and this irritated with men in general and Roberto in particular. "Mr. Silverstein, let me relieve your mind. I'm having lunch in a hot-dog place that I froze my rear off getting to because Mr. Bartolini wanted to walk. I am now stuck with Mr. Bartolini's company when I should be home trying to reorganize my vandalized apartment. And in case you haven't heard the gossip, my fiancé just married another woman." It did her heart good to use Alan just once to deflect trouble.

"Um, yeah, I did hear that. But that's really no excuse." Glenn didn't sound quite as forceful, though, probably because he was one of those guys who hated it when women cried.

If only he knew how far she was from tears.

Her phone beeped. She checked the number and said, "Excuse me, Mr. Silverstein; I have to take this. It's my landlord — hopefully with the news that they caught the man who vandalized my apartment." With a wicked glee, she put Glenn on hold.

"Miss Michaels?" Eric sounded brisk and efficient. "The insurance man has come and gone, and he took pictures of the destruction. The cleaners are done. I personally supervised them. The broken glass is vacuumed up. Your belongings, the ones that were unharmed, were put away — I know that not everything is in the right spot, but you can return and feel that you don't have to immediately unpack. I had the cleaners put into boxes things that I thought you'd want to distribute yourself. They're stacked on the wall between your bedroom and the living room. The crew cleaned the carpets —"

"The carpets?" What had been wrong with the carpets?

"Yes, there was an odor. We ascertained that the vandals —"

"Vandals? There was more than one?" She rubbed her forehead.

"The video shows two men. They were wrapped up with scarves and hats; there's no way to tell who they are."

"How did they get in?"

"It looked like they broke in somehow."

She took a long, frightened breath.

"But probably someone let them in. We're upgrading the security at the front. I'm so sorry, Miss Michaels; this has never happened before, and it won't happen again." He really did sound sorry.

She wrapped her arm around her waist and shivered. She supposed someday she'd feel secure again. "I appreciate that, Eric. About the carpet?"

"The vandals relieved themselves in the living room, so we cleaned all the carpets."

She changed her mind. She would never feel secure in that apartment. And she was never walking barefoot in there again.

Eric continued, "The painters have covered all the graffiti on the wall. Your clothes went to the dry cleaner's. The place looks great, and I took the liberty of replacing your mattress with a new one. Same brand, same style, and the cleaning crew made the bed. You can sleep here tonight without any worries." He was really putting himself out, trying to make sure she didn't take legal action against him or his corporation.

If he knew how bad her fortune had been lately, he'd take legal action against her for moving in and bringing all that lousy luck with her.

She glanced over at the long table where Roberto sat surrounded by men who looked like thugs. They were bent forward. Their voices rose, but she couldn't understand a word. In fact . . . Oh. They were speaking Italian.

"Thank you, Eric. I appreciate your help. I'll let you know if I choose to remain or if I've suffered too much anguish and wish to move."

"I certainly understand if you do want to move. Don't worry about breaking the lease." Eric sounded so hearty and approving she wondered if he *did* know about her bad luck.

"Thank you." She looked at the screen on her phone. To her surprise, Glenn had stayed on the other line. She thought he would have hung up in a huff. So she hit the line talking. "I just discovered my carpets had to be cleaned because the vandals peed on them. The police have no idea who they are. And the landlord would be happy if I moved. Now Mr. Silverstein — do you really believe I'm in the mood to be swept off my feet by an Italian hunk with no morals and light fingers? And would you be accusing a man, even a gay man, of dereliction of duty for saving Mr. Bartolini from jail?"

"Miss Michaels, I didn't mean —"

"No, don't apologize. Just remember that gender-based discrimination suits are difficult to defend." She hoped her kind-voiced reprimand would drive Glenn into a foaming-at-the-mouth fit. "I do have to put things away in my apartment again tonight. Can I depend on you to babysit Mr. Bartolini for me? I pay ten dollars an hour!"

TWELVE

At the table, the men heard Brandi's voice get more forceful.

"She's fiery, that one. She must be a handful." Mossimo turned heavy-lidded eyes on Roberto and switched to Italian. "So why did you bring her to our meeting?"

"I had no choice. She's my lawyer. We had trouble at the courthouse." And she was eye-popping, absolutely gorgeous and charming. She'd distracted the men and upset the Fosseras' strategy to bully Roberto. Of course, Mossimo was going to get his own way, but Roberto enjoyed derailing his strategy, if only a little.

"That's why you're late?" As if Mossimo had the right to demand an accounting of Roberto's time.

"I knew you'd wait for me." Roberto tipped his chair back, returned Mossimo's stare, and waited to see if Mossimo had taken the bait.

Mossimo gave a sideways grimace that doubled as an ingratiating smile. "We had a problem with our inside man. The feds got him on income-tax evasion."

"Classic maneuver on their part. Wasn't he smart enough to . . . No, I guess not." Roberto wanted to laugh at the frustration on Mossimo's face. His inside man had been his son, Mark. Roberto had just dissed him, and Mossimo needed Roberto too badly to take offense.

Oh, yes. Mossimo had definitely taken the bait.

"But you have other inside men." Roberto waved a careless hand at the men seated around him.

"Yes, of course, but not of his caliber." Mossimo winked in a heavy-handed attempt at coyness and lowered his voice to almost a whisper. "Not for a job like this one."

"Tell me about it." Roberto didn't expect Mossimo to talk. Not yet. Not until the terms had been broached.

But he lit up a cigarette. The ring on his little finger winked at Roberto. With seeming candor, he said, "There is a diamond at the museum. It's fifty carats or so, sort of blue, sort of purple, very famous. It needs to be liberated."

"The Romanov Blaze." Roberto glanced

at Brandi. She was still talking, but with less temper and more of a steely-eyed determination that boded ill for the person on the other end. She was paying them no heed. And he was glad, for he couldn't understand what game Mossimo was playing. What trump did Mossimo hold to give up his information so quickly?

"You know of it."

"Every aficionado worth his salt has heard about the Romanov Blaze. It's one of the top ten diamonds in the world." Roberto knew damned good and well that Mossimo had known nothing about the Blaze before it arrived in Chicago and he saw a way to make a profit off it. Nonno called Mossimo a thug; for sure he was a peasant who understood nothing about the finer things in life.

And Mossimo knew it, too. That was one of the reasons he hated Nonno so much. He always felt inferior — because he was.

Roberto rubbed a little salt into the wound, reminding Mossimo that Roberto traveled in the highest circles of society. "I saw it Saturday night at McGrath's fundraiser at his house. Surely if the stone needs to be liberated, it should have been liberated while on the road between the museum and a private home."

"Better the night before it leaves to visit the next city. When it's packed up, it will be easy to transport."

"Very good. Very clever." Mossimo was shrewd, so Roberto played the innocent. "But what has this to do with me?"

"You're an inside man."

"I haven't been convicted yet."

"A technicality." Mossimo laughed and coughed, then stubbed out his cigarette in his plate. "Your grandfather was the best in the business."

"Until you took him out of the business," Roberto said without heat. He had no reason to be angry. Not when revenge was within his grip.

"It was time for a change. Believe me, I hated to push him out. But he was old. He was getting soft. It had to be done. Yet I think" — Mossimo shook his finger at Roberto — "he must have taught you all he knew."

Roberto sliced a glance at Brandi, talking low and fast, giving Glenn Silverstein the facts and taking no shit. "My lawyer won't be busy forever. Get to the point."

"For this job, I want you to be my inside man."

Roberto laughed loudly enough to make

Brandi pull the phone away from her ear and stare.

Mossimo was unfazed. "It wouldn't be so bad, would it, to get a slice of that diamond?"

"I don't need the money." Roberto kept an eye on Brandi.

Her cheeks were flushed, her eyes hot, and she was snapping into the phone.

"You're a count. A really important man in Italy."

"In a few other places, too." Roberto realized he was enjoying himself.

"Yeah. In a few other places, too." Mossimo bared his yellow-stained teeth in what passed for a smile. "You never need the money, but you're stealing stones all over Europe and Asia. For a man like you, it's the challenge. The thrill. And think about it — taking down an important museum. You'll be famous among our kind."

Roberto toyed with the idea of denying he was one of their kind. But he didn't want to make Mossimo so mad he lost his temper. Roberto had seen the results of that. So he said, "I'll be dead. The security for that diamond is state-of-the-art. I'll be fried before I go two inches."

"You've looked it over."

Roberto shrugged noncommittally.

"So . . . it's a job that's going to get done with or without you." Mossimo talked faster as Brandi finished her conversation.

"Without me. I'm already going up on trial. Only a fool would do another job now."

"A fool with a grandfather."

"Ah. So that's it." Did Mossimo really think Roberto would fail to protect his own grandfather?

But Mossimo knew how Roberto's mind worked. "He's old. He's not leaving his house or his neighborhood, and he's not going to let you put a guard on him. If you don't cooperate, sooner or later we'll get him."

The waitress headed toward the table with their food.

"Sooner or later, Mossimo, someone's going to get pissed and take you out." Roberto's voice was so reflective it took a few minutes before the other Fosseras realized what he'd said.

Ricky and Danny stood up so violently their chairs hit the wall.

The waitress veered off and caught Brandi by the arm as she started toward them.

"Calmly. Calmly." Mossimo waved his men back into their seats. "There's no reason for threats. We're all friends here. We can work this out."

The stick and then kindness. Mossimo's grip on Chicago's lucrative jewel-robbery franchise was slipping, and he was desperate enough to try anything, no matter how risky, to keep control. Just as Roberto had hoped.

"We go way back, our families do. In Bernina for centuries the Fosseras and the Continis robbed together." Mossimo intertwined his fingers and showed Roberto. "A joining now is tradition."

"Not quite." Roberto put his hand palm down on the table. "The Fosseras don't know shit about being in charge."

Ricky and Danny stood up again.

So did Roberto. He placed his other palm on the table and leaned toward Mossimo. "Like having two of your guys follow me. That's stupid, and I want it to stop."

"I don't have my men following you." Mossimo managed to fake astonishment.

Before anyone saw him move, Roberto grabbed Mossimo's wrist and twisted it sideways. "Get them off my tail."

A collective growl rose from the Fosseras.

Cold metal touched Roberto's neck.

He let his gaze linger on the ring that decorated Mossimo's little finger. It was old, so old the design in the gold setting had worn off. The stone set into it, a flawed emerald with perfect deep green color, was not cut, but rounded and polished. That ring . . .

He hadn't wanted to seem eager to accept the job, but he hadn't expected the violent upsurge of emotion he experienced at the sight of his grandfather's ring. He wanted to wring Mossimo's neck. Instead he'd gone for his wrist. Without looking around, Roberto said, "Tell that son of a bitch to take that pistol off me or the doctors will have to cut the ring off your broken finger. It would be justice, yes?"

Mossimo's round face grew damp with pain and sweat. "Put the gun away. *Diavolo,* Danny, put it away before the cops see you. We don't need this kind of exposure!"

From the corner of his eye, Roberto saw Danny slide the gun under his shirt. *Yes.* "Now, Mossimo — get those men off my tail."

"I don't have men on your tail. You want me to take out whoever it is? I can do that." Mossimo was in real pain, so maybe he was telling the truth.

And maybe he was a lying sack of shit.

Roberto looked into Mossimo's mean little eyes, challenging him, letting him know that he had threatened an adversary to be respected. "I am so sorry for the unfair accusation. I should have known you, an old friend of the family, would not stoop to so dishonorable a practice." He released him. "So I'll take care of those two men."

"I can help you," Mossimo said.

"No help needed." Roberto smiled with all his teeth, and turned to Brandi.

She had hung up her phone, and now stared at him with wide, astonished eyes.

Well, of course. She'd thought he was a dilettante, an Italian count with light fingers, not a man capable of serving a generous helping of violence.

He tossed her her coat. "Put that on," he ordered.

She did, and her fingers were trembling as she belted it around her waist.

He gave the hovering waitress a tip, told her, "Put those kielbasas in bags," and said to Mossimo, "Thanks for the lunch."

"What about the job?" Mossimo sat nursing his wrist, and he'd lost that fake geniality. He looked like what he was — a mean, petty thief without skill or finesse.

"I'll be in touch."

THIRTEEN

Roberto caught Brandi's arm gently but firmly and shoved her toward the door.

She was torn. She wanted to unequivocally state that she didn't appreciate being pushed around. At the same time she wanted out of that restaurant before someone got hurt. Like her. Or Roberto. "What was that all about?" she whispered.

"A disagreement about who would pay for the meal." Roberto grabbed the lunch sacks from the waitress.

"Do guns always come out when you guys disagree?" She glanced behind her. Everyone at the Fossera table was on their feet, watching with narrowed eyes as she and Roberto strode for the door.

She faced forward again, the skin between her shoulder blades itching. Or maybe the sensation was cold sweat trickling down her spine.

"How did the conversation go with

McGrath and Lindoberth?" Roberto asked conversationally.

"The conversation with . . . Oh! With Glenn Silverstein." How could Roberto sound so normal when bullets could right now be winging their way toward them? "He wants me to check in every two hours."

Roberto shouldered his way outside. "Does he? What does he think that's going to accomplish?"

"That it's going to be a pain in my rear, which I believe is his goal." The cold air felt good after the stifling atmosphere — or maybe that was just relief. She took a long breath.

The car was nowhere in sight.

"Now where are we going to walk?" she asked sarcastically.

Roberto flipped open his phone and said, "Newby, we're ready."

She sidled away from the restaurant windows. Guns. Those people had had guns. Her father had a hunting rifle. Other than that, her whole experience with guns was watching Steven Seagal movies with Alan, and that only under protest. She knew she was naive, but she'd never seen a pistol used to threaten someone. Someone she knew. Someone like Roberto.

She glanced sideways at him.

Yet he looked unfazed, and she realized that during that whole scene, he'd exuded authority. Those men could have beaten him up, could have killed him, yet he'd been the one who had been in control of the situation.

Who *was* he? A jewel thief? A gangster? Or just a count?

He walked her to the entrance of the next building. Pushing her against the wall out of the wind, he handed her the bags. "Stay here." And he took off running — running like a man competing in a track meet instead of an Italian count/jewel thief in business clothes.

More to the point, those two guys who'd followed them from the courthouse were loitering at the corner, and when they saw Roberto flying toward them, they ran, too. Ran like they were guilty of something.

Roberto skidded around the corner.

He was out of sight.

Shit. She'd lost him already!

Brandi ran, too. The wind took her breath away. Her heart pounded with the cold, the activity, the fear he'd escaped her custody.

She rounded the corner. Roberto and the two men were nowhere in sight. She stared, feeling helpless and foolish . . . and alarmed for Roberto's safety.

Why? Why should she be worried about him? She should be worried about herself having to go back to Judge Knight and admit she'd lost Roberto Bartolini. McGrath and Lindoberth wouldn't be any too happy, either.

But she was worried that Roberto had gotten himself into trouble. Into *more* trouble. That he'd be hurt.

She was such a fool. She'd been clueless about Alan. She didn't know what was wrong between Roberto and the Fosseras. And Roberto . . . every time she thought she got a handle on his personality, he changed it.

Worse than any of that . . . mixed into her distress was the knowledge that the kielbasas smelled incredibly good.

How could she be thinking of food at a time like this?

Obviously the only thing she was good at was eating.

And, um, sex. She knew she was good at that. At one point over the weekend she'd reduced Roberto to begging.

She walked farther down the street, trying to keep warm, searching for him, hoping . . .

He came back around the corner at a run. "What are you doing here?" Again he grabbed her by the arm. He hustled her back to the corner. As Newby pulled up in the limo, Roberto shoved her toward the car.

"Would you stop pushing me?" She tried to shove back.

"I'm guiding you." He didn't wait for Newby to come around and open the door. He did it himself and "guided" her inside. He dropped into the seat beside her, shut the door, and Newby took off, all in one smooth motion. "Damn it, Brandi, I told you to stay put."

"I'm lousy at following directions." And sick and tired of being told what to do, shoved around, and generally made a scapegoat.

There must have been something about the set of her mouth that warned him he was in danger, for he said only, "Hm. Yes. I'll remember that." He took the sack out of her hand. "Good girl. You've still got the dogs."

"I'm glad I can do something right. I can't walk by myself, I get reamed out by Glenn for not keeping you 'under control' " — she made quotation marks with her fingers — "those men don't believe I'm a lawyer, I sl—" She shut her mouth. She must be tired. She'd almost referred to their weekend together, a topic of conversation she preferred not to pursue.

"You get peevish when you're hungry," he observed.

"I do not." Although the odor of the sausage, the onions, the sauerkraut was almost unbearably seductive, and that, coupled with her relief at being safe, at having Roberto safe, resulted in a huge belly growl.

Pulling a tray out of a hidden compartment in the side of the limo, he placed it on her lap. He ripped open the bag and handed her one of the warm, wrapped dogs. "Here, eat."

"Look. You have to tell me what's going on." She unwrapped the kielbasa with fingers that shook. "Who were those men?"

"The ones in the restaurant or the ones I was chasing?"

"The ones you were chasing."

"I don't know. I want to talk to them so I can find out why they keep showing up where we are."

She had to admire his skills in answering an interrogation. He didn't give away any more than he had to. "Do they have guns, too?" Then she bit into the kielbasa. She lost her train of thought. "That is so *good*," she said through a mouthful.

He smiled at her. Smiled at her the way

he had that night, that weekend, as if she were the most wonderful woman in the world.

Self-conscious, she reached for a napkin and met his fingers as he handed one to her.

Why would eating a hot dog make her think of sex with him?

Well, duh.

She rushed into speech. "Who do you *think* could be following you?"

"Just about anybody." He bit into his dog, too, and chewed reflectively. "The FBI, the police, reporters. I thought it was the Fosseras, but Mossimo says no. Of course, he lies like a rug."

So those guys could have guns. She knew she wasn't going to like the answer, but she asked anyway. "Why would the Fosseras follow you?"

"Professional curiosity."

Like a shock of electricity, she realized what he meant. "They're jewel thieves?"

"Mossimo runs the largest operation in the world right from his house."

"I could get in trouble for letting you anywhere near a criminal. Near a firearm!" The idea made her almost faint.

"I doubt Judge Knight would be angry if I got shot." Roberto grinned unrepentantly. "After this morning he's rooting for it."

"No, really. You were breaking that man's wrist." He had looked like he knew what he was doing, too. "They pulled a gun on you. That was not your everyday, run-of-the-mill lunch date."

"Perhaps not for you. Don't worry, *cara;* I won't let the ugliness touch you." He popped the top on a Coke and handed it to her.

"Why does there have to be ugliness?" She drank, and the sugar hit her system in a welcome rush.

"With the Fosseras, there is always ugliness." He took another bite. "I should have asked for deli mustard."

He was not taking her cross-examination seriously. "You have been remanded into my custody. If you'll recall, Judge Knight told you the penalties for screwing up, and he told me the penalties if you screw up, and I wish —"

"If I answer your questions, will you answer mine?" Roberto passed her the bag with the fries.

Instantly she was on her guard. "What questions?" The fries were those floppy, yellow, undercooked things, and she passed them back.

"Your fiancé has a wife?"

How badly did she want to know Roberto's secrets? "Only one."

He didn't laugh.

And really, what did it matter if he found out now or later? *Everybody* was going to find out sooner or later. That bastard Sanjin was going to find out — had probably heard from sleazeball Glenn. Yup, *if* she didn't have a year's lease on her poor trashed apartment, and *if* she didn't fully realize that quitting her first full-time position would screw up her resume big-time, and *if* she hadn't had Roberto remanded into her custody, she'd leave McGrath and Lindoberth and go home to Nashville. Right now, the thought of having Tiffany hug her, stroke her hair, and call her "poor baby" sounded like heaven.

Brandi's hand crept toward her purse, toward her cell phone.

But no. She couldn't talk to her mother. Not here. Not now. Not with Roberto watching her and waiting for his answer.

"Alan got his girlfriend pregnant and had to marry her." She wiped her hands on the paper napkin.

"Ahh." Roberto didn't act surprised, as though men did that all the time.

The bastards.

He looked her over, reflecting on some piece of information to which she wasn't privy. At last he passed judgment. "At least you didn't love him."

"I did, too!" She did, too!

"No, you didn't. You're not devastated; you're irritated."

"Because *you're* irritating!" And obnoxious.

"You haven't thought about your ex-fiancé all day. A woman whose heart is broken thinks of nothing else."

"Who died and made you the love expert?" Just because she'd jumped Roberto's bones without a thought of tomorrow, he acted like he knew stuff about her. Stuff she didn't know.

"Do you have questions you want to ask me," Roberto said, "or do you want to fight?"

"I don't fight."

He had the nerve to smile enigmatically.

She *didn't* fight. She was sensible and rational. So she grabbed at her fraying self-discipline and *focused.* "Yes. Yes, I've got questions. About the Fosseras — why did you go there?"

"They asked me to meet them." He didn't seem to care that the fries were underdone. He ate them with good appetite.

"Why? Why would you be so foolish as to go and meet people like that when you're awaiting trial?"

"No one says no to Mossimo."

Roberto's flat tone sent a chill down her spine. "Is he dangerous?"

"Very dangerous."

"Then why don't you turn him in to the police?"

"There are several reasons. First, the police aren't likely to take anything *I* say seriously. If you'll recall, I'm up for trial for stealing, and the police will believe it's a rivalry or a setup, or figure if he kills me, it's good riddance. Second, he hasn't done anything wrong that anyone has caught him at. He would take an investigation amiss and kill the person who started it." Roberto leaned close and looked into her eyes, and his were dark and stern. "Do you understand? You are not to speak to the police about Mossimo or the Fosseras. They don't care that you're young and pretty and a woman. They will kill you."

She didn't know what to say. She didn't know what to think. The stuff he was talking about . . . who was he? The passionate lover? The charming jewel thief? The imperious aristocrat? Or this grim-faced, intimidating man who . . . who perhaps was far too familiar with killing?

She hated being at such a disadvantage.

Somehow she had to investigate him. If only she had her laptop. She glanced around the car. "Where's the computer?"

"What computer?"

"The computer Newby said was in the car."

"You wish to send an e-mail to the police?" Roberto sounded polite and unyielding.

"No . . ." But she couldn't tell him why she wanted a computer, that she wanted to know all the details about him, his life, his occupation, his famous love affairs, and his infamous larceny.

"Sending an e-mail wouldn't get the information to the proper authorities," he said.

He was right.

But since the moment she'd left him less than twenty-four hours ago, her life had been chaos, and now she was in danger? Yes, she believed that, but who was she most in danger from? From the Fosseras, or from him? "I have to do what I think is best."

"Please remember, Brandi Michaels, that you are my lawyer, and any information about my movements or our conversations is off the record."

"I doubt if Judge Knight would look at it that way." Although he probably would;

judges and lawyers usually took a firm stance on lawyer-client confidentiality.

"Then it's a good thing I've been remanded into your custody so I can keep an eye on you." Roberto sounded quite pleasant.

Yet a chill slid down her spine. He wasn't threatening her with violence; rather it seemed he relished far too much their unremitting closeness. "What did the Fosseras *want?*"

"My head on a platter."

"What would that profit them?"

"You catch on very quickly." Then the exasperating man ate some limp fries.

"They want you to work for them, don't they?" She *did* catch on quickly. Putting her hand on his shoulder, she squeezed it and said, "Roberto, they want you to steal something, and if you get caught again you'll be in prison for the rest of your life, and the most talented law team won't be able to stop that." And she couldn't bear the idea.

"I swear to you, I am not going to do anything to put your job in jeopardy, and I am not going to do a job for the Fosseras." His deep voice vibrated with sincerity, and his dark eyes pledged much, much more.

"I depend on your word because . . .

Wait!" The limo slowly cruised through the narrow streets of an old-fashioned neighborhood. "Where are you taking me?" And why did her heart leap at the thought that Roberto was dragging her to his lair to have his way with her one more time?

"I thought you'd enjoy meeting my grandfather."

"Oh." How deflating. He wasn't dragging her to his lair.

How flattering. He wanted her to meet his family.

How stupid. This wasn't about her meeting his family. It wasn't even about his being remanded to her custody and having to stay close. This was about his convenience and his convenience only. He couldn't be bothered to take her back where she belonged. She was so insignificant he just dragged her along like extra weight.

Her teeth snapping, she ate the rest of the kielbasa. And enjoyed it, too, damn it.

"You'll like my grandfather. Nonno's a good man, a little eccentric, but if you can't be eccentric at his age, what's the point of living?" Roberto finished his dog, too, and the whole double batch of fries.

"And?" She waited for the other shoe to drop.

"He's a jewel thief."

Ah. The other shoe. Heck, a boot. "Why would you think I'd like him, then? I like honest people. People with some moral responsibility, who don't steal things for fun." She was deliberately offensive.

But Roberto only grinned. "He didn't do it for fun. It was the family business. The Continis —"

"Continis?"

"My mother's family are the Continis. They've been stealing from the rich for generations. We're from Northern Italy, up by the mountain passes. We used to rob travelers when they were weak from making the descent."

"How heroic," she said sarcastically.

"Poverty teaches you to take what you can."

She could hardly argue that. She knew very well what poverty did to a person. It helped you develop galloping ambition and made success not an option, but an imperative.

"Nonno's a legend. He's got the fastest hands you can imagine. He'll warn you he's going to do it, then take your wallet, your watch, your earrings, your handkerchief, your keys. I've seen him take the driver's license out of a woman's wallet inside her zippered purse and close the zipper on the way out."

"So he's a pickpocket."

"No, that's too easy for him. No challenge at all." Roberto grinned proudly. "He's an international jewel thief. When he was younger he was the inside man, the guy who went in and actually picked up the jewels. He was the man who disarmed the alarm before the alarm knew anyone was there. He could walk across a wired floor and never trip it. He was a ghost, the man hired for the big heists, and eventually the man who planned the big heists."

She hated herself for asking, but she had to know. "Is that what *you* do?"

"I hate to buck tradition," he said mildly.

She glanced at his hands — long, broad, capable of bringing a woman to ecstasy. . . . "You're good at stealing things."

"Yes, I am. But, Brandi . . ." His severe tone made her look up into his eyes.

Then she was sorry she did. For the first time since those nights in his hotel room, he focused on her with real sensual intent. "I never took anything from you that you weren't willing to give."

"If you'll recall, I'm the one who made the offer." She sounded sensible, but she blushed bright red.

Not that she thought he'd forgotten their weekend, but he'd made no moves on her. Until now, he hadn't made a single intimate comment. It seemed he was willing to pretend their relationship was and always had been totally professional. She'd been a little annoyed that he could so easily ignore what had passed between them, but she was grateful, too. Fending him off would have been awkward — especially since she thought she might succumb.

Of course, it wasn't as if they'd been together for a long time. She'd only officially met him this morning. It just *seemed* longer.

But she had to clear the air. "Look, you've got it figured out. I was angry at Alan. I wanted revenge, and I took it with you. You're probably feeling used and abused, and I'm sorry. I know I shouldn't have done it, but I made sacrifices for him and he . . . he just blamed me because I hadn't done enough. I was pissed. Do you understand? Asking you for sex was revenge, pure and simple."

Taking her hand between both of his, Roberto raised it to his lips and kissed it as if the smell of sauerkraut, onions, and garlic sausage couldn't offend him . . . as long as the aroma was on *her* skin. "You gorgeous creature, you can use me as often as you wish."

FOURTEEN

When Roberto called her a *gorgeous creature* in that Italian accent, Brandi was ready to attack him with scented candles and fresh flowers and . . . Oh, man, what did men like? With a '56 Chevy Nomad which had, so she'd heard, a really big backseat that folded down.

He kissed her hand again, then said briskly, "Here we are."

As he helped her out of the car, Brandi looked around. They were in a working-class neighborhood with two-story brick houses set close to the street. Tall stairs ascended from the sidewalk to the doors. From behind her lace curtains an old woman peered at the limo and at Roberto and Brandi.

"That's Mrs. Charlton." Roberto waved cheerfully. Taking Brandi's arm, he steadied her as she climbed the stairs. "Don't slip on that patch of ice."

The elderly man who let them in looked like a caricature of every Italian grandfather ever photographed. Deep wrinkles cut his cheeks and forehead. His thin white hair stood on end and waved in the breeze. His brown eyes twinkled. He was perhaps five-nine and, unlike Roberto, of a slender build.

"Hurry. Come in. It's colder than a witch's tit out there!" He shut the door behind them, closing them into a dim, narrow foyer with doors that opened into other rooms and a stairway leading up to the second level. He tossed their coats on a chair. With a broad smile that bared strong white teeth, he turned to his grandson, wrapped him in his arms, and gave him a bear hug.

Heartily, Roberto hugged him back. They kissed cheeks with such affection tears sprang to Brandi's eyes.

Man, she did need to call her mother. She was lonely for family.

"Who's this gorgeous creature?" Roberto's grandfather beamed at her.

Another *gorgeous creature* in a rich Italian accent. She could get used to this.

"This is Miss Brandi Michaels, my attorney." Roberto sounded proud.

She could get used to that, too.

"Brandi, this is my *nonno,* Sergio Contini."

"Eh, Brandi. What an intoxicating name!" Mr. Contini threw his arms around her and kissed both her cheeks, too. "What a beautiful woman you are. And so tall! Welcome to my home."

"Thank you, Mr. Contini." He smelled of soap and wine, he felt strong and wiry, and his accent was exactly like Roberto's. She'd bet he had the ladies lining up.

"Call me Nonno." The phone started ringing, an insistent summons. He ignored it, took her arm, and led her into a parlor decorated with brown brocade drapes, black-and-white photos, and tan lace doilies. "So how did you meet my Roberto?"

"We met at a party" — an understatement — "but we're working together on his case." She glanced at the cordless phone beside the gold recliner. It still rang.

Nonno still ignored it. "That's right; he said you were his attorney."

"One of his attorneys," she assured him. "He has a competent team at McGrath and Lindoberth."

The phone still rang.

"He's in trouble, my boy." Nonno glared sternly at Roberto, then broke into a grin. "But he'll get himself out."

"Nonno." Roberto's voice held a warning.

"No, no. I'm discreet. I say nothing."

The phone continued its pealing.

Finally Roberto asked, "Nonno, are you going to get that?"

"It's Mrs. Charlton, the old snoop. She'll give it another five rings and quit. Thank God it's cold or she'd be over here to meet our gorgeous little attorney." Nonno smiled at her. "Sit." With his hand on her shoulder, he pushed her onto a brown sofa so old the cushions slumped.

Apparently all the men in this family were into "guiding."

As he predicted, the phone finally stopped its incessant ringing.

"Wine?" He was already pouring three glasses from a cut-glass decanter.

All around her she noted touches of wealth interspersed with a general shabbiness. Cut glass and a slumping couch. A plethora of leather-bound books and an old-fashioned heat register that rattled in an unsteady rhythm. An oil painting by Marc Chagall that could be an original and a matted green shag carpet. The room was comfortable, yet neglected in the way of a place well lived-in and well loved.

Roberto sank down on the other side of the sofa and stretched back as if, for the first time since she'd met him, he could relax.

Nonno handed her the wine, and she noticed his hand. The skin was scarred and the fingers stiff, as if he couldn't bend them. An accident? Was that why he'd retired?

Nonno waited while she took a sip. "Do you like it?"

"It's wonderful." Red, rich, smooth, warming her belly and leaving the taste of blackberries on her tongue. She'd better not drink too much or she'd succumb to her exhaustion right here on the saggy old couch. Like Roberto, the warmth and the comfort of Nonno's home had already relaxed her.

"Have a cookie." Nonno passed a plate.

She nibbled on one. The scent of vanilla and the buttery taste of almonds filled her head, intoxicating her with the richness of flavor, the crumbly texture, the perfection that made her want to take the plate and shove every cookie in her mouth. "That is the most divine thing I've ever tasted. Who made them?"

"I did. I'm retired, my wife has passed on, so I keep myself busy." Obviously pleased, Nonno passed Roberto a glass, took his own wine, and sat in the recliner before the television. He reclined the chair, hooked the heels of his worn boots under the leg rest, and beamed at them. "My boy. He'd be okay in the business. He moves well and has the good hands." He wiggled the fingers on his good hand, then smiled slyly at her. "You know this?"

She blushed.

"Nonno." Roberto bent a reproving glare on the old man.

Unfazed, Nonno beamed at the two of them. "Roberto's too tall, too broad to be one of the really great jewel thieves. We professionals need to be able to hide in small spaces, to slip in and out of bedrooms unseen. But his mother didn't listen to me when she fell in love, huh?"

"Is the count tall, too?" Amused, she turned to look at Roberto.

He sat absolutely still, his eyes cold, fixed on his grandfather with an intensity that sucked the air from the small room.

Nonno threw up his hand as if warding off a blow. "Roberto, I tell you, I don't know!"

Still Roberto stared.

And still Nonno spoke. "I don't. You are my beloved grandson. I would tell you if I did."

Roberto gave an abrupt nod. "All right. I believe you."

What had happened? What had she said? Or rather . . . what had Nonno said?

Before her eyes, Roberto returned to his comfortable self. "We ran into the Fosseras today. Mossimo sends his regards."

"May he burn in hell." Nonno lifted his glass to Roberto, who returned the salute. Leaning forward with an intensity that caught Brandi by surprise, he asked, "Did you see the ring?"

"He wears it on his little finger."

"He dares." Nonno's mouth tightened.

Brandi remembered the ring Mossimo wore — it had been small, the gold rich and old, but the color of the emerald had been exquisite. Apparently it was the object of some rivalry, and she experienced the sensation of being caught between the proverbial rock and a hard spot. With her parents she had experience standing there, and it was never the best place to be.

"He flaunted the ring at me." Roberto smiled unpleasantly. "I taught him to be more cautious in the future."

"Where did you learn to do that?" she asked. "That move with the wrist, I mean."

"The count is a very wealthy man. My grandfather's business is stealing jewels." Roberto sipped his wine. "When I was a boy it was deemed a good idea that I have an elementary knowledge of self-defense."

She had come to know a little about Roberto's character, so she said, "How elementary?"

"Smart girl." Nonno nodded at her. "He has his fourth-degree black belt in jujitsu and a second-degree in karate."

"Wow."

"But you, Roberto. You challenged Mossimo?" Nonno leaned his head back against the cushion and looked at his grandson, his dark eyes glittering from beneath drooping lids. "I thought you were going to play the cowering pussy."

"I found the role was not to my taste."

Nonno gave a bark of laughter. "You've made your task all the more difficult."

"What is life but one difficulty after another to be overcome?" Roberto extended his hand in a gesture so essentially Italian, Brandi felt as if she'd been transported to the boot itself.

"So true." Nonno smiled fondly at his grandson. "Sitting on the couch beside you, Brandi, you see my only grandchild, the only child of my only child. We Continis, we steal, but only from the rich."

Her mouth quirked into an irrepressible smile.

"Yes, yes, it is true! We are the Italian Robin Hoods. We help the poor, we stand for justice, and for generations we are known for our passion for life, our impetuous decisions, our dancing, our drinking, our daring . . . our loving." He lifted his glass in a salute to his ancestors. "But Roberto was such a solemn little boy, and he grew up to be a somber, responsible man, and I was proud — of course I was proud! But I thought the Contini blood had at last succumbed to civilization. But no. It was only simmering in my boy's veins, waiting for the right circumstances to transform him into a man as mad and impetuous as the founder of our family, as old Cirocco!"

Brandi's frustration with Roberto made her sharp and bitter, and exhaustion stripped her tact away. "So he's a somber, responsible jewel thief? I don't think so!" Then she bit her tongue. No matter how disappointed Roberto had made her, she had no right to take it out on a pleasant old man who loved his grandson and served her wine and cookies.

"You'll break my *nonno*'s heart talking that way about our family vocation." Roberto chuckled indulgently and touched the lobe of her ear with his finger.

She jerked her head away. "Apparently you aren't very good at your family vocation or you wouldn't be facing trial."

Nonno cackled and slapped his knee.

"She's got you there!"

Obviously he was not at all offended, so Brandi warmed to her theme. "You should leave the illegal activity to professionals like Mossimo."

Nonno stopped laughing. In a reproachful tone he asked, "But Roberto, did you not warn the charming and beautiful Brandi about him?"

"Yes. She says she'll do what she thinks is right."

Both men turned to look at her as if she weren't very bright.

Nonno clicked his tongue in reproval.

"Nonno, I was hoping you would show Brandi your party tricks."

Nonno considered his grandson, then nodded slowly. "Yes, of course." To her he said, "Of course, I'm feeble and not as quick as I used to be. You'll excuse an old man for his clumsiness, yes?"

Brandi recognized that she was being set up, but what could she do? She had to play along. "What do you want me to do?"

"Stand up." Nonno got to his feet and, with his hands on her shoulders, guided her to a place by the window. "So. Here you have the best light so you can observe me. You should wear your watch." He handed her a serviceable, leather-banded Timex.

She stared at it. It looked just like hers.

It *was* hers.

"Put it on," Nonno said.

"But it was on." And he'd picked it off her wrist while moving her into place.

Roberto grinned.

"Wow, Nonno." She buckled the watch on her wrist. "You *are* good."

"I'm flattered, but you have no one to compare me with, do you? No." He handed her the ring her mother had given her for graduation.

"How did you do that?" He'd taken it right off her finger!

"Watch the watch," Roberto advised.

She glanced at her wrist. Her watch was gone.

Nonno handed it to her again. "They're slippery devils," he said cheerfully. "Here. You lost your keys."

They'd been in her jacket pocket.

"And your cell phone."

In her other pocket.

"Watch the watch," Roberto said again.

It was gone. Again. Her head was whirling. "How do you do this?" she asked again. She put her cell phone and her keys back into her pockets. She strapped on her watch without much hope that it would stay there.

"It's nothing," Nonno said modestly. "You

should have seen me before."

"Before what?"

"Before this." Nonno lifted his ruined hand and showed it to her, front and back. "It's my right hand. I'm right-handed. I'm not nearly as good with my left hand."

"What happened?" she asked.

Nonno's genial smile disappeared and he looked grim. Outraged. "Mossimo happened."

"What do you mean, Mossimo happened?" She leaned toward him, frightened and ill, remembering how Roberto had twisted Mossimo's wrist, not understanding how such a move could create such damage. "How could he . . . ?"

Roberto told her what she didn't want to know. "He used a ball-peen hammer to break every bone in Nonno's hand."

Fifteen

Brandi backed away, away from the image. A hammer, rusted hard steel, smashing again and again on the fragile bones of a man's hand . . .

"He wanted my business," Nonno continued. "I didn't intend to give it to him. But a man in the hospital can no longer lead his team, and a master thief with a hand like this can never work again."

"His men cried when they saw Nonno's hand. In his field, there was never anyone like Nonno before. There never will be again. He was an artist. Breaking his hand was like smashing the Romanov Blaze." Roberto watched her, his elbows on his knees, his hands clasped together.

She knew now why he'd started this. It wasn't a party trick; it was the best way to illustrate how dangerous the Fosseras could be. Not just killers, but men who enjoyed their work . . .

She surrendered, as Nonno and Roberto had known she would. "All right. I won't go to the police about them."

"Promise?" Nonno gave her back her watch, her ring, her keys, and her cell phone.

"I promise. I get it!" She sank down on the couch, her knees weak from the thought of such violence, such pain. "I'm not stupid!" But she flinched.

Was her father right? Was she stupid? She had landed herself in a stupid situation with professional thieves as allies and more professional thieves possibly threatening her life, and the lawyers who should have been her allies were her enemies, and one of the most prominent judges in Chicago scorned her for the company she kept. She rubbed the pain over her right eye and tried to ignore her father's derisive voice as it echoed in her head. *Brandi is stupid.*

She wasn't. She knew she wasn't. She was successful in school, and her friends valued her good sense.

But at times like this, when she was tired and in turmoil, it was almost easier to believe her father.

She attributed the familiar churning in her gut to worry about the situation. "Roberto, if you don't work for Mossimo, will he take a ball-peen hammer to you?"

"Don't worry about Roberto. He can handle himself. He isn't the thief I am, but he's one hundred times smarter." Nonno tapped his forehead and winked. "Well, not one hundred times, but he's a smart boy."

Roberto laughed. "Nonno, are you still dating Carmine?"

"No, she got possessive, you know?" Nonno flopped down in his chair in disgust. "Like when I took Tessa golfing, Carmine got mad. I've got no time for that."

By the change in conversation, Brandi knew they were satisfied with her promise. She leaned her head back on the couch and tried not to think about a hammer crushing Nonno's hand, or the guns and brutality, or her apartment being ransacked, or her precarious job. . . .

"Mama says you should marry again," Roberto said.

"Your mama should mind her own business," Nonno answered.

"She says she will when you do."

Roberto's voice sounded far away. She turned her head and looked at him. He was so handsome. Even his profile was gorgeous. He made her heart contract and the hair on her arms prickle, and when she remembered how deliciously they had made love . . . Whoa! She lifted her head. Of all the things she shouldn't think of, that was number one. Never, never should she reminisce about that night, that weekend. . . .

What were they talking about? It sounded like relatives now . . . in fact, she couldn't understand a word. Had her hearing failed her?

No. She smiled. They were speaking Italian.

She was warm, she was full, she hadn't had enough sleep last night . . . she was in trouble and she knew it. Tiffany wouldn't approve of her going to sleep on a visit, but she would close her eyes for a few minutes . . . just a few minutes. . . .

Nonno nodded at Brandi and smiled. "She's out."

"I knew she was going down for the count." Roberto stood up and looked down on Brandi, hunched into one corner, her chin settled on her chest. He moved her sideways so she was reclining. Nonno slid a pillow under her head while Roberto lifted her feet onto the sofa. She murmured and frowned, her nose wrinkling as if her dreams weren't pleasant.

Well, of course not. How could they be? She'd had one shock after another. Altogether, it had been one hell of a day.

"Get her cell, Nonno. We don't want her to wake up."

Nonno plucked the phone out of her pocket.

Roberto took the afghan Nonno offered and tucked it around her. He liked seeing her here, asleep in his Nonno's home, her golden hair spread across the dark upholstered pillow. He tucked a strand behind her ear, then turned to go with Nonno.

Nonno was watching him, hands on hips.

"You look like an Italian fishwife," Roberto said softly.

"Yeah. Sure." Nonno took the decanter and an extra bottle of wine and headed for the kitchen.

Roberto shut the door behind them. They settled down at the old table, glasses between them.

"So who is she?" Nonno demanded.

"A girl I met."

"A nice girl. What are you doing with her?"

His *nonno* could be damned cutting when he chose. "She picked me up. I let her. Then when I found out she was my lawyer?" Roberto spread his hands in a typical Italian gesture of resignation. "What was I to do?"

"You're crazy, bringing her along on a job."

"I'm not doing the job yet, and you should

have seen the Fosseras when I introduced her. They didn't know what to make of her — or me." Roberto laughed softly and poured the two glasses full. The men clinked them and drank. "They didn't know whether to believe she was my lawyer. They couldn't take their eyes off her. I won't put her in danger, Nonno, but I'm going to use her to blind them to what's really going on."

"What is really going on?"

"We'll know soon enough." Roberto glanced at the back door, then at his watch.

It was gone. "Give it back." He held out his hand, offering his grandfather a handful of change.

Nonno groped in his pocket, and a smile blossomed on his face. "Hey, boy, you're getting good. I didn't know you'd been in there."

"I've been practicing."

"Damned straight." Nonno handed over Roberto's watch. "For a job like this, you have to be the best. Tell me again why the girl is involved?"

Roberto took a breath that made him aware of his expanding lungs, of his swelling chest, of the blood pumping in his veins, of an excitement he barely understood and had never experienced before. "I want this job to go down perfectly. I want revenge for your hand. I want to show the world what I can do. I want those bastards who hold my feet to the fire to realize who they're dealing with. And I want her with me. I want her at my side."

Nonno nodded his head, a slow bob of acknowledgment. "Boy, for so many years you buried the Contini deep in your soul. But I see it now. You're as crazy as the rest of us."

"I don't like to be pushed into a corner."

"No. And I like the girl." Nonno bent a dark glare at Roberto. "Are you sure she's who she says she is?"

"No. Not sure. She could be a plant, from the Fosseras or the FBI, most likely." Anything was possible.

"Yeah." Nonno rubbed his chin. "According to gossip, Mossimo's in trouble."

"Why in trouble?"

"He's got no skills. All he's ever been good for is planning these jobs and bullying people to pull them off. And it's been a long time since he's successfully delivered a big payoff. Rumor is that the younger men are getting restless, starting to branch off on their own, setting up their own protection rackets, making trouble on the streets — fights and robberies. Big family. Big trouble. None of them have been caught yet, but I think maybe there might jockeying to see who replaces him."

"Fascinating." Roberto thought of the men around Mossimo's table today. Which of them would take Mossimo's place? Greg? Dante?

No. Fico, the man with the acne scars and the sharp, intelligent eyes. He'd watched the action between Mossimo and Roberto without emotion, as if he had no vested interest in who won and who lost.

"Mossimo's *got* to force you to work for him and *got* to pull this job off or he's going into retirement whether he likes it or not," Nonno said. "Make sure you have a care for the girl. Mossimo is in a corner, and a cornered beast is dangerous."

"I won't let anything happen to Brandi." Roberto would tie her up before he allowed her to step into harm's way. And he would kill before he allowed anyone to hurt her. "Anything else I should know?"

Nonno grinned. "I got the museum plans."

"I never had a doubt." Roberto grinned back.

"But they cost me a bundle." Nonno fetched a clean, crisp roll of blueprints from behind the chipped, green ceramic bread box.

"I'll pay you back." As Nonno unrolled them, Roberto stood and put his full glass on one end to anchor it.

Nonno put his glass on the other. "Ack, no. This is the most fun I've had since I landed in the hospital with this hand."

Their heads almost touched as they discussed the points of entry and exit, what they knew about security, the likely traps they didn't know . . . what the Fosseras had planned and how to thwart them. It was a war council, and it was missing only one of its generals.

A knock sounded on the back door.

Roberto picked up the plans and stashed them in the pantry. Walking to the bread box, he flipped it open and took out the loaded pistol Nonno kept there.

Nonno went to the door between the kitchen and the living room and checked on Brandi. He nodded at Roberto and shut the door again.

Roberto looked through the peephole at the two men standing there. Their collars were pulled up, their hats pulled down, but their faces were bare and they looked straight ahead, knowing they had to be identified before he'd let them in.

Not that they couldn't shoot their way in if they chose.

He disengaged the alarm, clicked the lock on the door, and held it open while silently they slipped inside.

Nonno stood beside the table, his lip curled, his back stiff with rejection.

Roberto locked the door behind them and reset the alarm. "Did anyone see you come in?"

"No. They're watching the house, but they didn't see us." The older man shed his coat and hat without consciousness.

The younger man kept his coat on, staring at Roberto as if he were a criminal. Which, Roberto supposed, he was.

No one shook hands.

The older man seated himself at the table. He gestured to the younger man. "Get out the museum plans and sit down."

Reluctantly, the young man pulled his laptop out of his briefcase. He opened it and the plans for the Art Institute were there — and they looked almost identical to Nonno's plans.

Almost. But not completely.

Roberto leaned forward and immediately identified the changes. Interesting — and more challenging.

"I never thought I'd be working with the likes of you," Nonno said to the strangers.

The older guy looked at Nonno. "I'm not

thrilled about this myself. Now let's get to work. We've got a jewel robbery to plan."

Sixteen

Brandi opened her eyes. She didn't know where she was.

Where was she?

She drew in a sharp, panicked breath.

Then, in a gush of memory, the truth was upon her.

Roberto. This was his grandfather's house — Nonno's house. His grandfather had suffered such a grievous injury by men she'd met today. And she dared not go to the police.

Her apartment had been vandalized, her treasured dragon broken.

Her first day on the job had turned into a nightmare.

She was in an unfamiliar town. She had nowhere to turn. No one could help her except Roberto, and he was a jewel thief — or worse.

Slowly she sat up and looked around. She was alone in the living room. The light in the corner had been turned on, the curtains closed. She'd been prone on the couch. Asleep. When had she gone to sleep?

Had she heard men's voices in the kitchen?

Where was Roberto?

She leaped up so fast her head spun. She dashed through the door into the kitchen, and stood swaying against the wall, staring.

Roberto stood at the stove. He had his white sleeves rolled to his elbows, wore a ruffled white apron, and stirred a pot with a wooden spoon. Nonno was looking into a pot and arguing with Roberto about the contents.

Head rush. She'd gotten up too fast. Gotten up too fast . . . and seen Roberto. Both could cause a head rush.

Only Roberto made her feel as if it would never stop.

Both men looked up, bemused, at her entrance.

"You all right?" Roberto placed the dripping spoon down on the red Formica counter and took a step toward her.

No. She didn't want him to touch her. She'd pitch over onto her face for sure. "I'm good." She looked him over. "Nice apron."

"My grandmother's." He winked at her and went back to stirring the concoction.

Puffs of steam rose from the pot carrying the aromas of garlic, onion, olive oil, and basil.

"Ah. She's awake, our little sleeping beauty." Nonno waltzed over to her, smiling, mellow . . . slightly tipsy. Tickling her cheek with his ruined fingers, he said, "We're fixing dinner for you, *cara.*"

"Thank you, Nonno." She smiled at the old man and thought, *Roberto cooks?* "It smells great."

"It's an old family sauce recipe. We put it on our homemade polenta, and the angels sing with joy." Roberto kissed his fingers.

She wanted to snatch the kiss out of the air, but she'd made enough of a fool of herself today. Instead she looked around the narrow, old-fashioned kitchen. The table in the middle of the kitchen was set with a red-and-white-checked tablecloth, three plates with silverware, and a large salad in a wooden bowl. Three places were set. . . .

A sleep-drugged memory surfaced, vague and uncertain. "Is someone else here?"

"Someone else?" Nonno lifted his brows, but innocence sat ill on his wrinkled face.

"While I was sleeping, I thought I heard men talking."

"We were talking." Roberto gestured between him and his grandfather. "We haven't seen each other for months. We had much to catch up on."

"Okay. I guess that was it." Although it seemed she'd heard different voices . . . it must have been a dream. She pushed the hair out of her face. "What time is it?"

"Seven o'clock. You slept four hours."

"Oh, no." She groped in her pocket. "I didn't call McGrath and Lindoberth and report in."

"I did it. Your phone's by your place setting." Roberto indicated the cell on the table. "Do you like mushrooms? Because we worship mushrooms, and if you don't like them, you're going to have to have bottled marinara."

"Love mushrooms," Brandi said automatically. "Who did you talk to?"

Roberto smiled a rather crisp smile. "I spoke to Glenn and cleared up a few of his misapprehensions about who's in charge in the monkey cage."

"Oh, no." She groped toward her chair and sat down. Glenn wouldn't forgive her for that.

"I assure you, *cara,* this was a fight about what I expect from him. It had nothing to do with you." Roberto comprehended too much.

"He won't care." She cradled her head in

her hands. "He'll take it out on his subordinates."

"But you won't be seeing him."

"What do you mean?" She lifted her head.

"I won't spend my days sitting in your offices, no matter how luxurious they are." He tasted the sauce, then offered the spoon to Nonno. "More parsley?"

"And a little more salt," Nonno said.

To her, Roberto said, "We are chained together by Judge Knight's ruling, are we not? All the time? Day and night, night and day?"

Somehow the details of Judge Knight's actions had previously escaped her. She'd been too exhausted, suffered too many shocks today to figure out all the ramifications, but now her brain was working. Sluggishly, but it was coming up to speed. "I *have* to be in the office. I just started work."

"I have work, too," he said. "I'm the head of a large corporation."

"You're a jewel thief!"

"It's a sideline."

"Damn it!" She slapped the table. The dishes danced. "Who are you really?"

"Exactly who you think I am," he shot back.

"I doubt if you could be that wicked." Her voice rose.

"I'm fixing the polenta right now." Nonno poured olive oil into a skillet and lit the burner.

"Where are we going to sleep?" she asked. "Huh?"

"I'm going to sleep at my hotel." Roberto had the gall to sound calm.

"I don't want to sleep at your hotel. I have to go to my apartment. I just moved in. I have things I need to do." Things she needed to put away — again — after the break-in this weekend. A break-in that wouldn't have happened if she'd been home instead of lolling around in indolent luxury making love to Roberto.

"All right. You sleep at your apartment and I'll sleep at my hotel."

"You'll run and I'll be holding the bag!"

"I already gave you my word that I would do nothing to harm your career." Now Roberto had the gall to sound insulted.

"Little Brandi, bring me the plates," Nonno said.

She stacked them and put them on the counter. "I can't believe we're going to have to sleep together. What was Judge Knight thinking?"

The two men exchanged glances.

She pointed her finger at them. "Not like

228

that. I am not sleeping with Roberto. Never again."

"Aha!" Nonno cuffed Roberto on the side of the head. "What were you doing? Brandi's a nice girl."

Shit. She couldn't even blame her exhaustion for her slip; she'd had a four-hour nap.

But she could blame it on her proximity to Roberto. He obviously blew the circuits in her brain or she wouldn't make those kinds of mistakes.

"She is a nice girl, and she'll be nicer when we feed her." Roberto looked meaningfully at Nonno. "Trust me. I know this."

"She has a temperament like Nonna, then." Nonno nodded wisely. "Dear Brandi, would you serve the salad?"

She narrowed her eyes and would have railed at them, but the smell of frying polenta mixed with the scent of the sauce and she was suddenly ravenous. She shook the glass jar filled with oil and vinegar and poured the dressing on the greens, then tossed them with the plastic salad tongs. Nonno put the plates on the table and seated himself on the end. Roberto removed the apron and seated himself on one side. She sat on the other side.

Nonno extended his hands to them both.

She placed her hand in his, then stared at

Roberto's broad palm extended across the table.

She didn't want to touch him. It was as simple as that. Hearing his warm, slightly accented voice was bad enough, but when she touched him, she forgot the trouble he'd made for her, his dubious honesty, and his unsavory profession, and remembered, in the hidden recesses of her body, how he felt beside her, inside her, on top of her. Touching him made her *want,* a want she didn't know if she could resist.

Roberto was no man for a woman with her feet planted firmly on the ground and her eyes on the goal. For a woman like her.

But the men were waiting for her to close the prayer circle, so reluctantly she placed her hand in Roberto's.

There. That wasn't so bad. She could deal. . . .

Nonno said the traditional Catholic blessing, and ended with, "Dear Lord, we implore your support with our ventures. Amen."

Both Nonno and Roberto squeezed her hand.

"Amen," Brandi murmured, surprised at the addition.

Taking her first bite, she barely restrained a moan of joy. This wasn't food; this was ambrosia. She took another bite, looked up, and realized the men were watching her. "It's good," she said.

They grinned, exchanged high fives, and settled down to eat.

Brandi had finished her first slice of polenta when Roberto announced, "I also spoke with your sister."

Brandi put down her fork. "You spoke to Kim?"

"She called and I answered your phone."

"Why didn't you come and get me?"

"You were sound asleep. Don't worry; we had a good talk."

"I'll bet." Today was one disaster after another. "What did you tell her?"

"That I would care for you."

"Oh, no." Brandi could imagine how Kim had responded to *that*. Kim was not the kind of woman who trusted a man to do what he promised.

Come to think of it, neither was Brandi.

"She wants you to call her." He caught Brandi's hand when she would have risen. "Show some respect for our cooking. You can call her after dinner."

"I am not grumpy when I'm hungry," she said in irritation.

"No, dear." Nonno sounded absolutely placid. Looking up, he caught Brandi glaring at him in outrage. "I'm sorry! For a minute you sounded just like my wife."

Roberto bent his head to try and hide his grin.

He wasn't trying hard enough.

"I think you two should spend the night here," Nonno suggested.

She wanted some time alone to try to figure out how her life plan had gone so awry. So she smiled and patted his hand. "Thank you, Nonno, but I don't have any clothes. I don't have a toothbrush. And after my meals today, I really need a toothbrush."

"I still have drawers of Mariabella's clothes up in her bedroom. Mariabella's my daughter. She's Roberto's mother. She wouldn't mind at all if you stayed." Nonno smiled coaxingly. "I'll make the bed and Roberto will go down to the corner for a toothbrush."

Brandi was delighted to see Roberto look truly pained. "Oh, man. Nonno, it's cold out there!"

"Wimp." With a single word Nonno dismissed his grandson.

"You've got a driver!" Brandi said.

"I'm not calling Newby to drive me a block." Roberto finished his meal.

She smiled. This would teach him to make her walk all over Chicago in this weather.

"Revenge is sweet."

"So you'll stay," Nonno said.

She really didn't want to. But her bed in her apartment was a new mattress paid for by the apartment manager. She wanted to go home — but not back to that place. She didn't want to smell the new paint and know the hateful message hidden beneath it, and see the couch with the cushions gone, and feel the damp carpet and hope the cleaners got every horrible thing out. Even with Roberto in the house, she would remember.

As she hesitated, Nonno sighed hugely. "I'm a lonely old man. So lonely. I would enjoy the company. Of course, you young people probably don't want to hang around with a feeble old man like me. . . ."

"Nonno, you're pulling my chain," she said.

"Why, yes." His eyes twinkled. "Yes, I am. Thank you for noticing."

She couldn't resist him. "I'd be delighted to stay."

Looking resigned, Roberto stood up and went to get his coat.

"Just for tonight!" she said.

"Of course, little Brandi." Nonno patted her hand. "Roberto, while you're at the store, pick up some eggs for the morning."

"Yes, Nonno." Roberto pulled on his leather gloves. "Anything else?"

"Milk," Nonno said. "And maybe some Bisquick."

"Yes, Nonno." He took a dark knit hat and pulled it over his ears. He should have looked nerdy.

Instead he looked boyish and sexy, and Brandi wanted to wrap his scarf around his neck, give him a kiss, and tell him to hurry. So she said, "About the toothbrush — soft bristles, compact head."

He looked at her. Just looked at her. He didn't smile, but his eyes were fond, as if seeing her sit with his grandfather satisfied something within him. "Soft bristles, compact head," he repeated, and headed for the door.

It opened and shut, leaving the two at the table smiling at each other.

"He's a nice boy. But he's spoiled." Nonno nodded wisely.

"He sure is." *Spoiled and breathtaking.* When he gazed at her like that, she forgot all his crimes and remembered only his charms.

"It's girls like you who spoil him. It's not good for you two to spend the night alone together." Nonno shook his head. "Things happen."

Things happen? They sure did, especially around Roberto.

"I know. I know. You young people are always sleeping with each other back and forth and you think old guys like me are out-of-date, but I'm telling you, my own daughter learned the hard way that men are louses who take their pleasure without a thought to the consequences!" Nonno's voice rose and his dark eyes sparkled with fury. "I had to send Mariabella to Italy to have her baby."

"Roberto?" Brandi had thought he was the son of a count.

"Yes, Roberto. He was born on the wrong side of the blankets. Then she married the count and he made all things right."

"Oh." She was confused and irritated. She needed to know more about Roberto. "But the count is his father?"

"In every way," Nonno assured her. "You stay here and drink a little more wine. I'll make up the beds."

"Actually, Nonno, do you have a computer I can use?" she asked impulsively.

"Of course. Roberto bought me a brand-new computer for my birthday. Come on, I'll show you."

Roberto walked down the dark street, his

head bent against the wind, as cold and uncomfortable as Brandi obviously hoped. The porch lights provided spots of light; the stars were far away and brittle-looking in the blackness of space.

Yet he smiled — she'd been so wickedly thrilled at the idea of sending him out into the cold.

She was not a woman with whom a man trifled. She was intelligent, she was quick-witted, she was passionate — and so, of course, she was vindictive. The last trait was not a permanent part of her character, but when a woman had offered a riches of femininity such as she had offered to her fool of a fiancé and had them rejected, she would seek revenge on the whole gender.

Roberto understood. He only hoped she understood that, when the time was right, he would take her to his bed again.

Come to think of it . . . he hoped she didn't. She was a strong-willed woman, and if she realized his intentions, her resistance would strengthen. He liked leading her on, giving her support in her new job while kindling the fires of her body. When their current situation was resolved, he would sate himself — and her.

His fists clenched in his pockets.

Yet waiting was proving more difficult

than he anticipated. Seeing her asleep on his *nonno's* couch, sweet and defenseless, had touched a tender chord within him and a fierce chord within him. He didn't understand this *need* to possess a woman with whom he'd indulged himself only a day ago.

Yet he would control that need. After all, Nonno was right: Roberto had always been the sober, responsible one in the family, and —

Behind him, someone coughed. Coughed as if he didn't want to, but couldn't hold it back.

Roberto's steps didn't slow. Nothing about him indicated that he'd heard. Instead he waited until he reached the darkest spot on the street and slid into the shadows beside the garbage cans.

The guy following him bumbled along, coughing up a lung.

The guy was really sick.

When Roberto knocked him off his feet he was careful not to kill him.

The boy struggled, punching wildly.

Roberto sat on his chest, pressing him into the icy concrete. "What are you doing? Why are you following me?"

The guy wheezed. "Not."

"Yes, you are. You and that other guy. What did you do, divide up the duties?"

"Had to." The kid started coughing again.

Roberto would have bet the FBI had put a tail on him, but the FBI didn't put their agents into the field with pneumonia. "You're with the Fosseras."

"Not!" The guy struggled frantically.

Roberto leaned close. "Bullshit." *Per Diana!* He wanted to put his hands around the guy's throat and interrogate him, but the kid was literally gasping for breath. Roberto would be lucky if he didn't die while he sat on him. Standing, he fumbled for his phone. "I'm going to call you an ambulance."

"No!" The guy stumbled to his feet and stood swaying. Then he took off down the street, weaving as he ran.

Shaking his head, Roberto watched him go. He was no threat. He would be lucky to live through the night.

Who the hell would send this loser to trail Roberto? Not Mossimo. Not the FBI.

So who?

Seventeen

Brandi sat at Nonno's tiny desk in his bedroom and stared in disbelief at the photo of a distinguished-looking Roberto on the nineteen-inch computer screen.

Roberto Bartolini, CEO of Bartolini Importers, speaks at the stockholders' meeting to report profits are up seven percent . . . The acquisition of Washington State's prizewinning Squirrel Run Winery is expected to add value to an already innovative company. . . .

She flipped away from the business news and to another page.

Count Roberto Bartolini, respected Italian-American businessman and heir to the ancient Bartolini estates in Tuscany, escorts Nobel Prize winner Nina Johnsten to the ball in her honor. . . .

Looking proud and happy, he stood back and allowed Nina Johnsten to take her bows, and he showed so much pride she might have been a supermodel instead of a woman about ninety years old and half his height.

Brandi shoved her hair off her forehead and went looking for the dirt.

Count Roberto Bartolini, known for his high-profile affairs as well as his discreet refusal to discuss his women, adds another notch to his belt with Chinese-American actress Sara Wong. . . .

"Wow." Brandi stared at the photo of Roberto with the tall, golden-skinned, dark-haired Asian woman. They were the most beautiful couple she'd ever seen . . . except for the picture of Roberto with English heiress Brownie Burbank. They were also the most beautiful couple she'd ever seen. And Roberto with German opera singer Leah Camberg. He had a way of making every woman more beautiful than she could be by herself.

Brandi looked down at her wrinkled suit. Except probably for her. Somehow she thought that, after today, she was the worse for wear.

But as much as she wanted to, she didn't dare linger over the photos of his various lovers. Nonno was making her bed, then coming back for her, and she needed to find out at what turn Roberto's life had gone wrong.

She found the stats in the most recent articles.

Count Roberto Bartolini, respected international businessman, has been accused of stealing his lover's jewelry . . . Mrs. Gloria Vandermere claims he took her eight-carat diamond after spending the night in her mansion . . . "He's good, but not eight-carat-diamond's worth of good," she is quoted as saying. When asked, Count Bartolini shrugged and said, "I'm a businessman, not a gigolo," but the still-discreet Italian nobleman refused to address the matter of whether he slept with Mrs. Vandermere. Count Bartolini is a descendent of American Italians on his mother's side, and his grandfather Sergio Contini was allegedly the head of a ring of jewel thieves in Chicago, but no whisper of dishonesty has ever before tainted his name. . . .

Brandi erased the browser's history,

turned off the computer, and sat loose-fisted in the ergonomic desk chair. If anything, her investigation had confused her more.

Roberto had never before been accused of a crime. He was rich, he was respected, he was a businessman, he was a lover. . . . Had he hidden his hobby from the press until the moment when he took one chance too many? Was this an aberration in character? Or was Mrs. Vandermere nothing but a disgruntled former lover?

Nonno tapped on the door. "All right, little Brandi, your room is ready."

At once she was on her feet and moving toward Nonno. She couldn't think of this right now. She now knew what the world knew about Roberto, and she was more confused than ever.

Nonno led her down the hall and opened the door to Mariabella's bedroom. "Here you are. The heat is on, but it's a little chilly still." He waved at the maple dresser. "Mariabella's pajamas are in there. She left a robe in the closet. Don't be shy; use what you need. Mariabella is a sweet girl. She'd want to share."

"Thank you, Nonno."

"The bath's at the end of the hall. You can spend as much time in there as you want — Mariabella always did. Hours and hours."

He cackled as if he were telling an old family joke.

Driven by impulse, Brandi kissed his cheek.

He patted hers. "I've enjoyed having a beautiful young woman visit, even if she is with my rascal of a grandson."

Downstairs, the door opened and closed.

"He's returned at last." Nonno headed back down the stairs. "I'll get your toothbrush."

"Thank you, Nonno." Brandi stepped inside the bedroom and felt as if she'd stepped back into the seventies. The carpet was lavender. The wallpaper and the bedspread were sprinkled with lavender flowers. A yellowing poster of Genesis featuring a young Phil Collins with hair that was a little longer but still thin was pinned on the ceiling. The heat register creaked and rumbled. Despite the chill, the room welcomed her with the generous warmth of a daughter of Nonno's, a mother of Roberto's. Brandi didn't hesitate to search the drawers for sleepwear. She found pajamas first and grimaced. Not surprisingly, Mariabella was shorter than Brandi — shorter by at least six inches. Of course, Nonno wouldn't think of that, and Brandi wouldn't hurt him by mentioning it. Instead she dug deeper to find a flannel nightgown. She pulled it over her head. It hit her at mid-shin.

She looked at herself in the mirror. Her arms stuck out. Her ankles stuck out. She looked like a gangly giraffe, and she felt sort of like Alice in Wonderland falling down the rabbit hole. All her perceptions were twisting, stretching, shrinking, and she didn't know which way was up.

She took out her PDA and opened it to her master list of qualities required in a man. She read them through. *Honest, dependable, goal-oriented, sober. . .*

Roberto was none of those.

It didn't matter. Or rather it shouldn't matter, because she didn't have Roberto. Shouldn't want to have him.

But . . . her stylus hovered over ERASE ALL.

Her cell phone rang. It was Kim, and with relief, Brandi put away her PDA and answered the phone.

"What are you up to?" Her half sister's voice blared in Brandi's ear. "Your mother keeps calling trying to pry information out of me. I'm pretending I know nothing — and you know how good I am at acting. Lucky for me, I can't figure out what you *are* doing. When I called earlier, that guy answered the phone."

"Did you think it was Alan?" Brandi buttoned the flowered nightgown.

"No, I did not think it was Alan. He didn't sound like a wimp who got spooked talking to a lesbian, so I knew it was the new guy. The new guy! The one you were supposed to leave after one night. Then after the weekend. What's going on?" Kim's voice got louder and louder. "Are you *crazy?*"

"I'm not crazy." Brandi moved to the window and squinted up at the night sky, trying to see the moon or the stars . . . or God. She had a few words she'd like to say to God. "But someone out there has it in for me."

"Whiner."

"Bitch," Brandi answered absently. "My apartment was vandalized."

"What? When?" One thing Brandi could always depend on — Kim responded fiercely to a threat to her younger sister.

"Last night. Then I went to my first day of work and my Italian lover was the defendant in my first case."

"The guy on the phone?"

"The very one." Brandi took the pins out of her hair. "Then the judge remanded him into my custody. Now I'm at his grandfather's, where I'll spend the night, and we're arguing about where we're going to spend the rest of the nights until the court case is over."

"He wants to spend them all in your bed, huh?"

"Nooo." Brandi got her brush out of her purse.

"C'mon! He'd have to be blind and an idiot not to be interested!" Kim sounded absolutely incredulous.

"Alan was neither blind nor an idiot, and he wasn't interested." Brandi brushed hard enough to pull her hair out by the roots.

"No, he was a self-absorbed son of a bitch who wanted all the guys to envy him for the babe he was dating, but hated that you were taller than him, smarter than him, and infinitely more interesting."

"Hey, thanks!" Kim was a gruff woman not given to compliments, and Brandi treasured this one.

"He was an abuser," Kim said flatly.

"He never hit me!" Brandi tossed the brush aside.

"He didn't have to. He made you feel bad about yourself. Now you've got another one who got what he wanted from you and is ready to toss you aside."

Brandi thought about the way Roberto looked at her when he thought she wasn't looking. "Not . . . exactly."

"Aha!" Kim sounded triumphant. "I knew it. I knew you were kidding me. The guy who answered the phone has the voice of a lover."

Amused, Brandi asked, "What, my dear lesbian sister, do you know about the voice of a man who is a lover?"

"You're not the only one who had an adventure this weekend." Beneath Kim's prim tone, Brandi heard suppressed excitement.

"Wait a minute. Wait. Wait. Wait." Brandi wanted to get this straight. "Are you saying you've found someone?"

"It's not impossible!"

"It is when someone's as picky as you are," Brandi retorted.

Kim laughed, a deep, satisfied laugh. "Yeah, well, she's special."

"What's her name?"

"We were talking about you."

"What's her name?"

"So this guy is interested in you?"

"I'll tell you when you tell me her name." Brandi grinned into the resulting silence. Kim could be stubborn. But not as stubborn as Brandi.

"Her name is Sarah."

"The vice principal you thought hated you?"

"I answered your question; now you answer mine." But Kim was laughing.

She sounded so happy, Brandi's heart warmed. Heck, if not for Kim, the events of the past fourteen years would have prostrated Brandi, but Kim faced the prejudices against lesbians and their father's scathing complaints to become a successful coach, and with an example like that before her, Brandi had to achieve her goals. She owed Kim a lot. "What was the question?"

"You going to be okay?" Kim asked gruffly.

"Sure. What else can happen?"

"Well . . ."

At that single word, Brandi's antennae quivered with suspicion. "What? Kim, what?"

"I just want you to know . . . I might have said too much to your mother."

"What?" *Oh, no.* "What do you mean, too much?"

"She was questioning me. She confused me. I didn't know what to say, so she started guessing stuff and — Hey, I gotta go. The pool tournament is tonight and it's my turn."

"Don't you dare hang up on me! Kim!

Don't you dare!" But the connection was dead. "Shit!" Now she had to call Tiffany. "Shit." But this time she was considerably less heated.

She should have called sooner. She knew it. There was no use blaming Kim because she'd tried to cover for Brandi and failed. It was just that this had gotten so complicated, much more than a simple jilting, and Tiffany would be so distressed — distressed because Brandi had been hurt, and more distressed that Brandi hadn't run to her mother for comfort.

But it had been years since Brandi had considered Tiffany capable of giving her anything, especially comfort.

Brandi's attitude didn't help their relationship, but what was she supposed to do? She'd tried to fake it, and all that had gotten her was hurt looks.

Taking a breath, she dialed her mother's home number. It rang and rang; then Tiffany's answering machine picked up. "I'm sorry I'm not home to receive your call. . . ." Brandi dialed her mother's cell. It rang and rang; then the voice mail picked up. "I'm sorry I'm not on the cell phone right now. . . ."

Where was she? At the movies? Somewhere with bad cell service?

Brandi tried Kim again, but of course she didn't pick up.

Nonno knocked.

Brandi put her phone in her purse. She slipped on the maroon velvet robe with the hem that exposed the ruffled hem of the nightgown. Walking to the door, she opened it two inches and peeked out.

It wasn't Nonno who inexorably pushed the door open; it was Roberto. He pushed her backward until he could look her over, and his smile blossomed.

Damn him. He didn't look amused. He looked . . . he looked the way he had when she'd finally put on the lacy nightgown and paraded enticingly before him. His black hair was tousled as if he'd just removed a cap. Tousled, with a lock that hung over his forehead that enticed her to push it back. His brown eyes held a kindling flame, and his lips . . . his lips were so very talented.

Not the best moment to think of that.

She fell back a step.

He followed.

She touched the buttons at her throat to make sure they were fastened. They were. She swallowed and asked, "Toothbrush?"

"Here." He pulled the plastic package out of his shirt pocket and handed it over. "I risked life and limb getting it for you. I deserve a reward."

"I risked life and limb going to lunch with you, so I'd say we're even." She cockily flipped the toothbrush into the air.

"So we both deserve a reward."

"None of that!" She waltzed backward, but somehow it seemed he was as good a dancer as she was, for she found herself wrapped in his arms. Driven by an inner rhythm, he moved her backward until, with a shock of pleasure, she felt his heated body before her and the cool wall at her back.

Burying his head in her hair, he inhaled as if the scent of her intoxicated him.

"Your grandfather would not like this." But *she* did. Oh, she did.

"I'm not doing anything except holding you." Roberto's voice caressed her.

"And sniffing me." Her body curved, settling into his as if it recognized its home.

He chuckled, a warm breath against her forehead. "I love the way you smell. Nonno would understand that."

Closing her eyes, she inhaled in her turn, but carefully, so Roberto wouldn't notice. He smelled like fresh air and rich passion, but something was missing . . . the scent of her on his skin.

"Besides, you like the way I smell, too."

Damn. He'd caught her. "Nonno warned

me against men like you."

"Did he?" He touched her cheek with his lips. "He should know. He *is* a man like me. Besides, who do you think sent me up with the toothbrush?"

Lifting her head, she frowned into his face. "Why would he do that?"

"He likes you. He wants me to settle down."

"Settle down?" Her breath caught. "Like marriage?"

"It's his fondest wish to hold his great-grandchild before he dies."

"You're damned calm about this!" In fact, Roberto was still holding her so that every inch of their bodies touched.

My God. Marriage. Who did Nonno think she was? For that matter, who did Roberto think she was?

"Nonno knows we respect him too much to go too far in his house." As he spoke, Roberto slipped his knee between hers and pressed until she rode it in a slow rhythm.

She hated the thrill that slid up her spine. "A good matchmaker knows the first and most important element of bringing people together is a common background and common values."

"Like you had with Alan?"

"What a despicable thing to say." She dug

her fingernails into his shoulders. "I told you that in confidence, not so you could fling my failure into my face!"

"It's not a failure." Roberto smiled, a slow, warm lift of his lips. "If you loved him, then it would be a failure."

He made her madder than Alan ever had. Ever could. "But I don't love you, either, and I'm not marrying a jewel thief."

"I haven't asked you." And Roberto kissed her.

Her hurt — if it was hurt — melted under the talented application of his lips and his passion, and the slow, relentless rise of her own desire.

How had this happened? At least in the matter of their affair, they'd behaved sensibly all day. He hadn't pressed her. She hadn't said too much. She'd been able to fool herself into believing they could work out their situation without squabbling. Now she knew the truth. Whether acknowledged or not, the passion between them irrevocably simmered and, with the slightest touch, came to a boil. She balanced on the edge of orgasm. . . . If he would only stop the motion of his knee, she could hold herself back. . . .

He didn't, and she couldn't.

He muffled her cries of fulfillment in his

shirt against his chest, and held her when she had finished and melted against the wall. When her knees could support her weight, he let her go. Leaning down, he picked something up off the floor. Taking her hand, he placed it in her palm and closed her fingers around it. His velvet voice whispered across her cheek. "Good night, *cara.*"

She stared after him in a daze as he walked out the door. Looking down at her hand, she saw her toothbrush . . . with the imprint of each of her fingers in the plastic packaging.

EIGHTEEN

As Brandi led him down the corridor to her apartment, Roberto stalked after her and wondered if she could feel his heat at her back.

"The place is a mess." She jingled her keys as she walked. "I moved in last week."

She displayed a charming skittishness, pretending that her explosive climax of last night had never happened.

And how dared she? Why wasn't she looking at him with adoration? Why didn't she demand the chance to wrap her long legs around his hips and ride him until they both burned to cinders?

"What is the number of your apartment?" *Three eleven, three twelve . . .*

"Three nineteen. Why?"

Because I'm keeping track of the numbers on the doors as we pass. Once we're inside, I'll press you against the wall and kiss you until you again fall apart in my hand. Then I'll take you to the floor and make passionate love to you until at last I am satisfied.

She must have read his mind, for her voice trembled slightly. "While I was gone this weekend, these guys came and —"

"Ah. Yes. *This* weekend."

"What?" She glanced behind her and jumped to see him shadowing close on her heels.

"Now we are going to discuss this weekend." *Three fifteen, three sixteen . . . Only three more doors . . .*

"N-no. No, we're not. Remember? Yesterday we agreed that if our relationship as lawyer and client was to work, we'd have to, um" — she turned and walked backward as if that somehow would stop him from leaping on her unaware — "concentrate on being professionals."

"I don't remember agreeing to that." But he did remember her riding his leg last night, and the soft cries she made as she came.

Memories like that had kept him awake far into the night . . . and gave him a hard-on big enough to warrant a line at the Navy Pier amusement park. He'd been confident he could taunt and tease her until she clawed his back in desire, and it was a tough realization that, where she was concerned, he had no restraint. He wanted her as desperately as he intended her to want him.

She'd turned the tables — and she hadn't even tried.

She stopped and glared at him. "Well, you did."

"Did what?"

"You agreed that we should act like professionals."

He was in no mood to be reasonable. "Are you trying to challenge me?"

"I'm *trying* to behave like a rational human being."

"Because I am definitely rising to the challenge."

He was pleased to see he'd left her speechless. With his hand in the small of her back, he turned her and propelled her toward her apartment.

"I am so tired of you guys pushing me around!" She hurried to get out of his grasp.

You guys? Jealousy caught at his throat. He caught up with a single step. "What *guys* are those?"

"You and your grandfather."

"Ah." His relief was huge, out of proportion, and another blow to the fragile structure of his self-control. Taking her keys from her fingers, he inserted them in the lock.

On the other side of the door, someone jerked it open.

Brandi screamed and leaped backward, slamming into his chest, knocking the air out of him.

A tall blond woman stood in the doorway. A tall, blond, toned woman who looked like a slightly — very slightly — older version of Brandi.

He recognized her. *Tiffany.*

"Mother!" Brandi quivered as her rush of tension dissolved.

"Darling, are you all right?" Tiffany held out her arms.

Brandi walked right into them and laid her head on her shoulder.

Roberto's drive to sexual satisfaction died an instant death. This was *not* the time.

"Why didn't you call me?" Tiffany walked backward, holding Brandi in her embrace. She gestured for Roberto to follow.

Roberto shut the door behind him, fascinated to see Brandi's display of weakness and her collapse into her mother's arms.

"I knew something was wrong — a mother's intuition, I guess — and don't yell at her, but I nagged Kim until she told me what happened." Tiffany rubbed Brandi's back in a slow, comforting circle. "Alan's a fool, darling, and you deserve better!"

Brandi lifted her head. Her eyes were slightly teary and she dabbed at her nose with the back of her hand. "I know. I'm not crying about him; it's just been a rough week."

"Well, don't you worry about anything anymore." Tiffany's voice was low and vibrant, with a dollop of a Southern accent and pure sex appeal. "I'm here to take care of you."

"Oh. Yeah." As if Tiffany had said the magic words, Brandi straightened her shoulders and stepped away from her mother. "Sure."

Despite Roberto's callous dismissal, he knew Alan's rebuff had hurt Brandi. She'd been told she wasn't good enough, and while Roberto took pride in his part in restoring her self-esteem, nothing could take the place of a mother's succor. Obviously Brandi loved her mother; why didn't she take what Tiffany offered?

And Brandi's rebuff clearly hurt Tiffany. She dropped her gaze and put her fingers to her trembling lips. For one unguarded second, she was the picture of dejection.

Then she recovered. Looking up, she smiled at him and extended her hand. "I'm Brandi's mother, Tiffany Michaels."

Taking it in both of his, he cherished it,

offering his comfort and appreciation. Bending, he kissed her fingers. "I'm delighted to meet you, Mrs. Michaels."

"Tiffany, please." The color came back into her cheeks as she warmed herself in his masculine admiration.

"You must call me Roberto."

"Mother, this is Roberto Bartolini. He's my client at McGrath and Lindoberth." Brandi gave them a disgusted glance, then went into the kitchen visible over the half wall.

"I'm delighted to meet you, too, Mr. Bartolini." Tiffany briefly tightened her grip, a gesture of thanks.

Up close, he could see the faint lines around her eyes and mouth, and the skin on her hands was thin and marked by slight spots. She had to be in her mid-forties, yet she was a beautiful, vibrant female who understood the art of flirtation as few American women did. And she liked him. He would bet she liked his entire gender . . . except Alan.

He observed Brandi as she moved around the kitchen. Grabbing a Kleenex, she blew her nose, then stood indecisively. With a sudden display of determination, she opened the trash, flung the Kleenex in, and slammed the lid back down. Very violent for

260

such a soft, inoffensive bit of paper.

He glanced at Tiffany. She watched Brandi, too, two lines between her finely tweezed brows, and the lines looked settled there, as if she worried more than seemed reasonable about such a sensible, studious daughter.

"Roberto, are you taking care of my little girl?" Tiffany asked.

"No, Mother, he's my client at McGrath and Lindoberth," Brandi called.

"I'm taking very good care of your little girl." He ignored the irritated flash of Brandi's sapphire-blue eyes. "And she's taking care of me."

Tiffany's gaze cooled. She took her hand back and stepped away. "That must be true, since you spent the night with Brandi." She was a mother demanding the explanation she considered her due.

"Tiffany!" Obviously appalled, Brandi came to the door. "What do you think you're doing?"

"Sh." Roberto went to her and put his finger on her lips. "This is your mother. She has the right to know where you spend your nights and with whom." *And,* his gaze warned her, *we do have something to hide.* "Tiffany, we spent the night at my grandfather's."

"At your grandfather's? Really? That's all right, then." Tiffany brightened. "Sometimes women do stupid things after a bad breakup, like get involved again right away, and I would hate to think you're Brandi's stupid thing."

If Tiffany had glanced at Brandi right then, she would have seen the truth. Brandi's pale cheeks and stricken eyes betrayed her, and he stepped between the two women. "I don't think Brandi could ever be stupid. Your daughter is a very skilled lawyer," he said, giving Brandi a moment to collect herself.

"I know. Isn't she wonderful?" Tiffany glowed with pride. "Do you know she said her first word at six months? *Cat.* She didn't say it right, of course, just *cka,* but she knew what it meant. My mother actually worried about her. Said that bright girls didn't stand a chance in this world, but Brandi proved her wrong. Proved everyone wrong!"

Brandi interrupted the intriguing glimpse into her past. "Let's sit down." She stepped around him and gestured him toward the chair.

Roberto seated himself, but he wasn't about to let the conversation drop. "Brandi has had a lot to prove to a lot of people, then?"

"Oh, yes." Tiffany tucked her arm through Brandi's. "As soon as she could walk she could dance, so she was wonderful at gymnastics and ballet. My husband only saw that; he never noticed that she got straight As in school, so when she graduated magna cum laude with a prelaw degree, he had to sit up and take notice!"

"Come on, Mother, let's sit on my new sofa. I think the color works well in here, don't you?"

Distracted, Tiffany sank down beside her daughter. "It does, but, darling, do you realize one cushion is slashed?"

Brandi had slept with him, but she didn't want him to really know her. She didn't want him to hear about her past. Because he was a jewel thief? Or because she wore masks she never discarded and kept secrets she wanted no one to know?

"Yes, I've taken care of the problem with the cushion." Brandi bit her lip as if she were accountable for something, although Roberto couldn't imagine what. "How did you get here, Mother?"

"I took a cab."

"From Nashville?" Brandi's sarcasm startled him.

"From the airport! The cabdriver was so pleasant, he pointed out the sights of Chicago, and he only charged me half the price on the meter. Wasn't that sweet?"

Roberto didn't doubt for a minute that Tiffany could charm a surly cabbie into digging into his own pocket to pay her fee.

"But . . . what about your job at the real estate office?"

"I quit my job."

"Mother . . ." Brandi sounded weary, as if she'd heard this too many times before.

"That disgusting man tried to sleep with me." Tiffany's heart-shaped mouth trembled. "I was being nice to his clients, and he seemed to think that meant I wanted to get in his pants."

"All right, Mother. All right." Brandi awkwardly patted her mother's arm. "I know it happens. Look at you. How could it not?"

"I don't ask for it!"

"I never said you did!"

"Your father said —"

"Oh, my father is a big fat jerk."

The exchange told Roberto far more about the family dynamics than a mere explanation could. Rising, he asked, "I'd like a drink of water. Would anybody like something?" When Brandi would have also stood, he said, "Let me do it. You want to catch up with your mother's news."

As he walked into her tiny kitchen, Brandi braced herself. She could almost have predicted what her mother would say and the tone of her voice.

"Darling, about Alan . . ." Her mother, who was never at a loss, seemed unsure what condolence to offer.

And obscurely, that made Brandi feel guilty. "I'm sorry; I should have called you when it happened, but —"

"You didn't want to talk about it. I understand."

Did she? When Tiffany had been dumped by Brandi's father, she'd talked about it endlessly with her friends, with her mother, with any stranger who would listen. Brandi had hated having everyone know their business, having everyone pity them, then watching their friends drift away because they didn't want to hear about it and know that at any time it could happen to them.

But that didn't excuse Brandi's neglect. She would have felt better if Tiffany were yelling.

Roberto dropped a glass on the floor and it shattered with a sharp, sudden sound.

Brandi jumped.

"Sorry!" he called. "Don't worry. I can find the broom."

"*That* is one gorgeous man," Tiffany

murmured as he rummaged around in the closet. "What a wonderful accent. He's Italian?"

Brandi needed to nip this blossoming mutual admiration in the bud. "Yes, and he's a jewel thief."

"How romantic!"

Of course, Tiffany would think that. "No, Mother, it's not romantic. He's a criminal, and there's a chance — a very good chance — he'll go to prison for the next twenty years."

"He doesn't look like any criminal I've ever seen. He's rich. That suit is Armani."

They heard the tinkling sound as he swept up the glass and tossed it in the trash.

"Even better, he knows his way around the kitchen," Tiffany added.

Something about Tiffany brought out the worst in Brandi. She always seemed to need her mother's shallow character confirmed, and she couldn't resist saying, "He's a count, too."

"Yummy!" Tiffany drawled the word with a Southern accent thick as caramel sauce.

"He's yummy because he's got a title?"

"No, he's yummy because he's sexy and rich and handsome. The title is just like whipped cream on chocolate zinfandel mousse. What a husband he would be!"

"Husband!" Brandi turned on her mother. "Why did you say that?"

Tiffany widened her lovely blue eyes. "That's the way I think, darling."

"So did his grandfather!" What was it with these people? Nonno and Tiffany didn't even know each other. Years separated them. They lived miles apart. Yet they had the same one-track minds! "I don't want a husband. I tried that, and you know how well it worked out."

"Roberto definitely doesn't match any of the requirements on your list," Tiffany agreed.

Brandi flinched. Alan had met all her requirements. . . . Was Tiffany being sarcastic? No, impossible. Sarcasm required a subtlety Tiffany didn't possess.

Besides, Tiffany wasn't looking at her. She was looking at Roberto. "There is nothing the least sensible about him, hm?"

Brandi made the mistake of glancing in the kitchen as he stretched up to get down some paper napkins, and her mouth dried. Husband? She didn't want to think about him like that. As if he were a man who was available and attainable. Because she'd already sampled him, she knew that he wanted her, and if she started thinking about forever she would make such a fool of herself — and there'd been far too much of that lately. "Conjugal prison visits are *so* much fun."

"Darling, you know he won't go to jail," Tiffany said with inborn wisdom. "Wealthy people never do."

Brandi wished she could come up with a pithy retort, but she didn't know the details of his case. Her first week at work, and she'd logged about an hour at the office working on the case. This morning she'd called Glenn's office, but Mrs. Pelikan had picked up the phone.

She'd sounded brisk and instructive. *On Mr. McGrath's instruction, we've restructured the team. You now report directly to me, and your job, Miss Michaels, is to keep tabs on Mr. Bartolini. Don't let him out of your sight.*

Do you believe he intends to leave the country?

Don't let him out of your sight, Mrs. Pelikan had repeated. She didn't have to explain herself to Brandi, and she didn't.

Brandi glanced at Roberto. *Don't let him out of your sight.* Too bad the instructions made her happy. "Mother, a husband at risk for a criminal record is definitely not on my list."

Tiffany glanced at Roberto as he filled up the glasses. "*Was* he your stupid thing?"

Her mother had an instinct about men and women that couldn't be denied.

"He's been remanded into my custody." A serviceable half-truth. "That's why I stayed at his grandfather's last night, and we've been arguing about where we're going to spend tonight. I want to stay here." Then realization dawned. They couldn't stay here. There was a bed and a couch with a slashed cushion, and she'd planned to give Roberto the bed because he wouldn't fit on the short couch — well, neither would she, but she figured she'd just put up with the discomfort to have her own way.

Now that Tiffany had arrived, her plan was not viable.

"So." With a charming smile, Roberto handed the ladies their glasses. "We go to my hotel."

"I'll sleep here," Tiffany said, "but can I trust you two alone?"

"Mother, you can't stay in the apartment!" Brandi still smelled the soap the landlord had used to clean the carpet, and the paint that covered the graffiti was a slightly different shade. She had never loved this place; it had been a temporary and convenient location to rest her head until she married Alan.

Now everything about it gave her the willies. No way would she leave her mother in an apartment that had been vandalized. If anything happened to Tiffany, she would never forgive herself. And she would be . . . so isolated.

My God. She shifted uncomfortably. She imagined a tragic end for her mother and all she could think about was herself. She was going to hell for sure.

Yet she desperately wanted to avoid Roberto's luxurious, memory-laden suite.

"Of course Tiffany will go with us to the hotel," Roberto said.

"That's a horrible idea!" Brandi said. Having her mother stay there in the suite where she and Roberto had made love? On every piece of furniture, on the floor, against the wall, in each bathroom? That was just . . . icky.

"There's plenty of space, two bedrooms and two baths —"

"Two bedrooms?" Brandi didn't want to contradict him — Tiffany didn't need to know she'd been in his suite — but in his fifty-eighth-story suite, there had been only one huge bedroom.

"Two bedrooms," Roberto confirmed. "I already called the hotel and told them I needed to move to a more family-appropriate suite. Newby is packing for me now. We're on the fourth floor, Brandi, in deference to your fear of heights."

"I don't have a fear of heights." How had he known? "They just make me a little . . . uncomfortable."

"Me, too. Thank you, Roberto, for letting us stay with you." Tiffany touched his arm. "That's so sweet."

"It's not sweet," Brandi said. "It's a bad idea."

"Do you have a better one?" Roberto asked.

She didn't. Of course she didn't.

So the other two ignored her.

"I just unpacked and I haven't spread out at all," Tiffany said. "Brandi, do you want me to pack for you?"

They were conspiring against her. "I can do it," Brandi snapped.

"Make sure you bring all your" — he waved his hand in circles over his body — "fancy dresses. I have many invitations. Many important people want to meet the notorious Italian jewel thief, and it would honor me to have you on my arm."

"The only" — Brandi imitated his gesture — "fancy dress I have is old and black, so I imagine we're not going to accept your invitations."

"No!" Tiffany bounced in her seat. "We

wear the same size, and I brought dresses with me!"

Incredulous, Brandi turned on her mother. "Dresses? You brought dresses?"

"Charles invited me to a party while I'm here." Tiffany watched her own hands as she smoothed them across her legs. "I can't go in some crummy old gown."

"That's nice of Uncle Charles, but you only need one dress!"

"Darling, when I left Nashville I didn't know which dress I'd want!"

Brandi worried that her mother had begun to make sense to her. She worried that her life had veered out of control and she would never get it back. And as Tiffany and Roberto rose together and headed toward her bedroom, chatting about their social schedule, Brandi worried that her lover and her mother had far too much in common.

After all, if they combined their forces, there was no telling what magnificent folly Brandi might find herself driven to commit.

But no matter what else happened, she was not going to go to any dinners or parties with Roberto. He knew too many shady men. He had too many shady connections.

She was going to put her foot down, and tell Roberto they were staying safely hidden in the hotel suite until she delivered him to trial.

NINETEEN

When Tiffany opened the bedroom door and Brandi stepped out, Roberto caught his breath in instant and painful masculine awareness.

In makeup done by a professional and a red dress that shouted *Take me,* Brandi was the epitome of allure.

But in cosmetics applied by the loving hands of her mother and clad in a blue velvet gown cut in the medieval style, she looked sexy, classy, vulnerable, and as if she needed only his embrace to be complete — although perhaps his libidinous imagination had produced that last bit.

He could no more resist taking her hand between his and kissing it than he could resist the sweep of events that carried him along. "*Cara,* you are the most beautiful thing I've ever seen."

"Yeah, thanks." Brandi's blue eyes glittered with the same cold frost as the sapphires in her ears. Snatching her hand away, she stalked away from him. She wore gold wedge heels that made her legs look a mile long from thigh to toe, and a gold belt that sat low on her waist and clanged softly while she challenged him with the sway of her hips. "Let's get this show on the road."

He lifted his eyebrows at Tiffany, who shrugged and mouthed, *She's sulking.*

Well. He supposed Brandi had the right — for a while. She'd lost the battle to stay in tonight. If he could, he would have indulged her, but he had no choice. His course had been set before he met her. He was seeking the truth about his past, and this operation was his way to find it.

She stood with the door of the coat closet open, staring into its depths with a frown. "Where's my coat?"

Ah. The tricky part.

With a nod at him, Tiffany picked the thickly quilted winter-white velvet coat off the chair and hurried after her. "Here, darling, wear this."

"What is it?" Brandi frowned as she examined the warmest Gucci he'd been able to find.

"It's mine," Tiffany said. "I knew it was cold up here, so I bought it before I caught the plane."

Brandi's frown grew thunderous. "But you can't afford this!"

"It's all right, darling," Tiffany said airily. "I got it on clearance from bluefly.com."

"Mother, you can't afford this coat whether it's on clearance or not. And it's white! How impractical can you be?"

Tiffany glanced at him as if apologizing for her daughter's bad manners. "But it's pretty, isn't it?"

"You can't afford this dress, or the other dresses, and you can't declare bankruptcy again." Brandi was truly distressed. "You have to cut up those credit cards!"

When had the roles of mother and daughter been reversed? Roberto thought their relationship had been askew for a very long time.

But in this instance, he'd bought the coat — he was tired of seeing Brandi shiver in the black London Fog — and he wouldn't allow Tiffany to suffer for his actions. Before Brandi could scold anymore, he said, "Brandi, thank your mother for her generosity in allowing you to borrow such a gorgeous garment."

Brandi turned on him in a heavy swish of skirts and a wave of indignation. But when she caught sight of his grim reproof, she stopped. She thought. Her innate good manners took over. "Thank you, Tiffany." She stroked the velvet. "It's fabulous, and I'll take good care of it."

"I know you will, darling. It gives me such pleasure to know you're going out. It's been far too long since you've had a good time." Tiffany beamed.

She was a kind and lovely woman, and why she wasn't decorating the arm of a rich man, Roberto didn't understand.

As Roberto helped Brandi into the coat, Brandi asked, "Mother, what are you going to do tonight?"

"Nothing. Watch a little TV. Read a little. I started a good book on the plane." Tiffany yawned and patted her mouth. "I'm a little tired from traveling. Maybe I'll just go to bed. How late will you be?"

"Don't wait up." Roberto bundled up in his own coat and scarf. "We've got three parties tonight."

"Three." Brandi pulled on her gloves and kissed her mother on the cheek. "I can't wait."

He flicked his finger against her cheek. "Sarcastic little witch."

They went out the door arguing.

Tiffany went to the window and observed as Roberto handed Brandi into the limo. She waited until they drove away, and she waited a little longer.

Then she returned to the bathroom, to the makeup spread out on the counters and the stylish emerald-green dress hanging behind the door.

By the time the car arrived to pick her up, she looked almost as good as her daughter. In fact — she inspected herself and the excited glow that lit her from within — maybe better, because she was happy, as she hadn't been for a long, long time.

The lights of Chicago cast alternating stripes of color and shadow in the back of the limo, but whatever the illumination, Brandi was beautiful — and offended. She looked away from Roberto and out the window, her proud chin tilted up, her neck a tempting length.

But she couldn't ignore him all night. He wouldn't allow it. Unerringly, he found her gloved hand. "Allow me to tell you what we will do tonight."

She swiveled to face him, her blond beauty cool and indifferent. "Since I have no choice, I really don't care."

"Indulge me." Peeling off her glove, he kissed her fingers. "First we'll go to dinner at Howard Patterson's. He's well-known for bringing in the finest chefs from around the world, and tonight he promises French provincial cuisine."

"Good idea. Feed me first. That'll improve my temperament."

"So true, although I think champagne also improves your temperament. Anyone's temperament, for that matter." He pressed his lips to her open palm.

She inclined her head. "How gracious of you."

She had the sharp bite of an asp and the brilliant wit of a dilettante, and the combination made him dodge and laugh, for he knew that she hid another guise behind the mask of sophistication. She was a passionate hedonist and a tender woman who had become a lawyer to set the world to rights.

God knew she was working hard enough to try to fix him. And while there had been a lot of women in Roberto's life, none of them had ever tried to save his sinful soul.

"After we eat and improve our temperaments, we're going to a party given by Mossimo." Roberto caressed the pad beneath her thumb.

"BYOG?" She pretended to be indifferent, but her heartbeat increased with each stroke.

"BYOG?" Roberto frowned. Seldom did his English fail him. "What is that?"

"Bring your own gun."

"Ah." He chuckled. "Yes, I'm sure there'll be enough firepower to start a small war. However, I will be unarmed."

Her hand convulsed in his. "I don't know that that comforts me."

"Trust me. I'll protect you."

"I know *that.* I was more worried that you'd do something stupid."

She was insulting, yet beneath her disparagement lurked an unthinking confidence that he would secure her safety, and that made him puff up like a strutting peacock. "I suppose it is forbidden to kiss your lips and ruin your glorious lipstick?"

"I'm wearing the lipstick that will remain on earth when all the glaciers have melted."

He leaned toward her.

And ran into her free hand. "However, there is another reason why kissing me is forbidden." She spaced her words for maximum impact. "I don't want you to."

"Champagne," he murmured, knowing how very much it would annoy her. "Much champagne."

She lifted her glossy, perfect lips in a delicate snarl. "Tell me the rest of the plan — we're going to Mossimo's?"

"Ah. Yes. I have to make an appearance, but I promise it won't be for long."

"I can't wait."

If Mossimo were smart, he'd stop worrying about Roberto and start worrying about Brandi. Roberto suspected she could take him down with a few well-chosen words. "I've saved the best news for last."

"I'll bet." Sarcasm, but she didn't take her hand out of his.

"Every year, Mrs. John C. Tobias gives a benefit ball for the symphony and a contingent of musicians plays for the dancing. It's a night made for grace and beauty. It's a night made for you, my Brandi, and I can't wait to take you in my arms to lead you onto the dance floor."

If his graceful sentiment impressed her, she hid it behind an impassive frost.

"Then, after we've waltzed together, you'll get your way."

"Get my way?"

"We'll return to the suite and stay there," he said in spurious innocence.

She stared at him in outrage — an outrage that slowly dissolved into mirth. Leaning back against the leather seat, she laughed loud and long.

He watched her, loving that she could laugh at herself without restraint.

"And tomorrow we'll do things your way again?" she asked.

"That's fair. At night you get your way. In the day, I get mine."

"You really are a case, Roberto."

"A case of what?" he asked cautiously.

"I'll let you know when I figure it out." She took her hand away from him. "We're here."

The limo inched up to the portico of the New England–style home, and the doorman ushered them inside. They greeted Howard and Joni Patterson, who insisted that Roberto appraise Howard's newest acquisition, a two-carat diamond tie clip created in the 1920s.

Roberto told them the jewel was worth only thirty-six thousand, but the setting put the value much higher. Howard was ecstatic, and in a little more than two hours Roberto and Brandi ate, charmed half of Chicago society, and excused themselves to go to the rival party.

"I have to go," Roberto told Joni Patterson. "To ignore a chance to dance with Brandi would be a crime against nature."

"Damn that Tobias woman!" Joni said. "Why she has to have her party on the same night I have mine, I never will know, but I certainly understand about the dancing. The two of you are made to dance together!"

As they descended the stairs toward the

portico, Roberto pointed out, "We're becoming quite the well-known couple."

"Wait until your trial," Brandi advised, "when we tell everyone I followed you around under court order."

"I wonder how many people will believe that?"

"All of them," she said crisply. "I'll make sure of it."

The dinner hadn't softened her ire quite as much as he'd hoped.

"I see you didn't tell Howard that we were leaving their lovely dinner to first go visit the Fosseras," she said.

"Sometimes I show a regrettable tendency toward lying."

"I suspected that."

"But not to you, my Brandi." Leaning close, he whispered in her ear, "Never to you."

He was delighted to note she hesitated before roundly saying, "And I've got a bridge I want to sell you."

Against all logic, she wanted to believe him.

When they pulled up to the Knights of Columbus hall, Brandi's mouth dropped. "Come on! The Fosseras can't afford a nice place for their parties?"

"They can." Roberto watched as Newby

carefully parked the limo in a way that guaranteed them a quick getaway . . . if they should need one. "But their nice places are for their wives."

"You mean it's a guy party?"

"Not at all. But I don't believe we'll meet any wives here tonight."

"They're partying with prostitutes? And we're going in?"

"Don't be ridiculous. I wouldn't expose you to prostitutes." He helped her out of the car. "They're with their mistresses."

TWENTY

The big room had been professionally decorated and the food professionally catered. The band that played could have performed in the best nightclub in the city. But the Fosseras had still held their party at a Knights of Columbus hall rife with cigar smoke and the faint scent of gym clothes.

Roberto counted the number of Fosseras over by the bar — twenty-two — and paid particular attention to the number of exits, including the windows. He noted the clump of females standing together near the dance floor, laughing shrilly and drinking everything from tequila shots to frozen drinks decorated with colorful little umbrellas.

"Oh. My." Brandi sounded amazed and impressed. "I didn't know about the contest." She handed her coat to the check girl.

"What contest?" Roberto smiled at the girl with special warmth, hoping that if he and Brandi had to make a hasty exit she'd remember which garments were theirs.

"The one where the woman dressed most like a slut wins. Yipes! Are any of these girls over twenty?"

Mossimo walked toward them, smiling, hand outstretched.

Brandi lowered her voice. "I assume the loser of the contest has to sleep with *him.*"

"It's whispered on the streets that his wife sends him into the arms of his mistress with a sigh of relief," Roberto said quietly.

"I'll bet." When Mossimo reached them, she dimpled and said, "Hello, Mr. Fossera, how good to meet you again."

"Hey! It's the lawyer," Mossimo said. "Whiskey, right?"

"What?" she asked in confusion.

"Your name's Whiskey, right?"

"My name is Southern Comfort," she corrected him smoothly.

She was smart-mouthing Mossimo Fossera, a man with no sense of humor and a damned touchy dignity. Roberto wanted to spank her.

Instead he chuckled indulgently. "Southern Comfort is also what she's been drinking." He patted her butt. "Run along and talk to the other girls, honey, and when I'm done here I promise to take you home and give you what you deserve."

"I'm so much more at ease with you, *darling*." Brandi gazed at him with wide-eyed and bogus adulation.

"As you wish." Roberto caught her fingers in his and kissed them. "She adores me and wants to be at my side always," he said — in Italian.

"I can see that." Mossimo watched her with a critical gaze and he, too, spoke in Italian. "But women need to seek their own kind, heh?"

"Well!" Brandi flounced with pretended indignation. "If you're going to be rude and speak Italian all night, I'm going to get a drink."

"Remember the special qualities of champagne," Roberto said.

Giving him a look that promised retribution, she headed off toward the knot of scantily clad women.

"She's quite the little firebrand," Mossimo said. "If you ever want someone to tame her —"

"I like wildcats."

"Your grandfather was the same way, but it's not good for a man to be under a woman's thumb."

"Ah, but you don't know what Brandi can do with her thumb." Roberto grinned. "Thank you for the invitation to visit you tonight, Mossimo. I especially appreciate the firm suggestion that I show up."

"Hey, I like to see my friends when I like to see my friends." Mossimo threw his arm over Roberto's shoulders and led him toward the men by the bar. "So . . . have you thought about the proposition I made you?"

"To steal the Romanov Blaze?"

"Sh!" Mossimo glanced at the caterers. "Don't be careless."

"Speak into the microphone, heh?" Roberto touched the flower in his lapel.

"Yeah. Speak into the microphone." Mossimo laughed weakly.

The Fossera men stood with drinks in their hands, watching Mossimo, watching Roberto, quiet, menacing . . . waiting.

"Ricky, man, good to see you again." Roberto shook hands with him. "Danny. Greg." His gaze swept the group. "But where's Fico?"

"He's around somewhere," Ricky said.

"Gone out for a smoke," Greg said.

"I hope I get to see him." How interesting that he had chosen to absent himself now. "But these guys I don't know." Roberto indicated the younger men, twenty to twenty-five, standing against the wall.

They were sullen; one even turned his

back as they walked up.

"They're boys. They're not important." With a gesture, Mossimo ordered them to leave. "Go dance with your girlfriends."

Roberto watched as they drifted away, muttering at being dismissed so lightly. No wonder Mossimo was losing his grip on his family and the business. Trouble brewed among the testosterone-driven youths.

Brandi had stepped into the girlfriends' conversation and now chatted animatedly, but he saw the glazed amazement in her eyes as the young men slouched over and, without a word, took the girls by the hands and led them onto the dance floor.

The older women still stood with Brandi; they were Mossimo's mistress, Greg's mistress, Ricky's mistress, Fico's mistress. Brandi couldn't have anything in common with them, and he feared that if he left her alone for long she'd try to rally the women to a revolt — and that would make the shit hit the fan.

They needed to get out of here, so he got right to the heart of the matter. "Mossimo, you said it yourself. To steal the Romanov Blaze from the museum is a huge challenge."

The men moved into a circle around him, protecting him from eavesdroppers — for all the good it would do them.

Speak into the microphone.

"Are you frightened?" Greg taunted.

"Of course. Only a stupid man faces death without fear." But Roberto didn't show fear now. He showed nothing but a polite interest in the proposition.

"Maybe you can't do it," Mossimo said.

Roberto dismissed that with a flick of his fingers. "Can your guys get me in?"

"They can get you in."

"Then I can steal the diamond. I have a plan already. I just don't know why I should do it for *you.*"

Before he could say another word, he found himself slammed up against the wall, Mossimo's forearm at his throat and Mossimo's gun pointed at his head.

So. Mossimo couldn't steal a jewel to save his ass, but he was still good with the strong-arm.

"Don't even think of betraying me." He shoved the cold pistol against Roberto's cheek. "I'll kill you. I'll kill your grandfather. I'll kill that pretty lawyer of yours, and damn it, I'll go to Italy to kill that whore of a mother of yours."

Roberto recoiled, ready to strike back.

But when he'd walked in here, he'd tacitly agreed to the deal and tacitly agreed that

290

Mossimo was his boss. He couldn't balk now. Not because this worthless asshole called his mother names. Not because he'd threatened Brandi or Nonno. In this operation, timing was everything.

Mossimo held him against the wall for one more moment, cutting off his air, letting him feel the threat, before stepping away and holstering the gun.

Roberto sucked in air, trying to clear his spinning head. Across the room, he saw Brandi stalking toward them, and shook his head. *No.*

She stopped.

No. Don't try to help me. You'll make everything worse.

She inclined her head, but as she walked back to the crowd of wide-eyed women, she made it clear she left him with greatest reluctance.

When Roberto could speak, he said hoarsely, "You misunderstand me, Mossimo. While you're known for many things, you're not known for your generosity. What can you offer me that will make this worth my while? And don't tell me prestige — I can't take that to the bank."

Slowly Mossimo's scowl cleared. Greed . . . he understood greed. "You're a famous jewel thief. To work with you is an honor.

Of course I know this. What do you want to do this job for me?"

"Tonight I dined at the home of Howard and Joni Patterson, and Joni was wearing a ruby on a chain around her neck. It was easily four point three carats and the color of fresh blood."

"I know of it." Mossimo bowed his head as if in shame. "But I can't get it. Their security is too good."

"Usually." Roberto examined his fingernails.

"What do you mean?" Mossimo asked alertly.

"Somehow, tonight their security in certain parts of their house was disabled," Roberto told him.

"Somehow, eh?" Mossimo began to smile. "Hey, you! Ricky! Get our friend Roberto some wine."

"Water." Roberto rubbed his bruised throat.

"Water." Mossimo pushed a chair under Roberto's ass, and they sat down for a low-voiced conversation.

When Roberto stood up again, the game was set. The bargain was made.

"It's a good deal," Mossimo said. "You bring the diamond to the Stuffed Dog, and I'll give you the Patterson ruby."

"Good." Roberto tapped Mossimo's belly. "Remember who has done you this favor, Mossimo, and give me and my *nonno* the respect and peace we deserve."

"Of course." Mossimo embraced Roberto, kissed both his cheeks. "This is a one-shot deal, profitable for both of us, and it's something to do with your time while you await trial, yes?"

Roberto nodded and noted how easily Mossimo gave him the kiss of betrayal. Judas would have been proud.

As Roberto strode across the floor, he crooked a finger at Brandi.

To his surprise, she obeyed him immediately and hurried to join him.

Taking his arm, she followed him to the hat-check. "Congratulations, you discovered the one way guaranteed to make me respond to your every command. I'd do anything to get away from those women."

Roberto chuckled, took their coats when the girl handed them over, and gave her a hearty tip. "Awful, was it?"

"Awful hardly begins to cut it." Brandi let him wrap her scarf around her neck. "Did you know you can discuss a Brazilian wax for twenty whole minutes?"

"God, no. I don't even want to think about it for one minute." He shrugged into his coat and took her arm. Together they went out the door.

They hadn't taken two steps when the scent of tobacco hit him. He stopped.

She kept walking. "Yes, as a subject of interest waxing is right between acrylic nails and acid peels. . . ." She peered back at him. "What's wrong?"

Fico stepped out of the shadows, a cigarette tucked between two fingers. "Roberto, good to see you. And you." He nodded at Brandi. "It's cold out for a skinny thing like you."

"Brandi." Roberto jerked his thumb toward the limo.

"Sadly, I'm getting used to this." Brandi marched away.

The two men watched her go, and when Newby had opened the door and helped her inside, Fico said, "So, my man, did you listen to Mossimo's offer?"

"I did." What did Fico have on his mind?

"You know you don't have to do it."

Interesting. "But I do. I am very fond of my grandfather."

Fico stepped closer. "I can protect your grandfather."

"That's a spectacular promise, considering Mossimo's reputation."

"Mossimo has my greatest respect, always."

No answer, yet all the answer Roberto needed. "And for my fee, Mossimo has promised me a jewel."

"A dead man can't collect payment."

"So he plans to kill me after I get the diamond?" Roberto already knew it, but that Fico told him was confirmation of all he suspected. Fico wanted to take Mossimo's place. He'd do what he must to prevent the robbery.

"I'm telling you that you would be better off leaving this job alone."

This was tricky. Trickier than Roberto had imagined, because he *had* to do the job. "But Fico, knowing Mossimo plans to kill me adds excitement."

Fico threw his cigarette into the dirt and gravel. "Do what you like, then. But don't say I didn't warn you."

"No, I won't say you didn't warn me. In fact, I never saw you here tonight. It's a shame we missed each other." Roberto stripped off his glove and offered his hand.

Fico looked at Roberto's outstretched hand, then grasped Roberto's arm at the elbow. Roberto reciprocated, and the two men shook hard, once.

Against all evidence, Roberto liked Fico.

The man wanted power, but not for the joy of inflicting pain. Fico was all about profit.

Taking a chance, Roberto leaned close. "Trust me. Fico, trust me."

Fico scrutinized Roberto's expression. "What would that gain me?"

"Exactly what you want, Fico. Trust me."

"Only a fool trusts anyone but himself."

"Then be a fool."

Fico considered Roberto for one more minute. "I will think."

"Do that."

They broke apart. Roberto headed for the car and hoped his instincts hadn't steered him wrong.

TWENTY-ONE

The cold wind swept into the car with Roberto, chilling Brandi more than the last hour — and that was saying something. When Mossimo had slammed Roberto against the wall and pointed that pistol at his head, she'd tried to scream. But one of the bimbos, one who looked about sixteen, had slapped her hand across Brandi's mouth and said, "No. You'll get him killed for sure!"

Brandi itched to get out of that Knights of Columbus hall, and she couldn't leave. Of course, she could have run out the door — but for some inexplicable reason, it never occurred to her to abandon Roberto.

What had her life come to that she was responsible for a jewel thief who went looking for trouble?

So as Roberto slid close and the car smoothly drove off, she snapped, "You're some kind of superhero black belt. Couldn't you have knocked Mossimo ass over tea-kettle?"

Roberto stared at her as if he regretted knowing her name. Sighing hugely, he said, "It's at times like this when I realize why the Fosseras keep their silly bimbos. Smart women are a pain."

"I thought so. You could have kicked his butt! Why didn't you?" She wrapped her hands around his wrist, felt the girth, the muscles, the tendons in her grasp.

"Did you happen to notice the number of sports jackets in that place? And the number of holster bulges underneath those sports jackets?"

"I know." But for some reason, his words didn't ring right with her. This powerful man had allowed a fat old bully to shove him around. He'd gone in there knowing Mossimo would probably do it, and he had submitted without a qualm.

Somehow, it felt as if she didn't know all the facts.

Well. She didn't. Roberto didn't confide in her, and she should be glad. This way, when she got put on the stand and asked about the crime, she could truthfully say she knew nothing.

She subsided against the seat. "What happened after he took his gun out of your face?"

"I saw you coming across the floor to rescue me and almost had a heart attack. Are you crazy?" Roberto's usually smooth tone grew harsh. "Do you know what those men are capable of?"

His aggressive display startled her. Alarmed her. Sort of . . . thrilled her. "I can guess. So why were we there?"

"If you ever see me in trouble again, don't you dare try to rescue me."

"You think I'm going to stand by and let someone shoot you?" Her voice rose, too.

Newby glanced in the rearview mirror. He must have heard them through the glass.

"What good will it do if you get shot, too?"

"At least I won't have to live my whole life knowing I'm a coward!"

"Damn, woman." Roberto caught her in his arms as if he couldn't bear to be separated from her any longer. "You scare the hell out of me. Don't you know the world is full of sharks, swindlers, and sons of bitches?"

"Yes, I've had one remanded into my custody!"

He kissed her.

She'd been waiting for this ever since she'd left him on Sunday evening. Every minute she'd been with him, breathing his scent, hearing his voice, watching him watch her, she'd wanted to taste him again. Now she reveled in his heat, in her arousal, in the motion of the car that carried her toward someplace where satisfaction waited.

When finally he lifted his head, she was sprawled across his lap, her fingers clutching his lapels. "Don't stop," she muttered.

"Have to." He sounded as unintelligible as she felt. "We're here."

"Where?"

"At the ball."

She stared up at him, his face a contrast of shadow and light. "What?"

"The dance. At Mrs. Tobias's dance. We have to go . . . dance."

"Now?" She had been lost in the darkness with him, and she wanted to stay lost. "Now you want to dance?"

He laughed, a sort of helpless-sounding amusement. "Since your mother's in our suite — yes."

Her mother. Tiffany. She'd forgotten about Tiffany.

"We could . . ." Could what? Get into Roberto's bedroom without Tiffany noticing? Have wild sex while her mother slumbered in the next room? Fat chance. Even as a teenager, Brandi hadn't tried that. "Oh, fine." She gave up and sat up. "Let's go dance."

The gust of cold air helped freeze Brandi's desire.

Unfortunately, the inside of the California-style mansion was bathed in the warm colors of adobe and earth, with blooming plants climbing every wall and birds singing in tall cages, and her appreciation of her surroundings and her pleasure in her companion started a rapid thaw.

She could hear music. She hadn't danced for months, and then only in a crowded bar with other law students . . . and Alan. There the Rule of Highly Ranked Law Schools prevailed; students good enough to qualify had no social skills and no ability to keep the beat.

That night, it had become apparent that the rule applied to medical students, too, and that went double for Alan.

Now, as a waltz played by world-class professionals filled the air, the ballerina within Brandi stirred, and she flexed her legs.

"This is not so bad, heh?" Roberto smiled as if he correctly gauged her rise of anticipation.

"This is good, and the other would have been . . ." Not *bad.* She couldn't bring herself to say that sex between her and Roberto would be bad. "Unwise," she finished.

"Definitely unwise."

He didn't have to agree.

A thin, old lady of medium height with dyed brown hair and bright brown eyes hurried to meet them. "Roberto, how good of you to come. You're exactly the rogue I need to make this party a success." She extended her hand and allowed him to kiss it, then stood on tiptoe to kiss both his cheeks. Turning to Brandi, she said, "And this young lady must be Brandi Michaels."

Startled, Brandi said, "Yes, but I'm sorry — have we met?"

"No. But when a woman reaches my age she has to have a hobby, and mine is gossip."

Brandi's mind leaped to the kiss in the car, to the affair at the hotel, to this infatuation with Roberto that led her to commit reckless acts of passion. She had known someone was going to talk, and apparently she was right.

But Mrs. Tobias tucked her arm into Brandi's and led her toward the source of the music. "First your fiancé runs off and marries some floozy, and you show the world how little you care by getting Roberto remanded into your custody!"

What a lovely explanation. Brandi liked it very much.

"You lucky thing! Of course, if I looked like you, jewel thieves would fight to be remanded into my custody, so luck had nothing to do with it, right?" Throwing back her head, Mrs. Tobias chortled with old-lady glee.

"Is that all your gossip?" Brandi stumbled in her relief.

Roberto caught her arm. "Careful, Brandi; don't fall now."

"Do you have more?" Mrs. Tobias peered greedily at her.

"No, but I do have custody of the one jewel thief," Brandi said.

"So far." Mrs. Tobias led them through the sunny, open rooms toward the source of the music. "I'm sure they'll all be knocking down your door. Good-looking attorneys — did I say good-looking? I mean *decent*-looking — are hard to find. And one who can walk and chew gum at the same time is even rarer. There!" They reached the balcony above a grand ballroom. She waved an arm. "Isn't it glorious? I use it for my tennis courts the rest of the year, but this night is the night it was built for."

It *was* glorious. The huge room had a gleaming hardwood floor, gold plaster walls, and a raised dais for the twenty-man orchestra. A hundred people mingled in small groups, the men somber in black and white, the women glittering with diamonds and elegance. The dance floor covered half the room, and couples circled, swooping and dipping, as the orchestra finished its waltz.

"It's so grand." Brandi clung to the rail and watched, enthralled, quivering with the desire of a much-thwarted dancer. "I've never seen anything like it."

"It's not for you to look at; it's for you to join!" Mrs. Tobias placed Brandi's hand on Roberto's arm. "Roberto, take this girl dancing!"

"With pleasure."

Ballerina Brandi had always loved her recitals, loved moving to the tempo, loved the grace and the flow of movement set to music. As they descended the stairs, the music changed to a tango and she gave an excited laugh. "Roberto, can you tango?"

"But of course. My mother insisted I learn."

As soon as they reached the dance floor, he put his arms around her and she knew she'd hit the jackpot. He could dance. Really dance. He'd been well trained, but more than that, the music recalled the skill and grace of his lovemaking. And the frustration of being always together yet always apart made the anguish of the tango real to her.

The violent rhythm caught them up, taking them back and forth across the floor, one fleeing, one pursuing in exclusive, desperate passion.

The other guests gave way, clearing them a space until they danced inside a circle of enthralled observers.

Roberto's dark gaze never wavered from hers.

Brandi concentrated on him, saw only him, knew intimately what move he would make next.

The room faded to nothing more than a backdrop to their movements.

They were sex set to music.

Then Brandi caught sight of a familiar face on the edge of the crowd. It sneered with such contempt, she missed a step.

Roberto pulled her back into him, absorbing the motion, but he must have sensed something was wrong, for he guided her with more force, ruthlessly taking her through the motions, allowing her the time to get over her shock.

By the time the music stopped, she had disciplined herself enough to smile engagingly at Roberto and clap as if she had nothing on her mind except her admiration for him.

He acknowledged her, too, bowing and clapping, but he leaned down and spoke in her ear. "What is it? Who's upset you?"

"It's nothing." But that was stupid. Roberto was going to find out. "There. It's Alan."

Roberto searched the crowd with his gaze and unerringly settled on the handsome man with brown hair, blue eyes, pale, freckled skin, and muscled, lanky body. "Ah. I see him. The extremely foolish fiancé has returned."

Roberto made her smile with a little more sincerity.

"He's not at all as I pictured him." He sounded perplexed. "I thought he would be . . . well, not necessarily good-looking, but certainly I imagined he would have an imposing presence for I hear he has a brilliant future. Instead he's . . . just short."

"He's not short. He says he's five-ten."

"He's shorter than you."

"Only when I wear heels."

Roberto snorted. "And when don't you?"

She didn't answer.

"No. Don't tell me you catered to his fragile ego and wore flats. Brandi! No!" Roberto started toward Alan. "I must meet the man who so crushed my Brandi's individuality."

She caught his arm before he'd taken two steps. "He didn't crush my individuality."

Roberto looked down at her.

"Okay, he mushed it a little. Oh, come on!" Deliberately casual, she strolled toward the edge of the floor where Alan waited, a petite and curvaceous redhead clinging to his arm.

She was all too aware of the speculation running rampant through the watching crowd. Chicago society now knew who she was, that Alan had jilted her and that she had become Roberto's companion. They anticipated a scene, but Brandi was determined to keep it civilized. After all, Alan had made it more than clear that he didn't care about her, and she . . . Well, her sapphire earrings had gone far to mend her broken heart. Her earrings — and Roberto.

"Alan." She extended her hand. "How good to see you here. You're back from your honeymoon in Las Vegas, then?"

He didn't answer. Didn't take her hand. Instead he stood looking up at her — in her wedge heels, she was two inches taller — and shook his head in what looked like disbelief.

The chill of humiliation started, but

Brandi would not allow it to control her. Alan had already controlled her through neglect and . . . oh, Kim was right. By an insidious kind of abuse. Lowering her hand, she smiled with quizzical amusement. "Come on, Alan, *you* walked out on *me*. You can be civil."

Alan looked as if she'd stung him like a wasp. "Don't be stupid, Brandi. We're not here to assign blame about who walked out on who."

She replied immediately, defensively, before she could stop herself. "I am not stupid, Alan."

Alan smirked.

"And I certainly hope you don't think I still care whether you walked out on me. I just think you should show some manners." But it was too late. Her fists and her stomach clenched.

Beside her, Roberto chuckled. Taking her hand, he smoothed her fingers and lifted them to his lips. "My darling Brandi, I deeply admire your ability to respond appropriately in any occasion."

Roberto had wrenched her attention from Alan's sour and offended face to him. To his warm appreciation, his generous support . . . his height.

"I would very much like to meet these

people." He smiled broadly enough to show all his teeth. "I'm sure it will be a pleasure."

They shared a moment of intense communication. He didn't think it would be a pleasure, but no matter what happened, he was there to support her. "Of course, Roberto."

When she had done the honors, Alan accepted Roberto's outstretched hand and shook it, then quickly took his hand back.

Obviously he would have liked to ignore Roberto, except Roberto was too important to ignore. And too big. And from Alan's point of view, that rather odd sparkle in his dark eyes might look dangerous.

Fawn looked up at Brandi with the helpless amazement of a toddler viewing her first giraffe. "Alan? Alaannn? Does she have the diamond? Because I want the diamond."

"I don't have the diamond anymore," Brandi told her gently. "I pawned it."

"Oh, no!" Fawn turned to Alan. "She's a rich lawyer. Let's sue!"

Alan ignored his wife. "Brandi! I don't understand how you could have done something so stupid."

Beside her, Roberto lurched forward.

She stopped him with her hand on his arm.

Stupid. That was the second time Alan had

called her stupid.

How had he come to assume he had the right to interrogate her and disapprove of her actions? Even now, when their engagement was over? Had she been so weak, so willing to go along with his dictates? Was she like her mother?

And if that was true, who did that make Alan?

Her father.

She stared at him. He looked nothing like her father, but he was the same. He was a manipulator. He was an abuser. And he'd done her a huge favor by dumping her.

Just as Roberto had done her a huge favor by showing her the way a man should treat a woman.

She glanced at him.

Roberto stood absolutely still, his laser gaze fixed on Alan. He might have been waiting for her cue.

But she could handle Alan. She turned back to him, to the short, petty, unhappy man she could now gladly walk away from. "You don't understand how I could do something so stupid? Like what? Pawn your ring? Spend the money on a day at the spa, a great dress, and some tall fuck-me shoes?" Her clear voice was carrying across the dance floor.

Wearing avid expressions, people pressed forward.

She continued: "Move into my apartment, start work, and get over you in less than a week? My God, Alan, when you got her pregnant" — she nodded at Fawn — "you didn't even have the guts to tell me not to come to Chicago. I uprooted my life for you, but you had to fly to Las Vegas and get drunk before you dared pick up the phone and admit what a weasel you are. I'm smarter than you, and unlike you, I'm not a coward, so don't you *dare* insinuate anything different."

In a clear, hard, carrying voice, Alan said, "No, Brandi. If you're over me so easily, it's obvious I did the right thing by marrying someone else. I don't understand how you can dance around the floor of an elegant ballroom draped across that man's arms like some kind of cheap whore."

TWENTY-TWO

Dressed in her best black suit with her most dynamic red blouse, her most sensibly hemmed skirt and her highest stiletto heels, Brandi marched down the corridor toward Uncle Charles's thirty-ninth-story office.

Behind her, Roberto sauntered like a man out for a summer stroll.

Uncle Charles's secretary's workplace was twice as big as Brandi's cubicle, and the double doors leading into his private sanctuary were polished black walnut and without a word declared his importance.

Right now, Brandi didn't give a damn about his importance.

She tossed her mother's warm Gucci coat on a chair. Planting her fists on his secretary's desk, she leaned over and said, "Tell Mr. McGrath that Brandi Michaels is here to see him."

The secretary, a petite young woman with a face carved out of ice and a nameplate that said, MELISSA BECKIN, was not impressed. "Mr. McGrath is very busy right now, but I'll be glad to pass him a message when it's convenient for him."

Brandi recognized the heat as Roberto walked up behind her. She knew he smiled at Melissa, because that ice melted so quickly she feared a flood. And she hated it when he said, "Brandi and I both need to see Mr. McGrath. Is there any chance you could get us in right now?"

"Who should I say is asking?" Melissa fluttered like a bird wounded by the arrow of love.

"Roberto Bartolini." His Italian accent deepened. "Count Roberto Bartolini."

Brandi had never heard him use his title, and she'd liked that. It seemed to indicate some modicum of humility. But obviously he didn't know the meaning of humility. Or of constraint. Or of the basics of good manners. Last night had proved that beyond all doubt.

"Let me speak to him." Melissa shoved her chair back a little too hard and almost toppled backward. "Oops! Sorry. So silly of me." She stood and sidled toward the door. "I'll just check and see if . . . Hang on a minute . . . don't go anywhere. . . ."

"I'll be right here waiting . . . for you,"

Roberto assured her.

She fumbled for the doorknob, turned it, and slid inside without ever taking her eyes off Roberto.

As soon as the door closed behind her, Brandi swung on Roberto. "Why did you do that? You ruined her coordination!" Like Brandi really cared. "Were you trying to prove a point?"

"You wound me, Brandi." For a man who had danced half the night, he looked remarkably fresh. "You seemed hell-bent on speaking to Charles, so I got you in to see him."

"Thank you very much, but don't do me any more favors! I can't afford them."

"As you wish." With his hand on his chest, he made a little bow.

Continental. Suave. Mad, bad, and dangerous to know. He was all of those things, and if Brandi weren't careful, she'd be road-kill beneath his wheels, because she found him just as irresistible as did poor Melissa.

But she'd learned her lesson, and irresistible wasn't nearly enough for her. She wanted respect, damn it, and she was going to get it if she had to wring it out of Roberto's thick neck with her bare hands.

Melissa opened the door and smiled at Roberto. "Mr. McGrath will see you now."

"Thank you." He strode toward her, his long legs eating up the space between them.

Brandi watched, sure of his intentions, biding her time.

"*Signorina,* you have been so helpful." He took Melissa's hand and bowed over it.

Melissa fluttered like a bird enthralled by a snake.

By Roberto, the snake.

Brandi moved closer to the door.

He lifted Melissa's fingers to his lips. *"Grazie molto."*

While he was gazing into Melissa's eyes, Brandi slipped past him and into Uncle Charles's office.

Roberto whipped around.

Melissa whipped around.

The two of them stared, appalled, as she smiled and shut the door in their faces. She flipped the lock and turned to face Uncle Charles.

The old guy was dwarfed by his huge leather chair and broad wooden desk. "I'm so glad to see you. Come and give me a kiss on the cheek." He cocked his head, his eyes bright like some inquisitive, baldheaded bird. "How is your mother this morning? As beautiful as ever?"

"I don't know. She wasn't up when we left." In fact, Tiffany had been only a lump in the bed next to Brandi both last night when Brandi came in and this morning before she left, and she hadn't stirred to even offer her daughter a good-bye kiss. Brandi didn't really blame her — she could probably tell Brandi was furious by the way she moved, and Tiffany never looked for confrontation.

"Ah." Uncle Charles smiled. "Then what are you here about?"

"I am here about that man." She pointed through the door at Roberto. "Do you know what he did?"

Uncle Charles leaned back in his chair and steepled his fingers. "You've got ten minutes to tell me." He sounded brisk, no longer kindly Uncle Charles but the busy head of a large law firm.

"Last night he took me to three different parties and he treated me like arm candy." She stalked toward the desk. "He showed me off to the businessmen of Chicago as his 'lawyer.' " She created quotation marks with her fingers. "He took me to a party with his low-life Italian gangster friends and their mistresses, patted me on the fanny, and told me to go talk to the other ladies because he had business."

"What did you do about it?"

"Do about it? First I said no. Mossimo

316

Fossera waited for him to . . . I don't know
. . . discipline me, I guess, but he instead
started talking in Italian. Fast."

Uncle Charles looked down. If he was trying to hide his smile, he wasn't doing a good
job.

"So I went and conversed with the ladies!
Who, by the way, were barely coherent in
any language except hair spray and contra-
ceptives." She leaned on the desk, hands
flat, and silently demanded Uncle Charles
look at her. When he did, she told him her
greatest fear. "Listen, Uncle Charles,
Mossimo Fossera wants him to steal something, and I'm pretty sure Mossimo is
threatening Roberto's grandfather. What are
we going to do?"

"Do? We're not going to do anything. If
Roberto Bartolini decides to do a job for
Mossimo Fossera, we can do nothing."
When Brandi would have interrupted,
Uncle Charles held up one hand. "Please
remember who we are. We're not policemen,
not FBI agents, not superheroes. We're
lawyers, and our job starts and finishes in
the courts."

"However, apparently I am a babysitter
who's going to be held responsible by Judge
Knight if Roberto does steal something."

Uncle Charles nodded. "Yes, if Judge

Knight deems that any misconduct of Bartolini's could be laid at your door, he could create problems for us in the future. Make sure you stick with Bartolini so Knight has no reason to doubt your vigilance."

"But I'm losing my reputation as a reliable lawyer before I even start work!"

"Miss Michaels, if you believe that, you underestimate the prestige of this firm."

Miss Michaels. Okay, so she'd annoyed him. "I'm sorry, but do you know what it's like fighting your whole life to be taken seriously and having that undermined in an evening?"

"No." Uncle Charles stood up, came around the desk, and took her arm. "But I assure you, you'll find the gossip around the office among the other young ladies most envious." He led her toward the entrance. "Now, Brandi, you go ahead and dress up for Bartolini; I know he enjoys seeing a pretty girl as much as I do. Anyway, I always thought you worked too hard. When this is over and you're buried in dusty law books, you'll look back and wonder what you were complaining about." He unlocked the door. He opened it. "If you're worried about not having the right clothes —"

"That's not it!"

"— ask Melissa where we keep corporate

accounts, and you can charge whatever you need on McGrath and Lindoberth." He patted her cheek. "That will be fun, won't it?" He ushered her out and shut the door while she stared at him in disbelief.

"Dress up for Bartolini?" she said to the solid oak. "Because he enjoys seeing a pretty girl?"

Dear God, Uncle Charles was a dinosaur. An insulting, patronizing, chauvinistic old dinosaur.

"Are you done?" Roberto asked.

Slowly she turned to face him.

He looked as charming as ever, but she detected smug satisfaction in his expression. *Jackass.* "I sure am," she drawled sarcastically. "Make sure you stick close. I'd hate to lose you in the crowd."

She stalked past the glaring Melissa, out the door, and down the hall. She punched the button for the elevator.

Roberto walked up beside her, their coats thrown across his arm, elegant in the latest of his endless Armani suits. He wore a white shirt, a red tie, perfectly shined black shoes . . . yet his hair was tousled and untidy, as if he'd spent the night making love.

Not with her, though. Not with her.

Damned if she was going to give in to their attraction just to get the same kind of satisfaction she could get from any appliance that took D-sized batteries. Not after that talk with Uncle Charles. Especially not after last night.

"What did he say that made you so angry?" Roberto asked.

"I was angry when I got here."

"Yes, but you were angry at me. Now you're angry at both of us."

"He made it good and clear what my function is in this firm. He wants me to charge evening gowns on him so I can look good for —" She choked rather than finish the sentence.

"Me. Hm. Yes. I can see that would be irritating." The elevator opened, and Roberto held the door while she stepped in.

"Like you care."

"Of course I care."

"No, you don't, or you wouldn't make me go to these parties!" She punched the button for the ground floor.

"I'm not *making* you go to the parties. I'm going, and you're going with me." He took her hand as the elevator doors closed. "Last night I loved holding you in my arms for our first dance."

"Yeah, I loved it, too — right up until the time Alan and his bimbo bride saw us."

"What did you expect me to do?" Roberto's mouth tightened. "Allow him to show you such disrespect?"

"I didn't expect you to punch him in the face!"

"He called you a whore."

Yeah, he had. She hadn't enjoyed it, but she was the kind of woman who thought it was better to shrug off that kind of humiliating public display rather than compound it by making a scene. "You broke his nose."

"Perhaps next time he sees a lady he'll think twice before insulting her." No matter what she said, Roberto wasn't backing off. His brown eyes were flat and cold, his features rocky with disdain.

But retribution fostered retribution, and Alan had shot her a glare that promised trouble. "I saw flashes from the crowd. Someone took photos of us."

"It happens."

The elevator began its descent.

"Maybe to you, but I'm not a glamorous Italian count, and you've been remanded into my custody, and I'm supposed to keep you out of trouble, and if Alan presses charges —"

"*Sh.*" Roberto gestured her to silence.

"What do you mean, *sh?* I'm just saying . . ." Then she realized why he was listening. The elevator sounded . . . funny. Like something was slipping.

And they were going . . . too fast. "Roberto?" She clutched at him. Thirty-three, thirty-two, thirty-one . . . the floors went whooshing past. The elevator was almost . . . they were plunging to the ground.

Roberto flung himself at the control panel, swearing, pulling emergency buttons.

And as abruptly as the drop started, it stopped.

Brandi fell hard.

When she opened her eyes, she found her cheek on the floor. She stared at the brown-and-teal industrial-grade carpet, at the expanse of polished wood wall, and at Roberto, sprawled beside her.

Stretching out his hand, he caressed her chin, but his fingers trembled. "Are you all right?"

"I don't know. How close are we to the ground?"

He lifted his head and looked. "We stopped on twenty-four."

"I'm awful." She was. She was sick with fear, her voice shaking.

"It could have started falling as soon as we stepped in."

That was so stupid she couldn't stand it. "Yeah, because if we hit the ground from twenty-four we'll be dead as hell, but if we fall from thirty-nine, they'll have to scoop us up with a snow shovel."

"Off the ceiling."

She didn't laugh.

In a reassuring tone he said, "Elevators have a lot of safety features."

"We just fell ten floors." Even terrified she could see the obvious.

"And stopped." He caressed her chin again. "That was no accident. There are governors that slow a plummeting elevator, and electromagnetic brakes —"

"And a really hard surface at the bottom if none of that works."

"The manufacturer guarantees the safety features will work. Plus there's a shock absorber at the bottom."

"If the manufacturer guarantees the safety features will work, why did he put a shock absorber at the bottom?"

"Ah, good. You're snapping at me. You are feeling better." He helped her to sit up. "Just a minute. Let me see if I can rouse anyone —"

A woman's voice blared through the speakers. "This is Officer Rabeck. Is there anyone in there?"

"Yes. Yes! There are two of us!" Roberto's Italian accent was deep and strong, as if the drop had shaken him back to his roots.

"What happened?"

"We don't know, but don't worry. We'll get you out."

"What do you mean, you don't know? You've got some idea, I'm sure." Roberto slashed her with a CEO's authority.

Reluctantly the officer said, "It seems that the computer is malfunctioning."

"Malfunctioning? How is that possible?" He got to his feet and addressed the speaker as if Officer Rabeck were standing before him.

"We've got a hacker. The cameras in the elevators aren't working, the safety measures are barely holding —"

Brandi found herself on her feet. "So this is malicious?" she shouted.

"We believe so, but let me assure you, we have our best men on this. . . ." Officer Rabeck turned away from the microphone. Obviously she didn't mean for them to hear, but her tone carried. "What do you *mean,* they're trying to cut off the speakers right now?"

With a frying sound the speakers went dead.

Too stunned for words, Brandi looked at Roberto.

He leaned against the wall, his jaw outthrust, his eyes angry. "I'm sorry, *cara.* This is my fault."

"Your fault? I know you have a huge ego, but how do you figure it's your fault?"

"It's the Fosseras. They're having a power struggle."

"And you're involved . . . how?"

"Mossimo is a man barely hanging onto his authority. He's planned a job. He wants the Romanov Blaze."

Roberto's casual revelation took her breath away. "Aim high, I always say."

"I'm essential to completing that job."

"So you agreed to do it?"

"I did. But if Mossimo doesn't get the diamond stolen —"

"He'll fall and the next man will step in." She got the picture. Her knees gave out and she slid down the wall. "So they want to kill you."

"There's a lot of money in reselling stolen jewels, and head of the syndicate in Chicago is a prosperous position."

As if to reiterate his theory, the elevator dropped another few inches.

Brandi screamed.

"It's all right." He sat next to her and slid his arm behind her shoulders. "It's all right."

"My God." She sat straight and stiff. "We're going to die. We're really going to die."

He nuzzled the nape of her neck. "Have I told you how sexy you look in black and red?"

In astonishment, she turned to look at him. "How can you be so calm?"

He smiled, a tender curve of the lips. A lock of his hair flopped over his forehead. His eyes warmed her with heat and admiration. "*Cara,* there is no one with whom I would rather meet my end than you."

She *was* going to die, but in the arms of the handsomest, sexiest, most noble man she'd ever met. It didn't matter that he was a jewel thief or that he paraded her through Chicago like arm candy or that he planned to steal the Romanov Blaze and, if he lived, would no doubt succeed. He was a marvelous lover who'd led her to ecstasy. He'd taken her mother under his protection without complaint. And for all her protests, when she saw Alan sprawled on the floor, blood spurting from behind his hand, she had experienced a burst of joy. He'd given her that — a taste of savage retribution because he wouldn't allow a petty, foul-minded little jerk to abuse her.

The elevator dropped another few inches.

She didn't scream this time.

She attacked him.

With her hands on either side of his face,

she held him still for a kiss that told him how desperately she wanted him.

He responded with an equal ferocity, thrusting his tongue into her mouth as if he needed the taste of her to survive. His fingers skimmed up her silky stocking to the lacy elastic around her thigh.

Her eyes closed when he touched the bare skin between her legs; she savored ecstasy while teetering on the sharp edge of disaster.

He pushed her back onto the floor and shoved her skirt up around her waist. From nowhere, a small knife appeared in his hand. His eyes narrowed; he looked cruel. He looked dangerous. He looked desperate. He looked like a pirate, and he sliced off her panties.

She almost came right then.

Instead she lunged for his zipper.

He unbuckled his belt.

Together they pulled his pants and underwear down to his knees.

She spread her legs and pulled him toward her.

He opened her with his fingers.

She whimpered. She was too sensitive. This was too intense. Too fast. Too driven.

Yet . . . she wanted more. She wanted him now.

He was so close she could smell the passion on his skin — an aphrodisiac that made her arch up to him. He placed his hips against hers. The head of his penis probed, then entered on a smooth, glorious glide.

And she came. And came. And came.

Roberto joined her, pounding into her, reaching deep.

One thought surfaced from among the chaos of sensation and glory.

If she had to die, this was how she wanted to do it. Entwined in Roberto's arms.

In love with Roberto.

TWENTY-THREE

"We've got it!" Officer Rabeck's voice blared across the elevator's speakers. "We've got control of the elevator! Are you two all right?"

All right? Brandi had never been so all right in her life.

But — *oh, God* — if the speakers were working, the security camera couldn't be far behind.

Roberto knew it, too. He touched his lips to hers and withdrew quickly. He dragged her skirt down, helped her to sit up. "We're fine," he called.

His voice was gravelly. Probably Officer Rabeck didn't know what that meant, but Brandi did. She recognized that sound. It meant he'd been well pleasured.

The elevator jerked.

Brandi gasped and clutched at him.

Then slowly the elevator rose, ascending as regally as a queen.

Officer Rabeck said, "We're bringing you up to floor twenty-five."

Roberto zipped up his pants, buckled his belt.

"There are emergency personnel here for you," Officer Rabeck continued.

Using the wall for support, Roberto worked his way onto his feet.

Brandi had drained him — and she was proud. And relieved to be alive. And . . . and she didn't know what she was.

He offered his hand.

She took it and let him help her stand. She pressed her trembling thighs together. He'd come inside her without protection. She had no panties. This was a disaster — and she didn't regret a minute of it.

She was alive.

She was in love.

She was such a fool.

"Don't hesitate to speak with the emergency personnel. They understand you've been through a trauma," Officer Rabeck said. "I'd recommend you go to the hospital, get checked out, and discuss your feelings with the doctors there."

As the doors slid open, Roberto leaned over, picked up a scrap of red, and stuffed it in his pocket.

Her panties. He'd gotten to them just in time.

A crowd of people stood staring at them — medical and emergency personnel, security, Uncle Charles and his secretary.

Roberto grasped Brandi's arm. He helped her out onto the solid floor.

She barely refrained from falling to her knees and kissing the carpet.

Uncle Charles grabbed and shook her like a parent who'd been frightened for his child. "Are you all right?"

"Fine. Really. Just stunned, that's all." She didn't want him touching her. She didn't want anyone touching her right now. She was still trembling with the aftershocks of violent orgasm. "I would like to go to the ladies' room."

He pressed a kiss on her forehead and let her go. "Of course. Melissa, would you go with her?"

"Yes, sir." Melissa moved to her side.

But before Brandi could walk away, Roberto slid his arm around her shoulders. In a low murmur meant only for her ears, he said, "*Cara,* we must talk."

She nodded. Melissa took one side of her, one of the medical personnel took the other, and they headed down the corridor toward the restrooms.

Roberto stood looking after her.

Damn! He'd fallen on her like a ravenous beast, taking her quickly, furiously, wanting satisfaction before he plummeted to his death. He'd demanded her satisfaction, too, and she'd given him that, but now she was avoiding his gaze. Avoiding him.

"Here." Charles handed him a clean white handkerchief. "Wipe the lipstick off your face."

Roberto stared at it, then into the knowing eyes of the older man.

"Don't worry. If I were in an elevator with a pretty girl and I thought we were going to die, I'd kiss her, too."

If you only knew . . . Roberto mopped his forehead as if wiping sweat off his brow, then cleaned his lips. He shoved the handkerchief in his pocket and buttoned his suit jacket to cover any other betrayals. Hell, as fast as he'd gotten dressed, his shirt might be sticking through his fly.

A policewoman with brown hair, gray streaks, and stern gray eyes stepped in front of him and offered her hand. "I'm Officer Rabeck."

"Officer Rabeck." Roberto smiled charmingly, but his gaze allowed for no prevarication. "Tell me what happened."

■ ■ ■ ■

By the time security let them out of the building, it was three thirty, the temperature had dropped to twenty below, and the wind was picking up. Brandi and Roberto hurried to the limo parked at the curb and slid inside the dim warmth.

The emergency and medical teams had, with the best intentions, questioned them and suggested all manner of treatment for their trauma. They'd proposed the hospital, a psychiatrist, but Brandi just wanted *out* of that building. She didn't want to talk about her fear and her feelings, because sex had triumphed over fear and her feelings were none of anybody's business. Heck, she didn't even know what her feelings were.

She knew only that Roberto's grim expression made her worry that he regretted that moment of madness in the elevator.

She should regret it, too. She knew it, but telling herself so made no difference. Her mind might not approve, but her body was still singing. As Newby slipped the car into traffic, she turned to Roberto. "You said we had to talk." Abrupt, but she needed to hear what he was thinking.

"Yes. I spoke to Officer Rabeck."

"Officer Rabeck?" *Oh, no.* The cameras had come back on while they were still sprawled together.

"She said they had video of the two guys who hacked into the computer that controlled the elevator."

"Really." And Brandi cared because . . . ?

"They followed us into the lobby, sat down, and hacked into the wi-fi and through that into the building computers. Apparently they watched the security cameras until they saw us enter the elevator, then tried to take it down."

Oh. That was why she cared. She'd almost been killed.

But she'd also had the best, wildest, most demanding sex of her life. With the best, most amoral, most powerful man she'd ever met. "We need to *focus.*" And not on this. On the two of them.

She brushed her hand across her face. She had it bad. She had it so bad.

"I know." Roberto's rugged face was grim in the dim light, and the lips she'd kissed so passionately were a thin, determined line.

She wanted to kiss him again.

He continued. "We've got to get this figured out, because it's the same two guys who've been stalking us. Officer Rabeck showed me the video. The guys had scarves wrapped high around their faces, but I recognized the one running the computer by the violence of his cough."

Something about Roberto's description anchored Brandi's drifting attention. "His cough?"

"He's got some kind of cold or bronchitis or something. I actually caught him last night when I went to get your toothbrush."

Now Roberto had her full consideration.

"He followed me. I caught him, but like an idiot I let him go. They hadn't moved on us, so I thought their instructions were to keep track of us. I knew who they were, and I figured, better the devil you know than the devil you don't know." The lines around Roberto's mouth deepened. "My carelessness almost got us killed."

"Two guys. Two computer hackers. And one of them has a cough?" Memory stirred. She leaned back against the cool leather seat, trying to capture the picture stirring in her brain . . . last Friday . . . "I wonder if they're the same guys as the ones in the pawnshop?"

"Pawnshop?"

"When I pawned my diamond ring, there were two guys in there, young guys. I didn't get a good look at them — they had their scarves pulled up and their hats on — but one of them had a cough. The shop owner said they were hackers. I was horrified, and he backed off and said they were just geeks." At the time, she'd been on the phone to Kim, so she hadn't been paying close attention, but she remembered that much. "He seemed scared, and I asked if everything was okay."

"Was it?"

"He said so."

"Think, Brandi." Roberto took her hand. "Why would guys you saw in a pawnshop stalk you?"

"I don't know. I pawned the diamond. I bought sapphire earrings. I got a check for the balance. They can't imagine I've still got the check, but . . . my apartment was vandalized when I got there Sunday evening, so . . ."

Roberto grasped her shoulders and turned her, fully facing him. "Your apartment was vandalized? Why didn't you tell me?"

"That note of incredulity doesn't cut it with me, buster!" She was starting to feel cornered. "I didn't tell you because we had agreed we wouldn't see each other again — although you *knew* better."

"All right." He rubbed her arms. "Why didn't you tell me later?"

"When, Roberto? At the courthouse, when

you were mouthing off to Judge Knight? At the Stuffed Dog, where Mossimo's men were threatening you with a gun? At your grandfather's?" She was getting wound up. "I actually meant to tell you yesterday morning, but Tiffany appeared and I didn't want to explain why I hadn't told *her,* so I kept quiet. Then we moved to the hotel, then we went dancing, then you hit Alan, then we came to McGrath and Lindoberth so I could yell at Uncle Charles, for all the good it did me, then we got stuck in a murderous elevator, and now here we are —"

"Buono!" Roberto held up a hand. "You're right. We've been busy."

"Busy? It's been one damned thing after another!"

"You suspect the men who sabotaged the elevator and the men in the pawnshop could be the same men, and your apartment was vandalized."

"By two men. The security camera in the apartment building showed two men."

"Did they steal anything?"

"No, they just tore things up. Dumped out all the boxes —"

"So perhaps they were looking for something."

"Perhaps, but they were mean. They

spray-painted graffiti on the wall, peed on the carpet, smashed my dragon . . ." To her horror, her voice broke.

Roberto noticed. Of course he would. The man, unlike most men, paid attention when she spoke. "Your dragon? It was special to you?"

"I bought it for myself before my parents broke up, and I've had it ever since. . . . Yes, it was special to me."

"My beautiful Brandi, you've been stalked. You've almost been killed." He ran his leather-gloved hand over her lower lip. "You don't need a dragon. You need a knight in shining armor."

"But I *want* a dragon." And she wanted Roberto.

"When this is over, I will find one for you. The best dragon in the world." He leaned forward as if to kiss her.

But the sexual flush was fading and logic was kicking in. They did need to discover who wanted to kill them, and the idea that she might be the target boggled her mind. She leaned away from him. "Don't be silly. The dragon's not important. What's important is finding out whether the same guys did it all."

Roberto straightened. "You're right, but *cara,* soon we do need to talk — about us."

Reaching into the inside pocket of his jacket, he pulled out a smooth, flat, black metal box about the size of his hand. He slid his finger over the miniature keyboard and the three-by-four-inch screen came alive with color.

"Whoa." She leaned over his shoulder and watched as he used his thumbs to type in a code. "That's your computer? It's seriously wonderful."

"You like technology?"

"Love it. I used my father's old laptop during law school, and kept it running through a couple of viruses, one worm infection, and a hard drive failure. The vandals smashed it, which is probably what it deserved, but I lost everything I hadn't backed up. When I get my first paycheck I'm going to buy the newest, best —"

"What's the name of the pawnshop?" Roberto's thumbs hovered over the keyboard.

"Honest Abe's Pawnshop on Brooker Street."

Roberto typed rapidly.

She continued, "The owner's name is —"

"Nguyen?" Roberto asked.

She stared at the photo of Mr. Nguyen staring out of the screen and read the headline: *Pawnshop Owner Killed.*

"He was such a nice guy," she whispered. And she could scarcely comprehend that, once again, the situation had skidded out of her control and into a murky area called *danger*. She pushed her hair off her suddenly sweaty brow. "This isn't about you? Someone's really trying to kill me? Me, personally?"

"Call your mother," Roberto instructed.

Brandi was already dialing her mother's number.

"Have her pack," he said. "I want her out of the hotel and somewhere safe."

Come on, Mother. Come on. Come on and answer.

"Hello?" Tiffany sounded crackling-bright and cheerful.

"Are you all right?" Brandi asked.

"I'm fine! Just fine! Why?"

Brandi heaved a sigh of relief. She nodded reassuringly at Roberto. "Listen, Mother, we've got a situation here and no time to explain. I want you to go to Charles McGrath's house. Can you do that?"

"Um, honey? That's where I am right now. In fact —"

"Good." Brandi collapsed against the seat. "Stay there until we get this cleared up."

The cheer drained out of Tiffany's voice. "What's wrong? Brandi, I know that tone in

340

your voice. What's wrong?"

Now Brandi polished her voice to a bright sheen. "I'm fine, but it seems that when I pawned Alan's diamond, I ran into trouble."

"Is Alan threatening you? Because I can talk to him." Beautiful, sweet Tiffany managed to make that sound like a threat.

"No, heavens no! Don't do that. It's not him, it's just . . ." Brandi tried to look back over the last week and pinpoint the beginning of the trouble. She couldn't. "Actually, Mother, when my pipes froze I would have been miles ahead if I'd licked them, gotten my tongue frozen to them, and stayed stuck until the spring thaw."

Beside her, Roberto chuckled. He brought up a blank e-mail. His thumbs flew as he typed a message.

Brandi tilted her head and tried to read it, but he hit SEND before she could.

"Is that Roberto with you?" Tiffany asked.

"Yes, Mother."

"As long as he's with you, I know you'll be safe."

When her mother said stuff like that, Brandi bristled. "He's just a man."

"Tomorrow I'll call and get you an eye appointment."

Brandi glanced at him in the fading light. Her mother had a point.

"Brandi Lynn, you let me know what's happening. Don't forget this time!" Tiffany ordered.

"No, ma'am. And you be careful, too!" Brandi hung up. "She's already at Uncle Charles's."

"His security is very good." Roberto held a memory chip in the palm of his hand. "If I show you the footage of the guys in the lobby, do you think you could recognize them?"

"I can probably tell you if they're the right age and size."

He slid the chip into a slot of the computer. "Officer Rabeck enhanced the picture for me. There we are, and there they are." He pointed at the door as first Roberto and then Brandi entered.

In a few minutes, the two young men followed.

The camera angle was high and to the right. The guys peeled off their coats. They wore black sports jackets and slacks. They kept their scarves high around their necks, but they looked respectable. One of them went up to the guard and spoke, gesturing at his friend and shivering graphically. The guard shrugged and gestured at a couch.

"While you were in the restroom, I talked to the guard." Roberto tapped the screen with his finger. "He said the boy — that's what he called him, a boy — told him they'd been waiting in their car for Jake Jasinski in International to come down so they could go to a family funeral. Jake had called them and said he was late and they were to come in and get warm."

"What does Jake Jasinski say?" She watched the two guys go and sit on the couch near a potted plant.

"That he's an orphan."

"I'll bet." She took a breath from a chest that felt tight and panicked. "Those could definitely be the men in the pawnshop. It's impossible to tell for sure, but —"

"The evidence is weighted in their favor."

"But . . . why did they kill Mr. Nguyen?" She took Roberto's wrist and looked into his eyes. "Why are they after me?"

"You said Mr. Nguyen was uneasy, so probably he knew they were going to hurt him, kill him." Roberto covered her hand with his.

"Why didn't he tell me something was wrong when I asked?"

"Maybe he was hoping to talk them out of it. Maybe he was a good guy who didn't want you to get hurt." Roberto's fingers clenched over hers. "But for some reason they're chasing you now, so I think there's a good chance he gave you something they want."

She touched her earrings. "I looked at them through the jeweler's glass. They're great stones, but those guys aren't coming after me for the sapphires. Not when they could have stolen them in the shop."

"So not the sapphires. How about the bag Mr. Nguyen wrapped them in?"

She spoke slowly, retracing that day in her mind. "I put them on in the shop. He gave me the case for them, but it's just one of those velvet jeweler's cases with the flip-top lid and the insert that sits in it holding the earrings, sort of, you know" — she gestured, trying to show Roberto the angle — "up for display."

"Where's the case?"

"In my coat pocket, which is why they didn't get it when they ransacked my apartment. Nothing's getting me out of my coat in this weather."

"Well . . ." His mouth quirked. "Something might."

At his reminder of their flagrant and reckless intercourse, heat washed through her.

She was being sensible. Yes, she was. But as always with Roberto, passion lurked close beneath the surface.

She'd changed since she met him. Had he

changed, too, or was his life one long kamikaze escapade after another? Had she truly fallen in love with a modern-day pirate?

Of course she had. He planned to steal the Romanov Blaze.

This man — this criminal — had no place in her life.

At the realization, pain hovered very near. When she had time, she was going to sit down and cry.

But right now they had a crime to solve. "I thought we were having a rational and very necessary discussion."

"We are, although it's not the discussion I would prefer to have with you at this moment." He sighed soulfully, as if he regretted every moment he spent not in her arms. Then he gazed at her wrapped in the warm winter-white velvet Gucci and said briskly, "This coat is not the right one?"

"No, it's the London Fog, and it's in the closet at the hotel. Roberto, do you suppose those guys are at the hotel searching the suite right now?"

"No. I just e-mailed the FBI and told them what was going on."

"You told the FBI?" She was horrified. "But shouldn't you be trying to keep a low profile?"

"A man in my profession has contacts. After all, I spent a lot of time with the good agents while they questioned me about stealing Mrs. Vandermere's puny eight-carat diamond. If I can't use the FBI in this situation, what use are they?"

"But you did promise to do the job for Mossimo, and if the FBI starts watching us —"

"Little Brandi." Again Roberto put his gloved finger to her lips. "Listen to me. I swear to you, I will do the right thing. Trust me."

When he said that, she wanted to die from joy that he cared and anguish that she couldn't — didn't dare — believe him. "Roberto, I want to trust you. I really do. But —"

His computer beeped. He glanced at the message that popped up. "The FBI is at the hotel now. They're guarding our suite. And the stalkers must have discovered that their plan didn't work, because they're loitering in the lobby."

Newby brought the car to a halt outside the hotel.

Roberto nodded toward a man under the awning bundled up in a doorman's outfit. "That's our FBI protection."

"How can you tell?" He looked like a

doorman to Brandi.

"I recognize him."

"Right." Brandi memorized his face. "Why doesn't he go in and arrest those guys?"

For a moment Roberto looked almost . . . guilty, and he sounded glib. "He can't do that until we know for sure who these guys are working for."

"What? Trying to kill us isn't a good enough reason to put them in jail?" Newby opened the door, and she got out of the car. "Do you remember when you were talking to Judge Knight, Roberto?"

Roberto followed her toward the hotel. "Yes," he said cautiously.

"I've decided you were right." As they passed the fake doorman, she spoke right to him. "The FBI really are a bunch of idiots."

TWENTY-FOUR

Brandi knew Roberto had promised to steal the Romanov Blaze. She just didn't know when.

Roberto knew.

Tonight was the night.

In a few short hours Roberto would be in the Art Institute of Chicago, in the innermost sanctum, lifting the giant sparkling stone from its display case. Afterward, accompanied by the Fossera men, he would go to the Stuffed Dog and deliver it to Mossimo, and then . . . ah, then the stain on the Contini family honor would be expunged, and Roberto would have the answers to the questions that had plagued him this past year.

But before he could steal the stone, he needed to discover the identity of the stalkers who wanted Brandi dead. He needed to know that when he left her alone, she would be safe.

At this hour, the hotel lobby teemed with guests. The concierge gave him a salute. The desk clerk greeted him by name. One of the female guests asked him for his autograph.

Brandi observed the parade of sycophants. "Everybody adores you."

"But of course. I'm a celebrity. Don't you find it amusing that notoriety gives me the same respect as wealth and respectability?" When she frowned, he grinned. She was predictable, his Brandi, charmingly so. "Now excuse me; I have to speak to someone."

Going to the bell captain, he leaned close and murmured, "Do you see the two boys hanging around by the potted plants?"

"Yes, Mr. Bartolini."

"They don't belong in here. Throw them out."

"Yes, sir." The bell captain touched his forehead in an informal salute and signaled security.

Roberto rejoined Brandi, satisfied he'd done his part to make sure the stalkers were miserable and cold. It was the least Roberto could do for them.

Brandi waited for him by the elevator, and if Roberto hadn't been watching, he wouldn't have seen the small hesitation as she stepped on board.

"We could walk up," he suggested. "After a life-altering plunge, it's all right to be afraid."

"If you can take the elevator, I can take the elevator." Yet as it rose, she leaned against the back wall with her head pressed against the paneling and braced herself as if waiting for the fall. "Besides," she said as if he'd made a comment, "the suite's only on the fourth floor."

The elevator stopped.

She jumped.

The doors opened.

Roberto put his arm around her back. "Let's go find out what's in your coat."

His touch seemed to galvanize her, and she hurried out and down the hall — away from him.

She didn't trust him, and while he supposed she showed good sense, still he hated to see the misgivings in her eyes. His every action was that of an adventure-seeking opportunist, yet he wanted her to see beyond his exploits to the man he really was. He wanted her to depend on him, confide in him, believe in him, and he had only two tools on which to rely — his touch and his words.

If she chose to doubt those, he could do nothing to change her mind.

In the suite she went right to the coat closet. Pulling out her London Fog, she dug her hand into the pocket and unerringly pulled out the white velvet jewel case.

He remembered it. It had fallen out of her pocket at the courthouse. He'd picked it up, handed it over, and she'd thrust the case into her pocket once more. Thank God it had remained there until they could get to it now.

She flipped open the lid, lifted the insert that displayed the jewels — and a black-and-gold video chip tumbled out onto her foot.

"My God." Scooping up the chip, she gazed helplessly at Roberto. "It's really here."

Taking it from her, he walked to the desk. He ran his fingers across the lock on his laptop, pushing the right combination, and the lid slowly lifted.

"You have the best gadgets," she said.

She sounded so awed that when this was over, he resolved to get her a laptop with as many bells and whistles as money could buy.

"Let's see what we have." He inserted the chip.

At once the screen came to life and played a typical day in a small neighborhood pawn-shop.

First they saw the counter and the cash register. They heard the door open and someone punch in the alarm code.

"There's probably another camera pointed at the door," Roberto said.

"Probably."

"When he first got the threats, he must have upgraded to a security system with sound."

"Probably," she said again.

They saw Mr. Nguyen come into the picture, go to the cash register with a bank bag, and fill the open till.

At the sight of him, Brandi took a pained breath.

Roberto understood. "It's a shock when you see someone who you know is gone."

"But I barely met him." She sounded bewildered.

"Death is always a surprise. About what time did you go in the shop?"

"Early. Probably ten thirty."

"Okay." Roberto fast-forwarded through Mr. Nguyen seating himself behind the counter and flipping through a magazine, and slowed when the door clanged. The shopowner looked up and flinched. Obviously he dreaded his visitors, but he called out, "Joseph and Tyler Fossera. What are you doing here? I told you to stay out."

Two young men swaggered up to the counter, and the oldest said, "Hey, you're nothing but an old gook. We don't have to listen to you."

"Yeah, man, he's a gook." The other boy laughed — and coughed.

"That's him; that's the kid I caught following me," Roberto said.

At the same time Brandi said, "That's them."

On the video, the oldest asked, "Are you going to take our offer?"

"I've checked around the neighborhood," Mr. Nguyen said. "You have no power here. It's your uncle who is the head of your family and if he knew that you were trying to set up your own protection racket in his territory —"

In a flash, the oldest punched Mr. Nguyen in the face.

Mr. Nguyen's head jerked sideways. He fell back, hitting the wall. Pictures clattered to the floor.

The younger guy said, "Joseph!" He sounded shocked.

"Shut up, Tyler." Joseph waited while Mr. Nguyen staggered up.

"Yeah, well, gook, we can protect you from *us*." Joseph thrust his head forward, a pugnacious little shit who needed to be taken out.

Mr. Nguyen put his hand to his jaw and gingerly moved it from side to side.

"I saw that bruise on his face," Brandi whispered. She couldn't take her gaze off the screen.

Roberto pushed the desk chair under her, and she sank down as if her knees could no longer support her.

"We're going to kill you if you don't pay us," Joseph said.

Mr. Nguyen shook his head as if clearing it, then rounded on Tyler. "And you! What are doing with this thug? You're smart. You program computers. You don't need crime!"

"He's with me!" Joseph grabbed Tyler around the neck. "Aren't you, man?"

"Yes, I'm with him." But Tyler didn't look happy. "You *have* to pay us. We're starting our own business. We're going to be rich, and everyone's going to pay!"

"Ask your uncle what he thinks of that, young Tyler!" Mr. Nguyen said.

Joseph pushed Tyler behind him and focused on Mr. Nguyen. "My uncle's old. He's lost his touch. Everyone says so. Someone new needs to step in. That's me."

"And me," Tyler said.

"No wonder they want the video," Brandi

said. "This would convict them."

Roberto nodded. "If Mossimo didn't get to them first."

"Would he kill those boys?"

"The ones who challenged his power? You bet."

On the tape, Joseph said, "Yeah, gook, Tyler is my second in command. So pay us" — he pulled a pistol and pointed it at Mr. Nguyen — "because I'm not kidding. We're going to kill you." His hand was absolutely steady, and he smiled as if anticipating the money or the kill.

Slowly Mr. Nguyen stepped back, his hands rising in the air.

Tyler was wiggling like a kid who needed to go to the restroom. "No, man, don't kill him; we'll get in trouble!"

"The weak link," Roberto said.

"Jesus, Tyler, you're such a chickenshit!" Joseph said in disgust.

"I'm not, either!" Without drawing breath, Tyler said, "Someone's coming. Shit, it's a girl."

All three heads swiveled toward the door.

"Didn't you lock it? You moron, what's wrong with you?" Joseph put his pistol in his coat pocket. He pulled his cap down and his scarf up. To Mr. Nguyen he said, "It's up to you. If you say one word, we'll kill her and you. Remember that before you say anything."

Mr. Nguyen nodded.

The boys moved down the counter.

The door opened, and Brandi heard her own voice saying, "It's cold outside. It's warm in here." She was talking to Kim, and in a second she appeared in camera range.

Roberto and Brandi watched as she pawned her ring and bought her earrings. They saw Mr. Nguyen take the white velvet case apart, then turn toward the camera. He looked into the lens and the expression on his face said it all. He faced death, but he took no one with him, and at the same time he hoped he brought the boys down.

He reached toward the camera. The chip went blank.

As the video ended, neither Roberto nor Brandi stirred.

She stood. "The little bastards!" she burst out.

He flinched at her vehemence. She called them bastards; if she knew the truth about Roberto, would she use that word so freely?

"They're not bastards," he told her. "They're Fosseras. Treachery is born and bred into their bones. Now let me copy this onto my computer and send it to the police." Pulling up the chair, he went to work, sending the video as an e-mail attachment to his contact at the FBI. Aiden would know what to do.

Walking to the window, she looked down. "I can see them from here. They look like a couple of innocent young boys shivering in the cold. But they killed Mr. Nguyen." She stared down at them, shaking her head as if she couldn't comprehend such violence. "I hope they get frostbite."

"They're going to get more than that." He finished the operation, then turned his attention to her. "But until they're in custody, they're dangerous men. Do you know how to shoot a gun?"

She faced him, exasperation clear on her face. "No, but I know how to do a flip on the balance beam."

"That's good, too." Going to the closet safe, he punched in the code and opened it. He pulled out his pistol, the small piece he kept handy for small jobs, and checked to make sure it was loaded.

Bringing it to her, he said, "Here's the safety. When you want to shoot someone, take the safety off. After that, point this end" — he showed her the end of the barrel — "at the largest part of the person you want to kill, and pull the trigger. It's not art. It's not science. It's security. Your own.

Don't take any chances. Until the FBI has those guys under arrest, take this pistol with you every time you go out."

She didn't argue with him. Taking the gun in her hand, she got familiar with the weight, clicked the safety on and off, and nodded. "Okay. I might not do a good job shooting one of those guys, but it won't be for lack of trying. Where do you want me to keep it?"

"Someplace easy to get to." He opened the top drawer of the desk.

She placed the pistol there and smiled uncertainly at him. "What happens next?"

That Roberto couldn't tell her — even he didn't know for certain what would happen next. For all the work he and his grandfather had put into the plans to steal the Romanov Blaze, there was still an element of uncertainty. Any robbery could go sour; this one, with enemies around every corner, could prove lethal.

More than that, when Brandi discovered what he had done, she would be angry. It might take him several days to get back into her good graces, and he didn't want to wait. He wanted her as he'd had her today, as he'd had her last weekend, in his bed for the slow, heated loving, for the impetuous, graceless matings. He wanted her . . . always.

"Brandi, we need to talk."

At his expression she caught her breath. Color bloomed in her cheeks, and her eyes dropped as if she were shy. Then they rose, and she said, "Yes, we do. Do you know what I discovered today in that falling elevator?"

"What?"

"That I love you."

He gripped the back of the chair hard enough to make the metal crack.

"I shouldn't," she said. "You're the wrong man for me. You fit none of my requirements. You're flighty. You want adventure. You're immoral. You don't respect the law. But I can't help myself. I adore you."

"As I adore you. Brandi . . ." She stunned him with her fierce courage. He had been anguished that she believed the worst of him, yet was it not braver to open her heart to him when she credited him with a notorious character?

Lust, shimmering beneath the surface, roared into the full heat of an Italian summer. He found himself beside her, holding her head in his hands and kissing her. Kissing her with a rough need he could barely rein in.

She responded. . . . Their impetuous need in the elevator was nothing to this. Her mouth sought his again and again.

He slid his hands inside her jacket, relishing the narrow width of her waist, lifting his hands to her breasts and knowing that inside her bra, her nipples had peaked.

She shed her jacket and pushed his off his shoulders.

What was it about this woman? He'd had other beautiful women, yet she tasted fresh, new, and something about the way she reveled in his response hinted at the desperation that drove her to this moment, this night, and her own confession.

Twined in each other's arms, they stumbled toward the bedroom.

In between kisses, he said, "Brandi, I promise . . . I will be everything you want. Honest . . . I will be honest."

For one moment she buried her head in his chest as if she cherished his pledge. Then she lifted her head. "Don't make promises you can't keep. You've never lied to me. I know who you are. I couldn't bear it if I believed you were a knight in shining armor and discovered . . . you weren't."

But he had lied to her. He'd lied to her about almost everything, and unless he bound her to him now, she would lash out at him for making a fool of her. "I'm not a knight in shining armor. I'm what you want

— I'm the dragon."

She laughed tremulously, pleased that he remembered.

Lifting her, he carried her to the bed. He laid her on the comforter. Leaning his forehead on hers, he said, "I promise to be the man you first imagined me to be. I *promise*."

She struggled to turn her head away. She didn't want to fall into his enchantment.

"Brandi. Listen to me. I promise my heart —"

"Your heart?" Her gaze leaped to meet his.

"My heart is in your keeping. Surely you're not surprised?"

"Why would I think you . . . you . . ."

Her uncertainty amazed him. "Love you? Do you think I take every woman I meet to my room? Do everything I can to keep her at my side? Insult a judge? Get remanded into —"

Brandi shoved him away and sat up. "You did do that on purpose!"

"But of course. I would do anything for you. Only for you." He grinned at her indignation. "I wanted to be with you. I wanted to see if fate had at last given me what I most desired — a woman of intelligence, of beauty, and of kindness."

She gazed at him as if he were a strange beast. "You're not like any man I've ever met."

"I would hope not." He pressed her down on the bed again. "I don't want to remind you of anyone else. When you think of love, I want to be the only man you can imagine. But I promised you my heart. Can't you promise me your trust?"

She surrendered. At last she surrendered. "I trust you, Roberto. No matter what happens, I trust you."

TWENTY-FIVE

A ringing noise woke Brandi out of a deep and satisfied sleep. "Roberto?" She groped, but he wasn't in the bed beside her.

The ringing noise continued.

Her cell phone. She fumbled, searching in the dark. Located it by the blinking red light that signaled a call. A glance at the clock told her it was midnight. Midnight. And — she stared at the caller ID — was that her father's phone number?

He never even called her in the daytime.

In a flash she imagined a heart attack. A car wreck. Some desperate need that made him want, at last, to talk to his middle child.

Flipping open the phone, she blurted, "Daddy. What's wrong?"

"What's wrong?" His wrathful voice blasted her ear. "What's wrong? I have a daughter who's a goddamn groupie, that's what wrong!"

"What?" She shoved the hair out of her

eyes, trying to comprehend what he was yelling about. "Who?"

"You didn't think I'd see the pictures, did you? Your stepmother couldn't wait to show them to me. My wonderful daughter, the one I always compare that pathetic son of hers to, cavorting with a jewel thief!"

Daddy was talking about *her.*

"Kissing cheeks with a bunch of gangsters. Dressed like a two-bit hooker!"

She straightened up. "What pictures?" She might be half-asleep, but she didn't need to hear him call her a hooker again.

"In the paper on the front page of the society section. The *Chicago Tribune* has been slavering over that creepy Italian ever since he showed up in your town. I knew McGrath and Lindoberth was representing him, but damned if I knew you'd decided to sink your law career to screw him!"

She had that sick feeling in her stomach, the one she always got when she talked to her father. "I have not sunk my law career."

"You'd damned well better not have. You owe me for your education. You owe me big. Vanderbilt wasn't cheap."

She had hoped this was some sort of nightmare.

His nagging about money convinced her it was real.

"I got into one of the best law schools because I'm one of the smartest people in the country," she reminded him sharply.

"Don't take that tone with me. You're as stupid as your mother."

She'd heard that a few too many times. "I am not stupid, and neither is my mother!"

"Who are you trying to convince? Your mother still can't add two and two and get four, and *you're* sleeping with a client! Didn't Vanderbilt teach you anything about ethics?"

"Just about as much as you taught me, Daddy." She had the satisfaction of hearing him huff.

The satisfaction was short-lived.

He took a huge, angry breath. "Right, and if I don't have a check for your tuition — the whole thing — on my desk tomorrow, I'll repossess your ballet lessons."

His rage was contagious. She stood up on the mattress and bounced with temper. "You'll get your money. I've got a good job. Tomorrow I'll go to the bank and take out a loan to pay you so I won't ever have to talk to you again. You're a controlling, abusive bastard, and I am done trying to please you."

She had to give him credit: He recognized what she'd done; she'd washed her hands of him. And he replied with all the spite and malice of which he was capable. "You're no better than your mother. A goddamned, stupid, spineless ballerina worth nothing. When I'm dead, you won't even have the guts to come to the funeral and spit on my coffin."

"You're absolutely right, Daddy. I'm not coming to your funeral to spit on your coffin. I don't like standing in long lines." She waited until he stopped sputtering. "Now, Daddy — you're the last person to criticize anybody for messing up their lives, so next time you want to shout at someone, don't call me." She almost shut the phone.

Then she brought it back to her ear. "And don't call my mother, either."

Then she hung up.

She hung up on *him*.

She rubbed her stomach and waited for the ache to start, that sick sort of roiling that told her she'd had another run-in with her father.

But it wasn't there.

She was angry, yes. Furiously angry at him for thinking that providing money for her college gave him the right to shout at her, and mad at herself for being foolish enough to fall into his trap instead of taking out a student loan.

But mostly she felt free, as if telling him off had released her from that spell of fear he'd cast the day he'd walked away from her and her mother. It didn't matter whether he called her stupid. It didn't matter whether he admired or despised her. She was done with him. She was an adult. He and his cruel words and his endless spite didn't have the power to hurt her anymore.

She took a long breath and released it slowly.

But in this world there was someone who did have the power to hurt her.

Roberto.

Where was he? Why hadn't he come back to bed to see what was going on? She needed to be held and praised, to be assured there was more between them than good sex.

Yet the suite was very, very quiet.

Slipping out of bed, she pulled on his robe and walked into the living room.

It was empty.

She checked the bathroom. Both bathrooms.

They were empty.

She looked in the extra bedroom. She looked under the bed.

She stood in the middle of the floor and took a long breath. This couldn't be happening. There had to be another explanation than the obvious . . . that Roberto had sneaked away from her and right now he was stealing the Romanov Blaze.

Picking up the hotel phone, she called down to the concierge. In her most charming, carefree voice, she said, "This is Brandi Michaels in room . . . oh, dear, I can't remember what room I'm in!"

"You're in room four-oh-three, Miss Michaels." The concierge sounded warm, entertained — and male.

Male. At least she had some luck tonight. "Oh, thank you. I never can remember numbers! Is this the helpful and handsome Mr. Birch?"

"You've guessed right, Miss Michaels."

"It's not a guess, Mr. Birch. I know *you.*" An older man, dapper and smart, good at his job and happy to be of service. The concierge should never give out information on a guest, but Mr. Birch liked women, and he liked her. If she struck the right notes, she could pull this off. "I am such a silly woman. I forgot to ask Mr. Bartolini if he would get me a bottle of my favorite nail polish while he was out. It's L'Oréal's Lollipop Pink; it's such a beautiful color, and it smells like candy! I just love it! Can you catch him before he leaves?"

"Just a minute." Mr. Birch put her on hold.

As she waited, she tapped her fingers on the table. The foolishness of her actions infuriated her. Looking under the bed. Calling the concierge and pretending to be a blithe, untroubled lady of leisure. But she couldn't stand not knowing the truth.

She had to know if Roberto was gone. She had to know if he had lied to her.

The concierge popped back on, and he sounded a little wary. "We're not sure if he left. There was a man, but he had his scarf over his face and his hat down, and he went out through the kitchen."

"He wanted a snack. I *told* him to order room service. He probably charmed some hapless cook out of a cookie." She lowered her voice and confided, "I swear, Mr. Birch, it's not fair that Mr. Bartolini can eat all the time and still be so thin!"

"So true." Mr. Birch sounded relaxed again.

"He's not here. He has to be somewhere. . . . I wish I could find his cell phone number!"

"He met three men behind the hotel."

"Yes, he went out to have a drink." If life were fair, she'd receive an Academy Award for Most Indulgent and Amused, when

369

actually she was Most Infuriated and Deceived. "With the Italian guys, right?"

"I couldn't venture a guess about that." Mr. Birch responded in the same spirit of amusement.

"Dark hair, dark eyes, all speaking Italian?"

"I believe that's right."

"Great! I do have Greg's cell phone number. I'll call him and catch Roberto that way. Thanks so much, Mr. Birch!" She hung up briskly — then flung the phone across the room. It thumped against the wall. It skittered across the table and bounced across the carpet. The antenna broke off with a snap. And that small act of violence wasn't enough — she wanted to stomp it to smithereens.

Roberto had sworn he wouldn't steal the Romanov Blaze. He'd promised her he would never steal anything again, that he would live on the right side of the law. For her. He'd said he would do it for her.

And instead the bastard had screwed her senseless, left her sleeping, and gone to do just what he'd promised he wouldn't.

Her father had called her a groupie and a hooker.

She was worse than that; she was a fool. She was as stupid as Daddy had insisted she was — because with her father and Alan as examples of what men could be, she had still chosen to trust Roberto.

She put her hands to her forehead.

Could she be any dumber? She had known Roberto was an international jewel thief with an eye for women and a way with words spoken in an irresistible Italian accent. Why was she surprised to discover he'd slipped it to her, then slipped away?

Her stomach didn't hurt, but her heart did.

She hated Roberto. She *hated* him.

Yet according to the courts and her boss, she was responsible for Roberto Bartolini. Her job depended on her keeping track of him, and if she was going to pay her father back — and by God, she was — she needed her job at McGrath and Lindoberth.

But how to find Roberto?

She eyed Roberto's laptop. She stalked toward the desk. She would do it like one of the big boys.

A touch on the keyboard woke the computer from hibernation. But the screen that appeared didn't hold a conveniently labeled PLANS FOR ROBBERY icon.

Yet not for nothing had she made it through law school with a decrepit computer prone to viruses. She knew a few things about searching for secrets hidden in the program code.

Settling down in the chair, she worked through the levels of passwords and encryptions until she had a file on screen that showed the briefest, barest of agendas for the robbery.

She had no time. No time to prepare. No time to plan.

Because if all was going as scheduled, Roberto was at this moment at the Art Institute of Chicago confounding the myriad traps and alarms around the great diamond and removing the Romanov Blaze from its case.

If all was not going well . . . he was dead.

She sat, her fingers still on the keyboard, frozen by the thought.

At this moment Roberto could be lying in a pool of his own blood, surrounded by the guards, by the police, by professionals pleased to have caught him before he laid hands on the diamond. He would be alone, with no one who knew his voice, his smile, his body, his mind. They'd call the coroner to put the body into a bag —

Brandi found herself on her feet.

She couldn't bear it. She couldn't bear the idea that she'd never see him again, that he'd be nothing but a noted criminal gunned down by the police.

Because she might hate Roberto, but she loved him, too.

"Damn it!" she whispered. She glanced at the rest of the schedule.

He was due to deliver the diamond to Mossimo at the Stuffed Dog in one hour and forty-five minutes. If she could intercept him, she could make him take the diamond to the police. He'd have to confess, but the courts would be lenient because he'd repented his crime.

Yes, she'd make him surrender the diamond if she had to shoot him to do it.

She opened the desk drawer and pulled out the pistol.

Aim at the largest part of the person you want to kill.

She'd aim at his fat head.

But she didn't have much time. Going to the window, she looked out. The Fossera boys were still there, waiting for her to come out. Worse than that, that FBI agent was watching the Fossera boys. Brandi knew she could ditch Joseph and Tyler, but she wasn't so sure about the professional skulker.

Picking up the phone, she called the one person she could always depend on. "Tiffany?" She could hear music and laughter in the background.

"Hi, sweetheart, how are you?" Tiffany sounded distracted.

"Not so good." Tears prickled Brandi's eyes.

"What's wrong?" Brandi had Tiffany's full attention.

"Mama, I need help."

Twenty-six

"Darling." Tiffany swept through the door of the suite dressed in a long dark coat with her blond hair hidden by a fuzzy hat and her face concealed by sunglasses. "I can't believe Roberto did this to you. This is an outrage!" She swept Brandi into a still-chilly embrace.

"I'll make him sorry," Brandi promised. She had the television on the local all-news channel, watching for a report of a break-in at the museum.

So far there had been nothing.

Roberto was still alive.

She'd make him sorry about that, too.

She gestured at the rolling suitcase Tiffany dragged behind her. "Did you bring the stuff?"

Tiffany inspected Brandi's face. "Yes, and you've done a wonderful job with the makeup and the hair. This is such a clever plan, Brandi. I'm so glad you included me!"

"No one else could possibly understand." Brandi rolled her eyes at her mother, but she couldn't tell whether Tiffany saw her.

Tiffany was still wearing her sunglasses.

Odd, because her mother had very strong opinions about a person who failed in the essential courtesies of removing her hat or her sunglasses, and while sunglasses helped with her disguise, it *was* nighttime. She didn't need them in here.

Peeling off her coat, Tiffany flung it at a chair. Kneeling beside the suitcase, she popped the latches. "I know you wanted one of my action outfits, but darling, I was packing for elegance."

"It's okay, Mama. Whatever you brought is fine with me." Brandi knelt beside her.

Tiffany took clothes out of the suitcase — a pair of Calvin Klein chocolate-brown wool slacks, a matching cashmere sweater, and Jimmy Choo stiletto heels in chocolate with an orange flower on the toe. Tiffany's tone was worried as she said, "This was the best I could do. The heels are last season's, but they're my favorites, and I think so kick-ass. Don't you?"

"It's all right, Mama. I know one thing — I might not be able to run in those heels, but running isn't what I do well. What I do well is walk and smile and make men forget good sense, and I'm going to need every weapon in my arsenal to pull off this diamond rescue without landing in jail." Brandi grinned, expecting her mother to appreciate her sentiment.

"You can do it," Tiffany said, but her mouth trembled.

"Did you break a nail on the suitcase latch, Mama?"

"No. Why would you think that?" Tiffany's breath caught, and her fingers trembled as she brushed her hair back from her face.

"Mama." Brandi carefully removed Tiffany's sunglasses. "What's wrong?"

"With me? Nothing! Right now, I'm concerned with *you.*" But her eyes looked as if she'd been crying.

With her own bad experiences to guide her, Brandi leaped to the logical conclusion. "Was Uncle Charles mean to you?"

"Charles? Heavens, no, he's the best man in the world. . . ." Tiffany choked a little. "It's just that you . . . you . . ."

"Me?" Brandi was taken aback. "What have I done?"

"You haven't done anything! It's just that . . . since the divorce . . . you've always called me *Tiffany* or *Mother.*"

"You *are* my mother," Brandi said, bewildered.

"Yes, but tonight you asked for my help. Oh, honey, you haven't asked me for help since the day Daddy announced he wanted a divorce." Tiffany sniffed. "You always treat me like some sort of imbecile."

"I don't think you're an imbecile." But Brandi stirred uncomfortably. She hadn't thought her mother was an imbecile, but she'd never seemed bright about anything but men and decorating.

"Tonight you called me *Mama*."

Brandi sat back on her heels. *Mother* or *Mama?* Shades of gray, unimportant in her eyes, or so she had told herself. But not really, because in her own mind she recognized the difference. *Mama* was the cry of an innocent, loving child. *Mother* was a teenage girl's criticism. "I hadn't realized you cared."

"I know you didn't," Tiffany hastened to assure her. "I know I wasn't any good as the head of the family. But sometimes I dreamed of the old days when you were ten and ran to me with your problems as if I could fix everything. You were such a sweet little girl!"

"Not so sweet as a teenager, huh?" Brandi remembered her disappointment as her mother went from one job to another and their income sank lower and lower, and she remembered, too, what a snot she'd been about it. What a snot she'd been ever since.

"I wasn't cut out to hold down a job. I knew it, but I wanted to make you proud of me, so I kept trying, thinking someday you'd remember you loved me and call me *Mama* again."

"My God." As Brandi viewed her mother's distress, revelation slapped her hard. "I'm turning into my father." And she'd been engaged to her father. The man she'd most despised in her life, and she'd been imitating him. Why?

Because he didn't feel. He didn't hurt.

"No, you're not! I didn't mean that. Oh, dear, I shouldn't have started this. I knew I'd mess it up."

"You haven't messed anything up." Brandi started to place her hand comfortingly on her mother's back, then chickened out. For a long time she'd barely touched her. The wall of their differences had seemed too high to breach.

But Daddy was like that. Touching no one. Connecting with no one.

Brandi couldn't afford to be like him.

Taking a breath, she put her arm around Tiffany's shoulders. "I have."

"No, you haven't!" Tiffany touched Brandi's cheek. "You're just a beautiful girl struggling to find her place in a world that thinks beautiful girls are stupid, like me. I'm so proud of you. You're so smart, like your father, but you're a good person, too, and I've wanted your approval for a long time."

"You're not stupid, and you don't need my approval," Brandi said fiercely. "You're wonderful just the way you are. Everybody thinks so. I've been a shit."

Tiffany laughed a little. "Maybe. Sometimes. But no matter how you act, I love you so much."

"I love you, too, Mama. I always have."

They hugged each other hard, in accord for the first time since the day they'd been left to face the world alone.

"You'll tell me when I say the wrong thing now, you hear?" Tiffany said.

"You mean stuff like, 'As long as Roberto's with you, I know you'll be okay'?"

Honestly bewildered, Tiffany asked, "What's wrong with that?"

"It sounds like you don't believe I can take care of myself."

"Oh, darling." Tiffany put her hands on Brandi's cheeks and looked into her eyes. "You are the most competent person I know. Of course you can take care of yourself. But two heads are better than one, and . . ."

"What?"

"I don't want you to have to spend your whole life alone. It's nice to have a man — or in Kim's case, a woman — to come home to. A bad relationship is just awful, but no relationship is very lonely." Tiffany sounded wistful and looked . . . well, lonely.

"You need someone."

"I have someone."

Brandi blinked. She knew her mother had refused one man after another all the time Brandi was in high school and college — men who wanted another trophy wife or, more likely, a trophy mistress. She'd been proud when, time and again, her mother refused.

Now, at last, Tiffany had taken a lover. "Who is it?"

"Charles McGrath."

"Uncle Charles?" Brandi shouted.

Tiffany tentatively smiled.

Brandi got a grip on her incredulity and said a little more quietly, "But he's . . . old."

"And he's rich. And kind. And he doesn't cheat on his wife," Tiffany pointed out. "He wants to marry me and shower me with clothes and jewels, and I want him to."

"But" — Brandi shuddered — "you have

to sleep with him."

"Love makes all things better."

"You *love* him?"

"Possibly. Maybe." Tiffany waved an airy hand. "But that wasn't what I mean. I mean, I know he loves me. He worships me. And when Roberto's old and gray, won't you still want to sleep with him?"

"Roberto? You mean . . . you know?"

"What? That you love him? Whew. Honey. If I weren't here, you could never sneak out of the hotel. You *glow.*"

"But Mama." Brandi took a breath. "What if he gets himself killed tonight?"

"Roberto? Get himself killed?" Tiffany laughed aloud. "I know men, and you could drop that man twenty stories and he'd still land on his feet."

"Actually, twenty-four stories," Brandi said reflectively, remembering the elevator.

"Honey, Roberto Bartolini is not going to get caught, and he's not going to get killed. Don't you worry about that. You just get yourself in and out of this mess tonight without getting hurt. That's all I ask."

"I'll be careful," Brandi promised. Tiffany's assurances made her feel better. Tiffany was right: Roberto did always land on his feet.

"Come on, then!" Tiffany said. "We've got

382

to get you ready to go. We don't have much time." Taking her makeup bag, she went into the bathroom.

"The dress is hanging on the hook," Brandi called. "Everybody saw me in it, and apparently the pictures were in all the papers."

"Yes, you're famous!"

"Infamous," Brandi corrected. Tossing the bathrobe aside, she donned her briefest thong and the beige slacks. She poured her boobs into her pointiest bra. She pulled on the beige turtleneck sweater. She looked down and grinned, then headed into the bathroom. "Look, Mama. Look at what I've got!"

"Oh." Tiffany put down the mascara wand and stared. "Oh, my."

Brandi surveyed herself in the mirror. "This'll knock their eyes out."

Tiffany giggled. "Or poke them out."

"Whatever's necessary." Brandi sat on the lid of the toilet and pulled on her trouser socks and her stiletto heels, then stood and stretched her arms over her head. "I'm ready for action."

"Not quite." Tiffany took off her large white-gold brooch sparkling with rhinestones, and pinned it on Brandi's right shoulder. "There."

"Thank you, Mama. It's perfect. It's so bright it's almost blinding." And not at all her mother's style. "Where'd you get it?"

Then together they said, "Uncle Charles."

"I'm working on his taste in jewelry." Tiffany put the finishing touches on her hair. "What do you think?"

Brandi turned Tiffany to face the mirror. She stood beside her.

Tiffany looked like her daughter, and Brandi looked like . . . well, she looked liked Brandi, but if all went according to plan, the Fossera boys would be miles away by the time she left the hotel.

Brandi handed her mother the velvet winter-white coat she'd worn last night and the video chip Mr. Nguyen had hidden in her earring case. "Now remember: Have the cabbie go to the police station, but tell him to take the long way around. Once you're inside you'll be safe, and if the Fossera boys actually try to follow you in, you can give the chip to the officers and tell them those were the guys who killed the pawnshop owner. That should fix them."

"I won't forget," Tiffany promised. "This will be fun!"

Picking up the long, dark coat Tiffany had worn into the hotel, Brandi pulled it on. She pulled on Tiffany's fuzzy hat and her sunglasses. She checked the safety on the pistol and put it in her pocket. With a brisk nod to Tiffany, she said, "Let's go."

Holding hands, they descended in the elevator. Tiffany tried to smile. "You're the smartest, prettiest girl in the whole world, and I have absolute confidence you'll make all the right moves."

And that was the difference between Tiffany and everybody else's mother. She didn't say, *I'll worry about you, so be careful.* Instead she said, *You're going to succeed.* In fact, now that Brandi thought about it, Brandi had been so successful not because she'd inherited her father's intelligence, but because her mother had always shown absolute confidence in her daughter's superiority.

And no matter how big a fool Roberto Bartolini had made of her, she still knew her father was wrong. She wasn't stupid. She was smart, she was ruthless, and she was coming out of this alive.

And she would make sure Roberto did, too.

"Thank you, Mama. I will succeed." Taking a leaf from her mother's book, Brandi hugged her hard and said, "You will, too, because you're the smartest, prettiest mother in the whole world. Joseph and Tyler

Fossera don't stand a chance."

As the doors opened into the lobby, Tiffany stepped out, shoulders back, dress clinging to every curve. She was the picture of insouciance with the white Gucci coat draped over her shoulder and caught on one hooked finger. She smiled at the bellman, the desk clerk, and every late-night reveler that she met, searing them with the heat of her beauty. As she approached the doors, the doorman leaped to open it for her, and she strolled out into the freezing cold wearing nothing but a blue velvet dress and a steely determination.

The doorman summoned her a taxi and helped her in.

The cab drove off.

The Fossera boys grabbed the next taxi.

The FBI man leaped for his car and followed them both.

Brandi grinned. The diversion had worked.

Her mirth faded. And she'd sent her mother into danger.

"Be careful, Mama," she whispered, her hands folded in prayer. "Please be careful."

TWENTY-SEVEN

Head down, Brandi strode toward the door.

Nobody in the lobby glanced twice at her.

She walked out and down Michigan Avenue and to the next hotel, where she caught a cab. "Take me to the Stuffed Dog," she said. "And hurry. There's a good tip in it for you."

"Sure, lady." Before they pulled up to the small diner, they'd been airborne three times.

She paid the cabbie, giving him enough to make him say, "Thank *you!*" She stepped into the street.

It was almost two in the morning, a clear night with stars so cold they looked brittle. Steam covered the windows of the Stuffed Dog. Inside Brandi could see a dispirited waitress sitting on a stool at the counter and two bedraggled customers hunched over cups of coffee.

Mossimo Fossera sat with his back against

the far wall. The table before him held an empty plate and dirty silverware shoved off to the side and a silver laptop. He was tensely watching a movie on the monitor.

But she knew it wasn't a movie. It was the real thing. Inside the museum the Fosseras were filming Roberto as he worked and sending the feed to Mossimo.

Mossimo faced the door so she couldn't see the screen, but she was able to read his body language. It was like observing a man watching a football game. He flinched. He dodged. Once he stood up, then sat back down. She knew everything was going well or he wouldn't still be there. Yet frequently his eyes narrowed and his lips moved in a disgruntled manner.

She could read that, too. No matter how ruthless or clever he was, he had none of Roberto's skills. Jealousy ate at him, greed kept him in his seat, and she was freezing to death waiting on the streets for Roberto to arrive.

She shivered as the wind swirled under her coat.

Unfortunately, she *was* literally freezing to death. She glanced at her watch. If everything went according to schedule, Roberto would be here in twenty minutes. Until then, she had to walk or she'd turn into a

Popsicle before she could even start to save him from prison for eternity.

She hurried down the empty street, then walked back to the Stuffed Dog and glanced in the window again.

Mossimo was on his feet, grinning, holding his arms over his head and shaking his fists.

Roberto had stolen the diamond.

Well. He had landed on his feet. He was still alive.

She paced away again. Her stiletto heels *tink*ed hollowly on the frozen sidewalk.

When she was at the end of the block, she heard a car coming. She turned.

The brown Infiniti F45 stopped at the curb, and two guys draped in coats and scarves jumped out and went into the restaurant.

She hurried toward the restaurant and arrived in time to see them peeling off their hats. She recognized them: two of the guys from Mossimo's party. They handed Mossimo a small case; he opened it, nodded, and put it in his pocket. The two men took chairs behind Mossimo, and they listened as Mossimo waved at the screen and told them what had happened. Then they faced the door in an attitude of waiting.

A woman's slurred voice spoke near her shoulder. "I didn't know they played football this late at night."

Brandi swung around.

What looked like a short bundle of rags stood there weaving in the wind, but when Brandi looked closer she discerned two bright eyes and a smiling mouth.

"It's probably a rerun," Brandi said. "It's awfully cold and late." And Roberto and Mossimo's men were coming with the diamond. Then the trouble would start. This woman needed to be well away. "Don't you have someplace to be?"

"Don't you?" The little thing was a foot shorter than Brandi. She smelled of whiskey and garbage, and she shoved at Brandi as if urging her to leave.

"I'm going to stay here until my boyfriend comes to pick me up." Which was not really a lie. When he saw her, he was going to pick her up and run with her out the door.

She hoped.

"You see, that's not a good idea." The woman's voice wasn't as slurred now. "This is a bad neighborhood at night, and a pretty girl like you shouldn't be out here. Why don't I call you a cab and send you back to the hotel?"

"What?" How did she know Brandi came

from a hotel?

"I can get you a cab," the rag woman said clearly. Then she jumped as if stung. She pressed her hand to her ear. "Shit. All right. I'll get in position."

Brandi stared as the woman shambled up to the door of the Stuffed Dog.

Had the voices in her head told her to go in?

A lone car drove down the street toward the restaurant.

Brandi stepped into the shadows to see if it would stop.

It did, and Roberto stepped out and headed for the door. Ricky, Dante, and Greg Fossera piled out and followed him.

Brandi slipped in on their heels.

Nobody paid any attention to her. The two Fosseras with Mossimo stood up and met the guys with Roberto, and the younger Fosseras laughed, slapped one another on the back, and generally acted like new fathers who had delivered their own baby.

Roberto stood in the middle, smiling and accepting their congratulations as if they were his due.

Stupid, lying, heartbreaking son of a bitch.

The old rag lady and two customers seemed oblivious to the celebration — probably drunk or hungover or just too smart to get involved.

Brandi wished she could be like them.

Mossimo sat at his table, watching and sneering, looking like a fat toad.

Brandi slid over close to the bar and the light switch, watching the scene, waiting for her chance, wondering if she really had the nerve to shoot someone and hoping that, if she did, it would be Roberto.

Putting his fingers in his mouth, Mossimo gave a shrill whistle.

The revelry died down at once, although the young Fosseras still grinned.

"Where's Fico?" Mossimo asked.

"He didn't show," Ricky said.

The men exchanged significant glances.

"The next time anyone sees Fico, kill him," Mossimo said.

The restaurant grew chilly and quiet. The customers slid low into their seats. The rag lady slipped behind the counter and crouched down.

Brandi slowly, quietly slid the safety off the pistol in her pocket.

"But we didn't need him," Dante said. "There was an alarm we didn't know about, but Greg here figured it out —"

Greg wagged his head.

"— and I disarmed it," Dante continued with a return of exuberance. "Then Roberto went to work. He's an artist. An artist, I tell you! No one even knows the Romanov Blaze is gone, and unless they look hard they'll never know, because the fake we replaced it with looks good!"

"Yeah, man," Greg said. "We were slick! We were clean! We got the diamond!"

"We did get it," Ricky pointed out.

"So where is it?" Mossimo snapped his fingers and pointed to his empty palm.

Ricky indicated Roberto while Greg and Dante pretended to prostrate themselves before him.

He drew out of his pocket a package about the size of his fist and wrapped in a black velvet drawstring bag.

Stupid, lying, heartbreaking son of a bitch. When Brandi finished this, she hoped the feds would give her a cell next to Roberto's so she could shriek her opinion of him for the next twenty-five years.

He started to hand it to Mossimo.

Heart pounding, Brandi drew her pistol.

Roberto stepped back. "But first, Mossimo, what about my ruby? You promised me the Patterson ruby in exchange for my work."

Brandi slid the gun out of sight.

Mossimo pulled the case out of his pocket and offered it to Roberto.

"Let me see it," Roberto instructed.

"So distrusting," Mossimo said in a chiding tone, but he opened the case and showed the gem to Roberto.

The setting glittered, and shafts of fire glinted off its glowing red facets.

Roberto nodded and smiled. *"Bella."* He accepted the case, snapped it closed, and stowed it in his pocket.

Then with the air of a showman, he cradled the diamond. He gave it a warm kiss.

Brandi wanted to shoot him so badly the hand holding the pistol started shaking.

He started to give it to Mossimo.

Again Brandi pulled her pistol. She pointed it at him. "Roberto!" she shouted.

Roberto wheeled around. At the sight of her, his incredulous expression gave way to terror.

"Give me the diamond," she said.

TWENTY-EIGHT

Guns appeared in every Fossera hand, pointing at Brandi, at Roberto, at one another.

Mossimo snatched the diamond away from Roberto. "Kill her!"

"Don't shoot," Roberto shouted. "For the love of God, don't shoot!" He ran toward her, knocking chairs aside.

One chair took Greg out at the knees.

Greg's pistol blasted. Ceiling tile and insulation rained down.

Another chair sent Ricky backward over a table.

In Roberto's hands, the chairs were weapons.

He raced halfway across the restaurant. One of the customers tackled him. They crashed to the floor and slid along the linoleum, hitting chairs like dominoes.

"Kill them all," Mossimo shouted.

He left Brandi no choice. She leveled the

pistol at Mossimo.

From behind, someone grabbed her by the hair.

She went down on one knee, the pain bringing tears to her eyes.

"I got her," the guy yelled, and twisted.

Her hat slid over her eyes. She shoved it off.

Joseph. It was Joseph, Mr. Nguyen's murderer, the little prick who'd tried to kill Roberto and Brandi.

How had he gotten here? Where was Tyler? What had he done to her mother?

Getting her foot under her, she stomped on his instep, sinking her stiletto heel deep into his shoe.

Yelping with pain, he let her go.

"Brandi, get down!" Roberto shouted. "Drop to the floor!"

So Joseph could kick her to death? No way.

"Bitch. I'm going to kill you!" Joseph grabbed for her again.

Ballerina Brandi performed a grand jeté that would have made George Balanchine proud. In stilettos. She hit Joseph right in the chest.

He went down, arms flailing.

She landed off balance, fell against the counter. She righted herself, but when she tried to put her weight on her foot, her ankle twisted.

She glanced down. Her mother's shoe. When she kicked Joseph, she'd broken the heel on her mother's favorite Jimmy Choo shoe. Furious, she turned back to Joseph.

Pandemonium reigned in the Stuffed Dog. Another chair smacked the wall. Fists hit flesh, and something cracked. Men and women were shouting, "Drop it! Drop it!"

Joseph's livid gaze had settled on Roberto. He lifted his knife, aimed it with the skill of a professional —

So she shot him.

The recoil slammed her elbow into the counter. The retort blasted her ears.

The knife whistled past so closely it sliced off a piece of her newly highlighted and beautifully cut hair.

Joseph screamed. Screamed like a little girl. He writhed on the floor clutching his thigh. Blood seeped through his jeans.

Incensed, gun raised, she turned back to the room.

The whole scene had changed.

The rag lady was pointing a pistol — not one like Brandi's, but a big long one — at Mossimo Fossera. The waitress held a shotgun. The two customers were pointing guns at the younger Fosseras, who were carefully putting their pistols down on the floor. People — agents — were pouring into the restaurant from the back and from the front, and they were all carrying guns. Shotguns and . . . well . . . some kind of really long guns.

Roberto leaned against a table, shaking his hand as if it hurt and glaring at Dante, who was flat on the floor and holding his bloody nose.

Brandi was a smart girl, but it didn't take brains to figure out that Roberto had never faced a threat here. He couldn't be any safer in a monastery.

The agent who had been guarding the hotel, the one Tiffany had lured away, walked in. He looked at her in disgust. "You and your mother. Couple of smart-asses."

By that she assumed Tiffany was fine. *Thank God.*

Roberto looked up at her. He sagged with relief.

Then his expression changed. He frowned, and a fire lit his eyes.

Yeah, she would bet he was mad. She'd interfered and screwed up his whole heroic operation.

Too damned bad. Maybe he should have trusted her, like he kept saying she should trust him. "Bastard," she said.

With the noise in the restaurant, he couldn't have heard her, but he read her lips. He walked toward her.

"You double-crossed me!" Mossimo shouted, clutching the diamond to his chest. "You bastard son of an Italian whore! You double-crossed me!"

Roberto stopped. He turned back to Mossimo. In a move so clean Brandi never saw it happen, he knocked Mossimo's feet out from underneath him. The whole restaurant shook as Mossimo landed flat on his back.

Roberto leaned over the wheezing bully. "The nice FBI agents are going to take you away now, Mossimo, and while you may not be happy to go to prison for two hundred years, I know one Fossera who will be glad to see you go."

"Fico. That turncoat Fico," Mossimo said.

"No," Roberto said, "I was talking about your wife."

The FBI agents laughed.

Brandi didn't.

"That jewel you're clutching? It's cubic zirconium," Roberto said. "The real Romanov Blaze left the country three days ago."

Mossimo unwrapped the stone. He held it up to the lights. The facets glittered with glory, mocking him.

Mocking Brandi.

As hard as he could, Mossimo threw the fake diamond at Roberto.

Roberto caught it, and in a gesture that celebrated his triumph, tossed it in the air. It landed in his open palm, and with a grin he closed his fingers over it.

Celebration. Sure. If Brandi had pulled off a sting this complex, with the faked theft of a phony famous Russian diamond, the real theft of an authentic ruby, and the fall of an entire family of his grandfather's enemies, she'd celebrate, too.

For the whole time she knew him, Roberto had been working for the FBI. Had been working to trap Mossimo Fossera and his men in the process of stealing and receiving the Romanov Blaze and put them away forever.

And like a cat in a fan belt, she got caught up in the plot.

All of this — the worry about her job, the unwanted socializing, Roberto's swaggering, her angst about having unethical and totally great sex with a client, her fear he would die and this wild chase across Chicago at night armed with a pistol and the resolve to rescue Roberto from his own folly, her mother's broken shoe — had been for nothing. For a sham.

The damned diamond she'd put her life in jeopardy to protect wasn't even the real thing.

Tonight, when she had woken up and thought Roberto had broken his promise to her not to steal the Romanov Blaze, she had felt like a fool.

Now she knew the promise he'd made, the one that had made her heart trill — never to steal anything again, to live on the right side of the law *for her* — was as big a fake as the cubic zirconium he held.

Because, hell, how could he steal the diamond out of the Art Institute when it had been out of the country for three days?

Carefully, before she could give in to her desire to shoot Roberto right in the chest where his nonexistent heart should reside, she placed his pistol on a table. She turned toward the door.

From the floor, she heard Joseph shout, "For you, Mossimo!"

Off balance, she spun and saw him aim a pistol at her head.

Roberto hurled the cubic zirconium.

With a thump it hit Joseph right between the eyes. He fell backward, unconscious, a huge, bloody welt on his face.

One of the FBI agents scooped up the pistol.

She stared at Joseph's prone body.

She was *so glad* she'd shot him.

Of course, he was only a substitute for the man she really wanted to shoot — Roberto.

Roberto, who again started toward her. He looked wary. He looked furious. He looked like a man who'd been hiding the truth from her almost since the moment she'd met him.

She held up her hand. In a clear, carrying voice, she said, "I'm going home now. I won't be seeing you again. I'd wish you a good life, but actually I hope you step outside and get hit by a flaming meteorite. That would be fitting retribution for what you've done to me."

Roberto continued to stride toward her.

She limped out the door.

A gust of wind hit Roberto in the face. It smelled of rain and felt almost warm.

The cold snap had broken.

Aiden grabbed Roberto by the arm.

Roberto turned on him, furious to be stopped.

"Let her go. She's pissed off and you can't blame her." Aiden was a stocky man with short, sandy hair and hazel eyes, and Roberto's collaborator for the whole operation.

They'd known each other for years, and when Roberto had heard the rumor that Mossimo Fossera intended to steal the Romanov Blaze, he took it to Aiden. Aiden had had the authority to make the deal Roberto wanted, and Roberto had the expertise Aiden needed. They had been a good team — until now.

"She can't walk around Chicago at two thirty in the morning looking for a cab," Roberto said impatiently.

"One of my guys is taking her back to the hotel. No, wait." Aiden put his hand to his earpiece. "She wants to go to Charles McGrath's. She'll be safe there. More than safe."

"Safe from me." Roberto knew Aiden was right. He was right, but Roberto hated it. She'd seen the whole operation go down, and right now she despised him. No explanation he made could change that. He had to rely on her own good sense to soften her feelings toward him.

Brandi was a rare, very rare woman — one who used logic on a daily basis. When she thought about it, she'd know he had had no choice but to lead her on. And she'd probably understand that he'd wanted her close as he went to those parties to be feted as an infamous jewel thief.

Hm. Perhaps it would be best if he took her flowers when he went to explain.

Mossimo Fossera was on his feet, his hands cuffed behind him, the rag lady holding a gun to his back. "This is entrapment! I didn't steal anything!"

"You accepted stolen goods," the rag lady said. "The Patterson ruby and the Romanov diamond."

"It wasn't the Romanov diamond," Mossimo screamed.

"Could have fooled me." The rag lady smiled.

"I want my lawyer," he brayed. "I want my lawyer!"

"Shut up!" Roberto told him.

So Mossimo changed to, "You're dead to us. You betrayed us. None of the thieves will speak to you again. Traitor!"

"Yeah, Count Bartolini here is really worried about that," the rag lady said.

"Count?" Mossimo laughed hoarsely. "He's no count. Everyone thinks he's so smart, so rich, so continental, but he's a bastard. Everybody knows it! The bastard son of Sergio's whore of a daughter."

"Get him out of here," Aiden said.

The rag lady and one of the customers

shoved Mossimo out the back door.

"I hate that guy," Aiden said.

"Yeah, but I got what I wanted from him," Roberto said.

"Revenge for what he did to your grandfather?"

"That, too." Roberto touched his pocket.

New agents entered with cameras and tape measures to document the crime scene.

Aiden kept a close eye on the proceedings. "Let me tell you, Roberto, when my man at the hotel realized he'd been suckered into following Miss Michaels's mother to the police station, and my agents here realized the woman watching Mossimo was Brandi, no one knew what to do. They were screaming in my earpiece like I could do something when I was following you."

"Couldn't they have gotten her out of here?" At least then she wouldn't have actually seen the sting.

"If we'd had another five minutes, but we didn't. We planned for everything except *her.*"

"That makes two of us." She'd worn the strangest expression when she looked at him. Angry, yes, he expected that. But pained, too, as if she'd been hit below the belt too many times and was bleeding internally. "I've got to go after her."

"Not right now. There's someone here you want to meet." Aiden nodded toward a tall, gangly young man who'd come in with the agents.

He sat in the booth, observing Roberto with keen curiosity.

"Who is it?" Roberto asked.

"He's the guy with the information you did all this for."

The news shook Roberto to the core. "He knows who I am?"

"He knows it all." Aiden shook his head. "The poor son of a bitch."

"He's here to tell me now?" Roberto glanced around. The fluorescent lights glared onto the upturned tables and shattered chairs. The agents worked, talked, and took pictures. Blood stained the floor. When he'd begun his quest, he'd never imagined it would end in Chicago in the Stuffed Dog at two thirty in the morning.

Aiden obviously saw nothing odd about the scene. "We made a deal, didn't we? You did your part, and I thought you wanted to know as soon as possible."

"I do." Yet Roberto wasn't ready. He didn't know if he'd ever be ready to know the truth about the man who had really fathered him.

A Chicago patrolman stepped in the door.

"What the hell is going on?"

Aiden shouted, "Hey, the restaurant is closed. This is an FBI crime scene!"

"The hell it is!" the patrolman bellowed.

Aiden walked over to fight with the indignant, pugnacious policeman.

He left Roberto to introduce himself.

The young man was about twenty-three, tall and broad-shouldered. His hair was as dark as Roberto's; his eyes were dark and intelligent. He watched as Roberto walked toward the booth, scrutinizing Roberto as Roberto scrutinized him.

"I'm Roberto Bartolini." Roberto extended his hand.

The young man shook it. He looked into Roberto's face as if seeking something. In a voice tinged with the accent of an East Coast aristocrat, he said, "My name's Carrick Manly. I'm your half brother."

Twenty-nine

The next day, neither Tiffany nor Brandi would answer when Roberto called. It took a trip to McGrath's mansion for him to discover the two women had moved back to Brandi's apartment.

Charles McGrath was none too complimentary about the way Roberto had handled the whole situation. "Damn it, boy, when I told you and the FBI I'd help with this operation, I didn't mean I wanted to lose my fiancée to a crisis with her daughter! I had Tiffany living here with me. I was buying her things, she was helping me decorate the house, we were going to parties. We were happy! Then Brandi comes to the door sobbing, Tiffany finds out I was in on the sting, and now neither one of them is speaking to me. Thank you very much!"

So Roberto loaded his flowers and his presents back in the BMW — Newby was an FBI agent, and now that the sting was over Roberto was driving himself — and went to Brandi's apartment.

When he rang the doorbell, Tiffany answered. "What lovely flowers!" She relieved him of the cheerful mixed bouquet of golden sunflowers and purple asters. "Are the gifts for Brandi?" She took them, too. "Not that any of this is going to work," she said cheerfully. "You'll have to do better!" She shut the door in his face.

He stood there, sure she would now open the door and announce she was merely joking.

She didn't.

After two days of leaving first reasonable, then abject, then angry messages on Brandi's answering machine, he finally had no choice. He called in an expert — Count Giorgio Bartolini, who had been married to Roberto's temperamental mother for over thirty-two years.

When the count heard the whole story, he sighed deeply. "All these years, and you still know nothing? This young woman, Brandi — you admire her intelligence, you love her independence, yet you used her."

Roberto was outraged. He had expected his father to take his side. "It wasn't like that, Papa."

"Most certainly it was. She has her pride,

and you made a fool of her." Roberto could almost see his father shaking his dark head in disgust. "Love that survives trial and strife withers at the sound of laughter."

"I did not laugh at her." Roberto was beginning to think this call was a mistake. "I phoned so we could talk sensibly about strategies to win her back. Instead you make it sound as if this rift is all my fault!"

Papa said nothing for a long minute. "If you were here with me in Italy, I would slap your face. Of course it's your fault! With a woman, you don't worry about *sensible*. With a woman, even if it's not your fault, you take the fault! That is what being a man is!"

"I have been a man for a long time, Papa, and no woman has ever required me to take the fault."

"No woman has ever saved your insignificant life before."

Roberto began to feel backed against the wall. "I saved hers in return!"

"That *is* what a man does. Do you love this Brandi?"

"Yes, but —"

"Then find a way to make her listen to you, admit you were wrong, and if you're lucky, perhaps she'll forgive you!"

"Roberto Bartolini crawls for no woman!"

"Good-bye, honey. You're going to make them all love you!" Tiffany kissed her daughter as if she were a girl going off to her first day of school.

In fact, Brandi was a woman going off to face the gauntlet of disgruntled McGrath and Lindoberth employees who now were sure her work ethics were lousy. "I'd settle for a little tolerance."

"I know it's going to be rough, but you have to go. You've got to pay off that loan from the bank!"

Ah, yes. The loan from the bank. The loan she'd taken out to pay back her father. The loan for which Uncle Charles had cosigned. "I've got three years to pay it back. Three years of working at McGrath and Lindoberth with people who will make my life hell." Brandi took a breath. "Three years isn't so long."

"That's the spirit!" Tiffany's cheerleader training was showing through. "Don't forget, you look great!"

Brandi did look great in a blue Dolce & Gabbana suit, a white cowl-necked sweater, and Donald J. Pliner pumps. Yesterday Tiffany had pulled out the credit cards Uncle Charles had given her and assured Brandi he had *begged* them to indulge in retail therapy. Brandi would have refused — knowing Uncle Charles had been in collusion with Roberto made her none too happy — but she had to do something about her hair. Joseph Fossera's knife had whacked off a one-inch-by-two-inch piece of her hair close to her scalp, and she desperately needed a professional to create a new style.

So Tiffany and Brandi had gone to the spa. Brandi's hairdresser had been horrified, then driven to a frenzy of creativity that resulted in an asymmetrical cut that made Brandi look almost French. A manicure and shopping had made both Brandi and Tiffany feel better about their lousy love lives.

Talking to Kim did *not* make either of them feel better about anything — Kim was madly in love, and while she tried to sympathize with their plight, it was clear nothing could penetrate her happiness.

But Brandi and Tiffany had had fun, and if Brandi was given to sudden bouts of tears disguised as temper, she never directed it at Tiffany.

Now, as Brandi entered the McGrath and Lindoberth building, the guard waved her in without checking her badge. "Don't bother, Miss Michaels; I know who *you* are."

She nodded and smiled, figuring that after the elevator incident every security guard in the place knew her name.

She closed her eyes as the elevator took her to the twenty-seventh floor and tried not to think about falling. The trouble was, when she emptied her mind, that opened it to the memories of lying on the floor with Roberto between her legs, coming with a desperation that shook her still. And to the memory of that moment when she'd realized she loved him.

But what good was love when the man was a lying creep?

When she'd posed that question to her mother, Tiffany had waved a hand at the presents and flowers and said, "He may be a lying creep, but he's a lying creep with excellent taste."

Brandi looked around at the open boxes filled with jewelry, glass objets d'art, and books selected especially for her. "We're not keeping that stuff."

Tiffany's answer left Brandi breathless. "But darling, we shouldn't let our dislike of him spoil our pleasure in the gifts. We want to hurt him, not ourselves!"

Even with their newfound accord, Brandi didn't know how to reply to that.

When the elevator doors opened, someone

yelled, "She's here!"

Brandi opened her eyes to see the hallway lined with people — attorneys, law clerks, the secretarial staff — staring at her. She braced herself for a ration of trouble and instead heard a sound she had never expected to hear from them — applause.

Were they making fun of her? Was this some kind of office joke?

Brandi stepped cautiously out of the elevator and walked down the hall past the gauntlet of smiling people.

Diana Klim was bouncing while she clapped.

Tip Joel punched the air as Brandi walked by.

Even Sanjin smiled and clapped — coolly, but he clapped.

When Glenn called, "Good work, Brandi!" she knew the elevator had dropped all the way to the ground and she was dead and in some kind of purgatory.

The sight of Shawna Miller standing outside her cubicle clutching a legal pad gave Brandi a measure of sanity. Shawna hated her. She would tell her what was going on without prettying it up.

"What's with everyone?" Brandi asked.

"We saw the pictures." Shawna said. "We read the story! Oh, my God, you must have been so scared, but you looked cool as a cucumber."

Brandi stared at the bubbling Shawna. "The pictures? The story?"

"We got the memo yesterday afternoon, and the story broke on the *Chicago Tribune* Web site this morning." She dragged Brandi inside her cubicle and indicated her computer. "You're in the *paper.*"

Front and center on the *Tribune* Web site were two photos of Brandi — one looking elegant and graceful in Roberto's arms as they danced the tango, and one in the Stuffed Dog looking intent and calm as she pointed her pistol at Joseph.

Brandi sank into Shawna's chair. "Where . . . ? How . . . ?" She started reading as fast as she could.

Brandi Michaels . . . new attorney for McGrath and Lindoberth . . . volunteered to assist international businessman Count Roberto Bartolini in a sting operation to thwart the nefarious plan to steal the Romanov Blaze . . . infamous kingpin Mossimo Fossera under arrest . . . FBI agent Aiden Tuchman said, "At great risk to her own life, Miss Michaels entered the fray and removed a threat to the operation with a kick to his chest, and when he again attempted to thwart us, she was forced to shoot him . . . cool under danger . . ."

"I don't believe it." Somehow Brandi had gone from dupe to heroine.

"That picture of you shooting that guy was so cool. You're my new hero!"

"Yeah. Thanks." The pictures must have been culled off the security cameras, or maybe the FBI agents had been wired. Brandi didn't know how this worked, because she hadn't been in the know. No matter what the *Tribune* said, Roberto had made a fool of her. But if the *Tribune*'s story smoothed her way at McGrath and Lindoberth, she would be ungrateful to complain.

"You'd have volunteered to help with the sting, too, if Roberto Bartolini was in on it," Brandi said as she stood. "It was no sacrifice on my part."

"You did get to go to parties with him, but no way. He's a hunk, but when the FBI told me there was going to be shooting, I'd have been out of there. He isn't worth getting killed over!"

"No, I suppose not." Brandi certainly shouldn't think so.

As she walked past Mrs. Pelikan's office, Mrs. Pelikan called out, "Miss Michaels, if I could see you for a moment?"

Mrs. Pelikan didn't sound nearly as infatuated with Brandi as the rest of the office, and she was shuffling papers when Brandi stepped in. "It would seem we need to assign you to a different case." She peered over her glasses at Brandi, and her brown eyes were cold. "Since this one was a front for you and Mr. Bartolini, and all the work we did on it useless."

From far off down the corridor, Brandi heard a rumble. Conversation? Laughter?

"Yes, Mrs. Pelikan. I'm sorry, Mrs. Pelikan." Brandi warmed to the woman who so greatly resented being lied to and used. Brandi could relate to that.

The rumble got louder. Definitely laughter.

Mrs. Pelikan relented. "I know you couldn't tell me, but what an immense amount of work for nothing!"

The sound of many voices carried more and more clearly into the office.

What was going on out there? "I promise, I won't be doing anything exciting ever again."

Mrs. Pelikan looked over Brandi's shoulder. She subdued a smile. "I don't know that I'd agree with *that*."

From the doorway, Roberto said, "Brandi, I'd like to speak to you."

Brandi stiffened. Slowly she turned.

And found herself facing a six-and-a-half-foot dragon.

THIRTY

The dragon was mostly green. Small green scales on his pointed snout, large green scales on his ridged back, green scales on his fat, three-foot-long tail, iridescent green scales on the ridiculously small wings that sprouted from his shoulders. Pointed white teeth grew from his long mouth. His black eyes, set deep into the sides of his head, shone softly. But it was the gem in the middle of his forehead that really caught her attention.

It was the fake of the Romanov Blaze, and it glittered with the same violet fire as the real thing.

Roberto looked . . . ridiculous.

"Brandi? Can we talk?" It was definitely Roberto's voice coming from inside the dragon.

"I don't talk to mythical fire-breathing reptiles." But she had to cover her mouth to hide her grin.

The whole floor, maybe the whole building, was watching. The men dug their elbows into one another's sides. The women giggled softly.

"You have to talk to me. I'm your dragon."

Her amusement died. "My dragon is broken."

"I know, and I'm sorry. I can't fix him, but if you'll let me, I can fix the things *I* broke."

"I don't want to talk to you." Brandi had been stomped by enough men lately. She didn't need to give this one a second run at her. Especially since this one was the only one who mattered.

"What did you break?" Shawna asked him.

"Her trust."

Brandi snorted. *And my heart.*

Roberto continued, "But if she'd listen to me for just a few minutes . . ."

"Brandi, you ought to be nice to the dragon," Diana said. "We don't want him to start breathing fire. There are a lot of papers in this place."

Their onlookers chuckled.

It wasn't fair. How had he gotten her whole office on his side? "Give me one reason why I should listen to you."

With his hands, Roberto opened the dragon's mouth and looked directly at her.

"Because I love you."

Their onlookers *ahh*ed.

The impact of his dark, intent eyes and firm declaration made her back up two steps. "Tell me why I should care."

He came toward her, claw outstretched. "Give me a chance and I will." Then his large backside caught in the door.

"As touching as this is, I've got work to do." Mrs. Pelikan looked over her glasses at the people crowded into the corridor. "As does everyone in this department. Sanjin, they're going to borrow your office. Show them where it is."

Sanjin stood immobile, his face blank with astonishment. "But I have work to do, too!" A jab in the side brought him to his senses and he said, "Follow me."

Roberto shuffled backward and gestured to Brandi to precede him. She walked down the hall, clutching her briefcase, acutely aware of the dragon shambling on her heels.

Damn Roberto. He made her want to laugh. He charmed her. And no matter how mad he made her, no matter how he hurt her, she still loved him.

Damn him. Damn him.

Sanjin opened the door to his office and gestured them in. He had a desk, a chair, a file cabinet, a view of the next building, and so little floor space the dragon made it a tight fit. He had to squish his tail sideways so Sanjin could shut the door behind him.

Even though most of Roberto was just a costume, she backed to the far side of the desk. "What made you think of doing *this*?"

"I wanted your attention." He opened the dragon's mouth again and looked at her. "My father told me I'd better crawl, and I said absolutely not, no woman was worth that, and he said . . . he said rather rude things." He winced as if they still stung. "He's a man whose opinion I respect very much, so I followed his advice."

"Because you respect him."

"No." He waggled that enormous, outrageous head. "Because every minute you're apart from me, my heart bleeds."

"Nice. Poetic. I'm not impressed." Although she sort of was, but he didn't need to think he could spout some romantic nonsense in that deep Italian voice of his and she would roll over like some kind of dragon groupie.

"In your absence, I wanted to know everything about you, so I begged Charles for photos and stories about you. I saw your baby picture. I saw ballerina Brandi in her first recital." He reached out a claw. "I heard all about your father."

She opened her briefcase and fussed with the contents, arranging the already neatly arranged notebook, pen and pencil, PDA, and shining-new laptop. "How nice of Uncle Charles to tell you *that.*"

"But I am not like your father."

"No, you're a whole different bag of beans."

"Nor am I the son of Count Bartolini."

She looked up. She shut her briefcase. She placed it on one side of the desk and seated herself on the other. "Okay. You win. You have my complete attention."

"Two years ago, my mother was diagnosed with breast cancer."

"I'm sorry." And why was he telling her *this?*

"She got very ill, and she believed — we all believed — she was going to die. So she called me to her bedside and told me the secret of my birth." Roberto clasped his clawed hands across his scaly chest. "My father is a man she got involved with while at college, a man who got her pregnant and left her. She came home to Nonno, who sent her to his family in Italy. Before she gave birth to me, she met the count. She married him, I was born, and I grew up believing he was my father."

"No one told you differently?" That was

hard to believe.

"Except for my mother and the count, no one knew the truth. Everyone thought they'd had an affair during his visit to the States. Gossip said that they fought and my mother, in her pride, refused to tell him of her pregnancy, but when she went to Italy, they found each other again and married."

"Look, I hate to dispute you, but Mossimo knows. He called your mother a . . . he called your mother names."

"Mossimo suspected the truth, and probably there are rumors. But really — does anybody believe Mossimo when he spouts venom?"

"No. No, it never occurred to me to pay attention to him." She swung her foot and watched the motion. "What has this to do with you and me?"

"My mother would not tell me who my father is."

"Ah." That would grate on Roberto. He would need to *know.*

"She says she sinned. She says she's ashamed. She says that he isn't a good man, and she would not tell me his name. I would make a scene, but thank God she's in remission, doing very well, and I don't want to upset her."

"What about your father? The count, I mean."

"He's in every way a good parent to me. I can't tell him that I need to know" — he shook his dragon head as if his own emotions bewildered him — "to *see* this man who begat me. What was it about him that made my mother reject him and flee in such horror?"

Brandi began to understand the events of the last week. "But you had to know, so you searched for a way."

"And I found it. I'm not an international jewel thief — not usually — but I know the family business and I keep up the Contini contacts. Nonno called and said that Mossimo Fossera intended to steal the Romanov Blaze. I used my contacts. I went to the FBI and told Aiden Tuchman that if he would find out who my father was, I would help him bring down the Fosseras." The dragon shrugged his massive shoulders. "It's as simple as that."

"As simple as that — for you. For me, I made a mistake. I saw you at Charles's party and I thought it was fate."

"That was no mistake. It was fate, for once I saw you, made love to you, I wanted you with me. When I discovered you were one of my lawyers, I thought fate had given me the woman of my dreams." He touched his claw to his chest. "I was wrong."

"Not the woman of your dreams, huh?" For a man who was good with words, he was lousy with words.

"Definitely the woman of my dreams, but not *given* to me."

"Oh." Better.

"Not given to me. I had to earn her. Still have to . . ." He shut the mouth. He looked down.

He bonked her in the head with his snout. "Ouch!"

"*Cara!* I'm sorry!" He tried to get close and got stuck between the wall and the desk. "Are you all right?"

She rubbed the bruise. Green glitter drifted onto her shoulders. "I'm fine, but I think you mashed his nose."

Roberto felt around and found a misshapen nostril. In a mournful tone, he said, "Now when I breathe fire, I'll singe myself."

"You're ridiculous." He made her want to laugh again, and that would never do. Laughter would indicate softening, and if there was one thing Tiffany had taught her, it was that a man should work if he wanted a woman, and then work some more. Besides, Brandi might still love Roberto. She might still want him. But he had lied by omission . . . although now she understood why . . .

Hastily, before she could think of more reasons to become sympathetic, she said, "So you trapped Mossimo. Did Aiden come through?"

"Yes. The night of the sting, after you went storming out the door, I met my half brother."

She leaned forward, her interest well and truly caught. "Your father's child by another woman?"

"Carrick Manly. He's the only legitimate son of billionaire industrialist Nathan Manly."

Memory stirred. "Nathan Manly. Didn't he steal all the capital from his collapsing industry about ten or fifteen years ago and flee to South America?"

"That's the rumor. I thought that on my mother's side I was the descendent of an ancient clan of jewel thieves. It turns out I'm also the son of the corrupt man who stole the livelihood of thousands of his employees and stockholders." Roberto laughed bitterly. "He also, before he left, spread his sperm throughout the land, impregnating young women indiscriminately and without conscience. I'm one of who knows how many of his children. Of his *sons* — apparently he fathered only sons."

"So you have a whole family spread out across the country and you don't know who they are?" She could almost hear her mother's voice in her head. *Don't feel sorry for him, Brandi! Don't you dare! He hasn't given you a single gift today!*

But he sounded so grim and sad. He was a man who had known his place in the world. Then his identity had been whisked away and replaced by uncertainty. Being Roberto, he hadn't moaned or complained; he'd taken action, and now the mystery he had sought to solve had deepened.

"Carrick is tracking down my brothers. He wants whatever information they have about his father."

Brandi noted that Roberto didn't call Nathan his own father. His father was the count.

"Carrick's mother has been accused by the federal government of being in collusion with Nathan to steal the money. Carrick says she's innocent. Certainly she has no money. I don't know, but I told him I would help him find my brothers. For him. And for me." Roberto tried to squeeze closer to her. "No one else knows the whole truth, Brandi. Only me . . . and you."

She stared at him, trying to resist the appeal of a man who *did* trust her enough to confide in her.

"Tell me, did I forever ruin my chances to love you as you deserve to be loved?"

Don't let him seduce you with green scales and big white teeth! "Take off that stupid dragon suit."

"I have sworn to wear this until you agree to marry me." He put his claw over his heart.

"That is the dumbest thing I've ever heard." Which it was. Also the most romantic.

"So tell me you'll be my bride."

"Tell me one reason I should marry you, Roberto." *Oops.* Impatience had driven her to indicate how very much he charmed her.

He knew it, too. "I have two. I love you. How can I not? And when you thought I was in trouble, you came to rescue me. No woman has ever done that before."

"I was an idiot." That was the real problem. She'd gone off to rescue a man who didn't need rescuing.

"No. You were a woman in love." His voice took on that warm, intimate tone he used during sex.

"Like I said — an idiot." When she thought about how humiliated she'd felt when those FBI agents poured into the restaurant, she could . . . she could shoot Joseph again. The little weasel. "But I'm not going to be an idiot anymore. You made a fool of me, and I don't trust you."

"How can you not? I've told you what no one knows. I trust you with everything I am." As he took a step toward her, his large, scaly foot kicked over the trash can. It clattered against the desk. Wadded-up papers rolled across the floor. "Can you learn to trust me again? I'll spend my life making you happy." He scooped up her hand with his claw and raised it to his teeth. "I beg you, Brandi, please marry me."

She looked at her fingers. They were covered with green glitter. She looked at him. He was an insensitive jerk who never stopped to think that he might be hurting her by dragging her along on his adventure. Yet he flattered her because he had been unable to leave her behind.

And he was sensitive enough to recognize the importance of a dragon in her life. . . .

"Just a minute." Opening her briefcase, she located her PDA in its pocket. With her stylus, she flipped through her lists until she found *Qualities Required in a Man.*

1. Honest
2. Dependable
3. Goal-oriented
4. Sober . . .

She pushed ERASE ALL.

The list disappeared forever.

Carefully she placed the PDA back into her briefcase, shut it, and turned back to Roberto. "Take off the dragon costume and we'll *talk* about the *possibility* of marriage."

He crowed like he'd already won.

Man, he was irritating. "I said *talk.*"

"I have a gift for you."

Irritating, but he knew just the right words to say. "What gift?"

"Can you see the zipper under the dragon's arm?" He twisted sideways.

"Yes. What do you have for me?" She pulled it down.

"A ring."

"I threw the last diamond ring at the toilet." She hoped he realized what that meant, coming from Tiffany's daughter.

"It's not a diamond. Open the zipper wide. Can you see my pocket?"

"Yes." He was wearing a T-shirt and jeans that fit like a glove.

"Get the ring out."

So she had to grope him. He was a very

clever strategist. Slowly she slid her hand into his pocket. His hip was firm against her hand, tempting and warm, and she just stood there a minute, her eyes closed, as she relished the chance to touch him once more.

She was so easy.

"Are you having trouble finding it?" He sounded amused and pleased.

"Yeah! I mean, no, it's right here." She delved all the way to the bottom and felt the small, smooth circle. She drew it out, then stared at the old, worn yellow gold and the polished stone in puzzlement. She'd seen this before. On Mossimo's hand. "It's Mossimo's ring."

"No." He touched her cheek with his claw. "It's the Contini ring, stolen by one of my ancestors so many years ago its origins are lost in myth. The head of the Continis wears that ring. My *nonno* wore it until he married; then he gave it to Nonna with love and honor. She wore it until she died; then my *nonno* put it back on his finger. It should never have left him until the moment he passed on the mantle as head of the Continis."

"How did he lose it?" As if she couldn't guess.

"When Mossimo smashed Nonno's hand,

he stole the ring."

When she thought how she and Roberto had faced off against that beast, she wanted to faint from fear and beam with pride. "And how did you get it back?"

Roberto opened the dragon's mouth and grinned at her. "At the Stuffed Dog, I lifted it off Mossimo when I threw him."

He looked so pleased, so mischievous, she couldn't hold it back anymore. She laughed. "You are so bad!"

"Nonno told me to give the ring to you." Roberto put his scaly arm around her shoulders. "I would be honored if you'd wear it and add my name to yours."

She carefully placed the ring on the desk. She laid her head on his scaly chest. "I do like dragons, but I like Roberto better."

In a flash the two of them started tugging, trying to free him from the costume that encased him.

They thumped around Sanjin's office.

"There's got to be another zipper."

"Don't you know how you got in here?"

"The person at the shop dressed me, and I didn't know if you were ever going to let me out." As they struggled to free his head, his tail repeatedly hit the door.

"You liar. You knew all you had to do was bat those beautiful dark eyes at me and I'd melt." She found another zipper. "Here. Right here. That's it!"

"That's not true." He almost tumbled over.

She caught him. They teetered on the verge of falling. "You just don't want to admit it until we've got you out of the costume."

"Shouldn't you be glad to marry a wise man?"

She jerked on the ridge on his back, and suddenly his head was free, his shoulders were free, and she could see his face without gazing through white pointed teeth.

The tussle suddenly stopped. They stared at each other, and Brandi could think of nothing but how much she loved him.

"Give me the ring," he whispered.

Without looking down, she groped until she found it. She handed it to him.

Taking her left hand, he slid it on her third finger.

She looked at the smooth green stone and knew she held the weight of Roberto's history in her hand. Slowly she said, "It doesn't matter who your father is, or your grandfather, or your mother. I treasure them all, but only because they brought you into this world. For me. Just for me."

"Yes, I am just for you. And you are just

for me." Still half in the dragon costume, he caught her in his arms and kissed her. "The ring . . . do you know what they call the Contini ring?"

She kissed him back. "What?"

"The dragon's scale."

She laughed. And laughed.

Fate had an interesting sense of humor.

They fell over in Sanjin's office.

In the corridor outside, Sanjin heard the sound of Brandi's mirth and again heard the rhythmic thump of the tail against the door. With an exasperated sigh, he walked away.